THE MASTER OF CASTLELEIGH

Clarissa turned and knelt upright, so that the front of her body was exposed to her maid. Once again, Lucy hovered uncertainly.

'Well, carry on, girl. Do I even have to instruct you on how to wash?' Clarissa chided her.

Tentatively Lucy began stroking the sponge from shoulder to shoulder and then rinsing off the soap with clear water, sending a cascade flowing down Clarissa's breasts and stomach. Nervously, she started rubbing the sponge around the top of her mistress's breasts, but Clarissa soon stopped her.

'That is far too rough. Use your hands.'

Lucy put down the sponge and rubbed the soap between her hands until they were gloved in a rich lather. Reaching out, she began to massage the thick, scented foam into her mistress's right breast. Clarissa closed her eyes to help her savour as deeply as possible the tingling feeling created by every touch of the girl's fingers. She shuddered at the spasm which shot through her as Lucy began to wash her nipples. She realised that Lucy must know her mistress was being aroused by her work, but Clarissa had long since ceased caring what the girl thought.

THE MASTER OF CASTLELEIGH

Jacqueline Bellevois

This book is a work of fiction.
In real life, make sure you practise safe sex.

First published in 2001 by
Nexus
Thames Wharf Studios
Rainville Road
London W6 9HA

www.nexus-books.co.uk

Typeset by TW Typesetting, Plymouth, Devon

Printed and bound by
Clays Ltd, St Ives PLC

ISBN 0 352 33644 7

One

The fog cloaked moon and stars. It hung like a heavy yellow shroud above the roof tops and smoke-belching chimneys. The only illumination in the narrow, cobbled lanes came from the windows of houses and taverns and the occasional guttering lamp beside a doorway. It was a dangerous place to be on such a dark night, but Richard Buxton felt no fear. Over six feet tall, broad shouldered and in his late twenties, he knew he was the match of any man he might encounter in the streets of Whitechapel that night. He also had more than just his athleticism and strength to rely on. One twist of the silver nob of his cane would send three feet of the finest, sharpest steel slicing the air towards any would-be opponent, and in the pocket of his long frock coat lay a small pistol, primed and waiting. But it was not just his build and his weapons that would deter any footpad. It was also the stern-set countenance and the pene-trating, fixed stare. Richard Buxton was angry, very angry. He would have welcomed any such opportun-ity to assuage his feelings by giving full vent to his temper. Many eyes watched him as he strode the filth-littered streets, but the brains behind them appreciated the danger and the men shrank back into the protective shadows of doorways and alleys. He would release the tensions within soon enough.

The girl who awaited him would be shown no mercy.

A narrow passage brought him into a spacious square of tall, terraced houses. The air was cleaner here than in the labyrinth of cramped, fetid lanes behind him. Lamps were lit beside almost every door and the pavement was broad and even. Buxton walked diagonally across the square and rapped with his cane on the door of number 32. His knock was answered within seconds by a small, young girl in a crimson dress, which was cut as low as possible to reveal her more than adequate charms. Her blonde hair was curled and piled high on her head, secured by a tortoiseshell comb. At the first sight of her visitor she held the door wide and curtsied as he entered the hall.

Buxton did not look at her as he placed hat, gloves and cane on the side table. 'Tell your mistress I am here.'

With a 'Yes, sir' the girl hurried away as fast as the thin length of gold chain linking her ankles would allow.

Buxton was standing before the gilt-framed mirror, brushing dust and specks of soot from the shoulders of his coat, when the mistress of the house answered his summons.

Maxine Brandside was a tall, slender woman in her mid-thirties. Her black hair was cropped and her long deep-purple dress severely cut. She wore no jewellery or make-up. The first lines, thin as spiders' threads, had begun etching the corners of her eyes and mouth but in a way that added extra character to her beauty. Her eyes were as dark as coal and never showed the slightest intimation of her thoughts. When she smiled she displayed perfect teeth, so even and white that they seemed to sparkle in the candlelight. When she

2

spoke her voice was soft and eager, as if the man before her was the only man in the whole world.

'Richard. How good to see you again. I was beginning to think you were not coming. Come with me; there is something about your manner which tells me you need a drink.'

Buxton followed her along the hall and through double doors into a large, square room, sumptuously furnished in the French style with red velvet chairs and sofas and ornately gilded marble-topped tables. The flock-papered walls were festooned with gilt-framed landscapes and seaviews, except for one across which hung a ceiling-to-floor curtain.

Buxton settled himself in a corner of one of the sofas beside the marble fireplace. Maxine went to a sideboard which occupied half the length of one wall, and upon which were arrayed bottles, decanters and glasses.

'Champagne?'

'Brandy,' he replied. 'And don't mind the measure.'

She poured several fingers of Cognac into a glass for her guest and a tulip of champagne for herself. She handed him his glass before settling herself in the chair opposite. Buxton downed half the fiery liquid in one synchronised movement of hand and head.

'Better now?' Maxine enquired as he lowered the glass.

'It will take more than all the bottles of brandy you have in the house, and even all the girls too, to make me feel better,' Buxton replied gloomily.

'You are welcome to both, Richard, you know that. You are more than just another client to me; you are a friend. What has put you in such an ill temper?'

Buxton took another gulp of brandy. 'My father. Isn't it always my father?'

3

Maxine smiled. 'Don't tell me, let me guess. You are a wastrel. A libertine. You are a disgrace to the family. It is time you grew up and accepted responsibilities. When he was your age he –'

Buxton too allowed the smallest of smiles to twitch the corners of his lips as he completed the sentence for her.

'When he was my age he already owned two mills and was a partner in his first coal mine. He worked from six in the morning till twelve at night. He saved and invested his money. But then, of course, he didn't have an allowance like me. Only two years' schooling, before being sent out to work on the carrier's wagon. But by the time he was eighteen he had six wagons of his own, and five grown men working for him.'

Buxton paused to empty his glass and Maxine went to the sideboard and returned with the bottle, which she placed on the table beside the sofa. Buxton filled half his glass. He was beginning to relax now in the warmth of the brandy, the heat from the fire and the presence of his friend. He sat further back on the sofa, stretched out his legs and gazed at the ceiling.

'Had it been the same old litany, I would not have minded. It is a game we have played for years. He rants and raves and vents his spleen. I stand humbly and admit that I have failed him, but that I will mend my ways. He mellows and I touch him for some more of the old wherewithall. But not this time. This time it was serious and there was no moving him. I am to be married.'

Maxine could not suppress her laughter. She could imagine no man more unsuited to the constraints of holy wedlock than Richard Buxton.

'Married! You Richard? I somehow cannot picture you sitting beside the hearth and bouncing your son and heir on your knee. So does your father have any suggestions as to who the unlucky bride should be?'

'More than suggestions. It is already arranged. I am to marry the Honourable Lady Clarissa Fitzhumphreys, no less.'

'And what is the Honourable Lady Clarissa Fitzhumphreys like, may I ask?'

'Eighteen and never been kissed. I have only met her the once, just briefly at a party a few months ago, but she came across as wetter than the Thames at high tide. Pretty enough, I'll give her that, but terribly shy and dull. The thing is her father's a bloody Earl, the tenth Earl of Brackenhurst, no less. Family tree the size of Hyde Park, but poorer than a church mouse. She's got three older brothers you see. The heir is concentrating on gambling away what's left in the family coffers in every gentlemen's club in London that will still let him through the door. The second son is in the army where, apparently, his mess bills always exceed his allowance, and the youngest son is a rector in some God-forsaken parish up north, where the stipend doesn't allow an Earl's son to live in the style to which he was once accustomed.'

'And if there is one thing your father does have it's money, and an eligible son and heir,' commented Maxine.

'Absolutely right. He might be rolling in money but he has no pedigree, no social standing, you understand. For all his millions he is, and always will be, the son of a farrier. But marry into the family of an Earl who can trace his lineage back to Hastings, and suddenly he becomes more acceptable in the circles he wishes to move in. As a member of the family, the good Earl of Brackenhurst will open doors for him after, naturally, my father has cleared his debts.'

Maxine leaned over and took his hands in hers. 'Richard, it's not the end of the world. Wed her, bed

5

her and leave her to run the house. You can continue then as you do now.'

Buxton shook his head. 'If that was possible I wouldn't mind. But there's a catch. The Earl is giving his daughter a dowry. A rundown pile in the wilds of Essex called Castleleigh. My father insists I go and live there and take on the responsibilities of squiredom. Apparently, it will make a man of me. If I don't, he'll cut me off without a penny, and this time he means it. He likes the idea of his son being a Lord of the Manor. Can you imagine it? Me having the parson to dinner, worrying about yields of corn or barley or whatever, and sitting on the magistrates' bench?'

Maxine looked at him thoughtfully for a moment and then stood up, still holding his hands so that he had to follow.

'No, Richard, I cannot imagine you as some rosy-cheeked country Squire. But I do not have to imagine what will drive such images from your mind for tonight at least.'

She led him to the far wall and pulled the sash of the curtain which covered it. The drapes swished back to reveal not paper or panelling, but a mirror. A mirror in which they could not see themselves, only the two people in the room beyond.

The girl was kneeling on the bed. Her wrists were cuffed together and from the thick leather which bound them a chain rose to the ceiling. Her legs were splayed as far apart as possible. Her chestnut hair spilled over her shoulders, her breasts were large but firm, the nipples jutting proud and stiff. Her stomach was smooth and no hair disfigured or hid her sex. She knelt, suspended and helpless, staring at her reflection in the mirror at the head of the bed and, unknowingly, directly into the faces of the two who watched in the adjoining room.

The man was in his fifties. He was tall and, in his youth, must have been strong, but the muscles had long since turned to flab and his belly drooped down to the point where it almost obscured his erection. In his right hand he held a tightly tied bundle of birch twigs. Buxton and his host watched as he put down the glass of champagne he had been sipping when the curtains were drawn back and returned to flogging the girl.

'He's a Member of Parliament. One of the leading advocates for clearing the city streets of prostitutes, and very outspoken about the need for moral reform,' Maxine informed Buxton as she slid back a small grill beside the mirror so that they could both hear, as well as see, what was happening.

The birch whistled through the air landing with all the man's strength on the girl's buttocks. She cried out and swung forward on her chain. Her eyes were shut tight and her mouth opened wide as she gulped in air while she waited for the next blow. It was not long in coming. The man wielded the birch with practised efficiency. Now across the back of her legs, now the buttocks, now ripping into the skin of her back, now her shoulders, and then back to her legs and buttocks.

The girl screamed with every blow and sweat began to pour down her face and stream from her armpits, cascading down her breasts and falling like teardrops from her straining nipples. And, as the ferocity of the beating gained momentum, so did the rhythmic swaying of her body. Forwards, backwards, side to side, she moved as far as the constraints of the chain would allow. Her glazed eyes were fixed on her own reflection in the mirror. She stopped crying out with the pain that each swish of the birch brought, and began to pant and shake like an animal on heat. Her voice was hoarse, her tone desperate.

'Please, Master. Please, Master. Please, kind Master. Please . . .'

The man threw the birch aside. He clambered on to the bed, lifted the girl's right leg and slid beneath her, positioning his erection directly beneath the moist and swollen lips of her sex. With a look of the purest joy on her face the girl sank slowly down on to him. She rotated her hips as she rose and fell, gently at first and then with increasing speed and vigour. The man gasped and the girl screamed, but it was not the scream of pain of a few minutes before, rather an outpouring of total ecstasy.

Maxine pulled the sash and the curtains closed. She ran her hand down the front of Buxton's trousers, cupping them over the bulge which distended the cloth.

Buxton smiled and turned to her. 'A nice little filly. Why have you never introduced us?'

Maxine gently stroked the bulge, which grew and strained further against the fabric with every caress.

'She enjoys it all just a little too much for your taste, I think, Richard. And she comes so quickly you would find no sport in her at all. I keep her for my older, less physically demanding clients.'

'So, what have you got planned for me tonight, Maxine? If I am to forget for a while the trials of the day, it will need to be something special.'

Maxine ran her hand up Buxton's trousers and over his chest until her fingers were stroking his cheek.

'Her name is Violet. I have been saving her especially for you. I acquired her a couple of months ago and I have been training her myself. She is coming along nicely. She vows she will do anything for love of me. But tonight will be the biggest, and hardest, test she has yet faced.'

Buxton took her hand from his cheek, kissing her lightly on the lips as he did so. 'Then let us not keep the lovely Violet waiting any longer. Lead on.'

They walked side by side into the hall, up the staircase and along a corridor. Muffled cries of pleasure and pain escaped from the rooms they passed, but there was no noise from the one at the far end of the passage.

Violet sat on the edge of the bed and stared at the candle, which had melted down almost to the stick. She did not know how long she had sat there, waiting. There were no clocks in the room and, even if there had been, she would have been unable to see them, for the dying candle cast only the very smallest pool of light. It had been late afternoon when she had been summoned and, she reckoned, it must now be about nine or even ten, but she had no way of telling for sure. She had been told to sit and wait, and so she was sitting and waiting; waiting for whatever the night would bring. The flickering stub of the candle would not last much longer, and then she would be alone in the darkness. Violet was scared by the thought, but though there were oil lamps in the room she dared not light them, for she feared the punishment such an act would bring even more than she feared the dark. All she could be certain of was that, eventually, her mistress would arrive, and the thought made her both excited and afraid.

Violet's parents could hardly have picked a less appropriate name for their daughter. She had luxurious red hair which tumbled to her shoulders, framing a freckled, elfin face that was exquisitely pretty. She was barely five feet tall and though her body was slim to the point of thinness, her small but perfectly formed breasts pushed enticingly against the tight confines of her blouse. In addition to her white blouse she wore an ankle-length black skirt from beneath the hem of which protruded two dainty black-stockinged feet.

She looked up as the door opened and light from the corridor flooded the room. Then, remembering what she had been taught, immediately cast her eyes down and stared at the floor. Her heart leapt with delight that her mistress had returned at last. But then, she realised, her mistress was not alone.

Maxine closed the door and lit the oil lamps before speaking.

'Stand up, Violet. Let us look at you.'

Obediently Violet rose, but still kept her gaze fixed on the carpet. She felt a strong hand under her chin, lifting her head, forcing her to look into the face of her mistress's companion. She shrank back as Buxton's pitiless eyes stared into hers. A man! What could her mistress be thinking of, bringing a man here?

'Delightful, my dear. Absolutely delightful. I congratulate you,' said Buxton, releasing his grip and strolling round her, appraising her as he might a thoroughbred at the yearly sales.

Violet looked uncertainly at her mistress. She had been waiting eagerly for her mistress to return. She had been told tonight would be special, that she would be able to provide new services for her mistress. The past hours had been spent in anticipating, half hopefully, half fearfully, what those services would be. But she had expected her mistress to return alone and now she was confused.

Maxine addressed her sternly. 'As I am your mistress, so this man is now your master. You will do everything and anything he commands. I have instructed you in the pleasures and pain of obedience and disobedience, but there is still much you need to

10

learn, and your master will help teach you. Do you understand?'

She could only look at the floor and mumble 'Yes, Mistress'.

Her mistress's voice cracked like a whip. 'Louder, girl. Louder.'

'Yes, Mistress,' she almost shouted.

Buxton again raised her head and then bent down and brushed his tongue along the line of her lips. She shuddered at his touch, but dared not try to resist.

'I wonder if the rest of you tastes as sweet,' he mused aloud as he let go of her and stepped back.

'Take off your blouse,' he commanded.

Violet hesitated, looking questioningly at her mistress. Maxine merely took two paces forward, raised her arm and sent the back of her hand smashing into the girl's cheek. Violet cried out and staggered back, almost losing her balance and falling on to the bed.

Her mistress's voice was the temperature of icicles and her stare would have sliced steel.

'This is the last time I will tell you. Have you learned nothing? Obedience is all. Disobey your master and you insult me.'

With trembling fingers she fumbled the buttons in her haste to undo them. She tugged her blouse from the waistband of her skirt and slid it off her shoulders. She looked from her mistress to her new master as she held the thin cotton in her hands, her arms crossed to hide her naked breasts, uncertain what to do next.

Buxton answered her unspoken question. 'Throw the blouse on the bed, Violet, and stand up straight with your hands on top of your head.'

She did as she was told. Eyes cast down, she waited nervously for her next instruction.

Buxton placed a hand over each breast and gently rotated her small, ginger-ringed nipples with his

11

palms. His hands moved slowly downwards, stroking across her stomach and then he walked behind her and firmly, but not uncomfortably, massaged her shoulders and back.

'Good muscle tone,' he observed. 'She'll bear the whip well, that's for sure. Remove your skirt.'

Violet had expected the order and this time she did not hesitate to comply. She had never stood naked in front of a man before. Only once, many months before she had met Maxine Brandside, had she known sex with a man. Starving and living in a basement hovel, she had sold herself for a shilling to a drunkard who had accosted her outside a public house. He had led her to an alleyway and taken her roughly on the cobbles, tossing his payment into the gutter as he adjusted his clothing and walked away. She had felt what a man aroused was like, but she had never actually seen one excited. Now, standing in the centre of the room, unbuttoning her skirt as this stranger watched, she felt more ashamed and humiliated than she had ever felt that night.

Yet, there was also a different sensation building inside her. A kind of fluttering in the pit of her stomach was tingeing her embarrassment with excitement. She was conscious that her mistress too was watching, and she would do anything to please her mistress. The skirt slid to the floor and she stepped out of it. Dressed only in knee-high black woollen stockings, she shivered with fear as she waited.

Her master, for that was how she was now coming to think of him, traced his index finger along a line from navel to the small, but thick, triangle of red pubic hair. He looked at her trim, lithe body as he spoke to her mistress.

'Not shaved I see.'
'You disapprove?'

'On the contrary. To remove such beautiful red curls would be a sin.'

He reached out and once again pulled her head up and back so that he could look directly into her eyes.

'I wish to see you serve your mistress. On your knees and let that tongue of yours put a shine on her boots.'

Quickly, almost gratefully, she sank to all fours and crawled the two yards to where her mistress stood.

'Open your legs,' the man commanded and, obediently, she did so.

'Wider. As wide as they'll go.'

She spread her legs as far apart as she could, conscious that, with her face pressed against her mistress's feet, and her buttocks raised, her sex was fully displayed for her new master's scrutiny.

'Get on with it.'

She began to lick the knee-high leather boots. She had done this before. It was a sign that she agreed to her servitude. She enjoyed doing it because it demonstrated that she was obedient. But this time, a man was watching who could see into every part of her body. She was sucking her mistress's right heel when the next command came.

'Stand up.'

Violet stood.

'Turn round.'

She turned.

Buxton had removed all his clothes and now stood facing her. She gasped as she looked at him, unable to tear her gaze from the massive, throbbing, cock which thrust proudly towards her. The man seemed amused.

'Don't try to tell me you've never seen one before.' He beckoned her forward. 'No? Well, we will have to get you better acquainted, shan't we? Kneel.'

Once again she sank to her knees, her face hardly an inch from him.

'Lick.'

He held his erection so it was level with her mouth. Tentatively she poked out her tongue until it touched the tip and began licking the area round the slit in the swollen head.

'Open wide.'

She parted her lips and he slid into her mouth. She gagged involuntarily as he pushed towards the back of her throat.

'Suck.'

She began to suck, instinctively moving her head backwards and forwards along the shaft between her lips. The taste was of salt and sweat but not, she decided, unpleasant. The flutterings inside her intensified and she felt her juices beginning to flow in the same way as they did when she pleased her mistress.

'Perhaps some encouragement?' he queried, and in almost the same moment there came the crack of leather as the lash scored a vivid red line diagonally down her back. Unable to scream, she involuntarily fell forward as the whip tore into her, impaling her throat on her master's manhood. Tears stung her eyes as the searing pain of the unexpected punishment tore through her body. She drew her head back and resumed sucking the monster organ which filled her mouth, her body tense as she waited for another blow.

Once more, the thin leather slashed across the small of her back, but not for an instant did she stop sucking. She compressed her lips as tightly as she could around the shaft, her tongue tantalising its entire length. She brought up her right hand and began, ever so gently, to stroke and massage his balls and then rub the base of his penis. The lash landed again, cutting into her buttocks and then the top of her thighs. Her back was on fire from the severity of the whipping, but so too was every nerve in her body, and she felt the trickle of her juices merge into a river that flowed down the insides of her thighs.

'She learns quickly,' Buxton remarked approvingly as he placed both hands behind her head. With his fingers tightly gripping her hair he began to push in and out of her mouth with the power of a piston.

Suddenly, she felt the rod filling her mouth jerk and the first explosion of cream hit the back of her throat. She tried to pull her head away but his grip made that impossible. She choked as the thick, salty liquid forced itself down her throat, and she was made to swallow spurt after spurt until she feared she would drown.

It seemed an eternity before he finally withdrew, wiping the last drops of come across her lips as he did so. She sank to all fours and retched.

'Bring any up and I'll make you lick it off the carpet,' she heard her mistress say and, somehow, she managed to keep the cream inside her, except for a thin sliver which dribbled from the corner of her mouth and ran down her chin.

The man towering above her spoke again. 'You have pleased me. Now it is time to please your mistress once again. Get on the bed.'

She turned and, still on hands and knees, crept towards the bed, where her mistress lay naked, legs apart and knees raised. She climbed on to the bed, positioned herself between her mistress's legs, and lowered her head. She did not need to be told what to do. This was what she had been longing for during all those lonely, gloom-filled hours. Feverishly, her tongue darted inside her mistress's sex, pausing only occasionally when she raised her head and gently

15

licked and nibbled the swollen clit. Her mistress's body rose and fell and swayed from side to side in rhythm with the sensations pulsing through her.

Out of the corner of her eye she saw her new master select a thin willow cane from the selection of instruments laid out on the table. She tensed as she saw him raise his arm. He brought the thin cane down across her buttocks with every ounce of his considerable strength. Her face buried in her mistress's sex, and her head clamped securely between powerful thighs, meant she could not scream or cry out.

He slashed again, this time leaving a second red line exactly one-quarter of an inch below the first. Clearly pleased with his marksmanship, he repeated the process until she felt as if her buttocks were on fire.

The stinging of the cane hurt even more than the cutting of the whip. Tears filled her eyes and ran down her cheeks to converge with the moisture oozing from her mistress's sex. After twelve powerful strokes of the cane he tossed it aside. She could see that, doubtless because of the sight of the two women and the exercise he had just enjoyed, he was fully erect again. He positioned himself directly behind her and drove his full length into her, until his balls were hard against her pubic hair.

Her eyes opened wide at the sudden, brutal invasion of her body. She felt as if she were being split apart and feared that this monstrous thing inside her would tear her in two. But now her juices were flowing uncontrollably, lubricating her passage and easing the pain, while her muscles stretched to accommodate, and then constricted to clamp, the intruder.

Ruthlessly he rammed into her, and the greater his force, the more urgent the sensation inside her

16

became. It seemed to fill all her senses until there was no yesterday or tomorrow nor even today, only long seconds filled with the sensations climaxing within.

Maxine's whole body quivered as she came. In the same instant, Buxton let loose, gasping as he shot jet after jet of his seed inside the girl. She reached her own peak and would also have cried aloud had she not been drinking the rich-tasting waters gushing from her mistress.

There were a few moments' silence, as each regained their breath and let the sensations subside, before her master withdrew and her mistress relaxed her thighs and released her grip. While they dressed she remained kneeling on the bed, waiting for instructions as her master's spunk dropped from her and stained the counterpane.

At last, her mistress condescended to address her. She looked at the weals down her back, the lines across her buttocks and the damp patch on the counterpane between her legs and smiled.

'You did well, Violet. You have served your first master and you have pleased me. You may go to bed now. I have no further use for you tonight.'

Buxton did not speak until he was once again lounging on the sofa in the salon, brandy glass in one hand and cigar in the other.

'A fitting farewell to the pleasures of London,' he remarked. 'Who knows when I shall be able to enjoy them again.'

Maxine settled herself next to him and ran her fingers tenderly through his hair.

'You will find a way, Richard. If there is one thing I am certain of it is that you are quite unable to forsake the delights this house provides.'

'And the pleasure of your company, Maxine. Don't forget that. You are the one person I know who not only understands, but also enjoys, my particular tastes and requirements. Yes, somehow I will find a way to return. But when or how I do not know. In just over one month, I shall be married and the Squire of Castleleigh.'

Maxine laid a comforting arm round his shoulders. 'None of us can foretell the future, Richard. Who knows, perhaps Castleleigh will bring you much more than, at the moment, you could ever imagine.'

Buxton sighed. 'Yes. Who knows?' He raised his glass. 'Here's to Castleleigh.'

Two

Clarissa awoke as the first thin shafts of sunlight slanted through the gap between the heavy velvet curtains. She lay still, staring at the ceiling as the dawn gradually pushed back the darkness of the night. Beside her, she felt Richard stir in his sleep and, careful not to disturb him, gently ran the back of her hand along his thigh. Was it really only yesterday that the very thought of such an action, even the idea that she should lie naked next to a man, would have disgusted her? In a few short hours she had crossed the threshold from childhood to womanhood and now, as she recalled all that had happened, she once again relished the transition.

Although she had dimly recalled the name Richard Buxton as someone she had met fleetingly at a party in London some months before, they had not been formally introduced until after her father had informed her that she was to become his wife. The Earl had been totally honest with her because he expected, and received, no argument. The family was in dire need of money and, though he regretted that she would be marrying out of her class, there was no alternative. There were her brothers and the estates to consider, and what these new industrialists lacked in breeding and manners they compensated for with wealth. And so it had been decided. Together with his father, a stocky, swarthy man with a rough voice and awkward graces, to whom Clarissa had taken an instant dislike, Buxton had visited the family seat at Brackenhurst where the engagement was officially announced. He had been polite, but cold and distant, and had left as soon as possible after the formalities had been completed. She had not seen him again until her father had led her up the aisle of the village church at Castleleigh and she had found herself standing before the altar beside the man she had promised to comfort, honour and obey for the rest of her life.

Her brother Oliver had conducted the service, much to the obvious chagrin of the Reverend Pimms, the local vicar. Throughout the service, Buxton had had an air about him more in keeping with a prisoner stoically accepting his sentence than a groom eager to enter a new life of matrimony. After the service, they had returned to The Hall for the wedding breakfast.

The party which seated itself around the table was small, just her, her parents, Richard's parents, his brother Peter, who had acted as his best man, and her brother Oliver. Lucy, her personal maid who had followed her down the aisle and held her flowers was not, of course, allowed to join the family at table. It was a sober, almost sad gathering, more suited to a funeral than a wedding. It was nothing like the wedding Clarissa had always dreamed of. She had imagined a cathedral, or at least a minster, filled with all her family and friends. She had cherished a vision of herself in a white satin gown trailing yards of lace behind her, and of being escorted by numerous bridesmaids and page-boys. The wedding dinner she had always expected to be held in the magnificent dining room at Brackenhurst Court, and after it there would be a grand ball. Then, she and her lover would leave for a long honeymoon in some romantic destination, such as Venice or Rome. Instead, her father had decided that as little fuss as possible should be made about the affair. She appreciated that he felt humiliated by being forced to marry his daughter to the son of a common tradesman, and understood why he did not wish his friends, and the rest of the Brackenhurst family, to witness his humiliation. Also, despite the loans secured from Richard's father, the Earl remained as penny-pinching as ever. Denied the wedding of her dreams, she was also not to enjoy the romance-filled holiday she had always wanted, but immediately assume her role as the mistress of the house.

After the meal, which comprised in the main merely a selection of roast meats, overcooked vegetables and stodgy puddings, came the speeches. The Earl spoke of his pleasure at the union, even while he looked disdainfully at his daughter's new father-in-law. Buxton spoke of looking forward to his life as the Squire of Castleleigh, but said nothing about his new wife. At last the meal ended and the women retired, leaving the men to their port and cigars. Her mother and Buxton's made polite conversation, but it was evident to all that there was no real point of contact between them. How could there be? One the wife of an Earl, the other the daughter of a tavern-keeper. As soon as she felt it proper, Clarissa summoned her maid and retired.

As she entered the master bedroom, the nervousness that had made her stomach quiver all day was instantly replaced with a fear which brought sweat to her brow and seemed to sap all the strength from her legs. She stood in the centre of the huge room at a loss as to what to do next. Lucy could barely disguise her amusement.

21

'Would you like me to help you undress and prepare for bed, Madam?'

The girl's words penetrated slowly. Undress? She would have to undress. He would see her undressed. Of course he would. How silly. He was her husband. That was part of being married.

'Yes, thank you, Lucy,' she finally replied and stood, awkward and silent, while her maid unhooked her dress, removed the layers of petticoats and then unlaced the tight corset that pinched her waist while lifting her breasts. While her maid carefully put the clothes away, she pulled on a silk nightshift which covered her body from shoulder to ankle. She sat in front of the ornate dressing table with its three mirrors while Lucy vigorously brushed her long, golden hair.

'I'll be going then now, shall I, Madam?' Lucy said when she had completed her mistress's toilet. Clarissa nodded her assent and heard Lucy stifle a giggle as she left the room.

Why did these common girls always know more about such matters than people like herself? Probably, Clarissa told herself, because they came from overcrowded hovels where privacy was impossible.

Once the door clicked shut behind her maid, Clarissa realised that she had never felt so alone or so frightened. She had no concept of what was to befall her during the coming night. All she knew was that she must obey her husband in all things. She remembered her mother's words of the previous evening when they had sat together in the drawing room. 'When you become a wife you have only two duties. One is to run the house efficiently and the other is to obey your husband. Men have their needs and, however distressing, even repulsive, we may find them, it is the lot of womankind to endure them.

22

When your husband makes demands upon you, you must submit to them. You will not enjoy them because women are not meant to enjoy them. While you yield to his pleasures of the flesh, try to concentrate your mind on higher things. I always found reciting the Psalms in my head very effective.'

When Clarissa had pressed her for more information, her mother had simply shrugged off the questions as not being fit for a lady to ask and had talked instead about the wealth of her husband to be.

After many minutes sitting on the stool, staring at her reflection, she pulled back the richly embroidered quilt and slid between the sheets. Turning down the oil lamp on the table beside the bed she had waited, trembling, for the arrival of her husband. She did not have to wait for long.

The door opened wide and he strode into the bedroom, almost tripping as he did so and banging his knee against a small table. His voice was harsh and she was shaken by his anger.

'Damn it! It's like the Black Hole of Calcutta in here. What are you trying to do? Cripple me?'

He proceeded to light all the lamps in the room. She shrank from their brightness, pulling the sheets further up so that they touched her chin and all that could be seen was her face, framed by her golden hair which spread like a fan across the pillow.

For a few moments he stood beside the bed just looking down at her and then, without a word, he began to undress. She watched him remove his coat, but as he began to pull his shirt over his head, she averted her gaze.

'Well, don't you want to look at your new husband?'

She was not sure whether he was laughing or sneering. She turned her head and looked at the man

23

standing at the side of the bed less than a foot away. She had never seen a naked man before and the sight scared her. She had seen labourers in the fields, stripped to the waist as they toiled to bring in the harvest, but she was totally innocent as to what lay below. She saw the thick mass of curly black hair at the base of his stomach from which protruded a thick penis resting on two testicles which seemed to her as big as cricket balls. She had seen the private parts of dogs and horses on the estate, but somehow it had simply never occurred to her that men were similarly endowed. She felt her cheeks redden at the sight and the realisation but, try as she might, she could not stop staring at them. He bent and threw the quilt aside. His tone was mocking as he regarded the long white shift.

'You look more ready for a funeral than a wedding night. Such attire will impede our pleasures. Remove it if you please.'

At his command, she swung her legs over the edge of the bed, reached down and pulled the shift up over her head, tossing it into the corner and then quickly rolling back, grabbing the quilt and cloaking her nakedness. She shut her eyes tight as she felt and heard him climb into bed beside her. As he reached for her she tried to remember a Psalm and when that failed, a hymn, but no words penetrated the wall of fear that encircled her mind. She simply stayed still and tensed herself to suffer, as bravely as possible, whatever fate had in store.

He lay on his side, his right elbow on the pillow, his head resting on the palm of his hand, and just looked at her for a while before she felt his other hand stroke her hair. His fingers traced the contours of her face before sliding beneath the sheet and coming to rest on her right breast. His hand cupped

24

it as his thumb and forefinger closed on her nipple, gently squeezing and flicking the tender skin.

His breath was hot on her cheek before his face loomed over her and his lips began brushing hers. His arm reached under her head, pulling her tighter to him, and he kissed her roughly, forcing her lips apart and driving his tongue into her mouth. And all the time he continued massaging her breasts, while his fingers tweaked and pulled at her nipple. And then, as his tongue continued to flick and dart within her mouth, his hand left her breast and slid down across the flatness of her stomach to force her legs apart. His fingers toyed with the soft, golden hairs as they prised open the lips and found their target. Two fingers squeezed the secret button at the top of her sex and she shuddered involuntarily as a strange sensation, like a thousand tiny needles, tingled through her body. He brought his arm up only momentarily to sweep sheet and quilt aside before his fingers returned to their task. She shuddered again when he rubbed his fingers up and down between the slowly swelling lips of her sex and then her whole body jerked as first one finger and then another slid inside her. His mouth left hers and his tongue traced the line of her neck until his lips encircled the top of her breast and his teeth began teasing a nipple that was now gorged and erect. And all the time his fingers drove backwards and forwards, while his thumb flicked at her clit, each contact sending shock waves rippling through her entire being.

The tenseness slowly ebbed from her body, and with it went fear. Her head spun as her senses reeled under the torrent of new sensations that threatened to drown her. She still trembled, but now not from fright but from delight. She felt herself grow wetter and wetter as his fingers pushed ever more forcefully in and out, and instictively she spread her legs as wide as possible.

And then he raised his head, withdrew his hand and smiled down at her. She looked up at him, studying his expression, trying to discover whether something she had done had caused him to stop.

'What's good for the goose . . .'

He left the saying unfinished, simply taking her hand and placing it at the base of his stomach. Her fingers closed around his erection and for a moment her old fears returned. Surely, nothing could be this large, and this rigid, and not contain a bone. Then his lips were once again hard against hers, their tongues entwined and all she cared about was pleasing him and being submerged by these wonderful feelings she had never even dreamed existed.

She held his manhood gently but firmly, massaging the throbbing shaft from base to tip. His breathing quickened and a small moan of pleasure escaped his lips as he brushed her arm aside and rolled on top of her. She felt the tip of his cock push aside the thickened lips guarding her sex before he thrust inside her. She cried out with the pain as he rammed into her body and destroyed her virginity. But as he began to move, slowly at first, and then with increasing urgency, the pain disappeared, to be replaced by a deep inner fire spraying sparks of pure delight to every part of her body. Suddenly his movements quickened still further and then his body tensed. And, in that same moment, her whole being seemed to disintegrate and she almost fainted as her senses exploded.

Panting, he withdrew and lay beside her and she held him close, her head on his chest, her arm across his stomach, and wondered how anyone could have thought what had just happened was something which had to be endured but never enjoyed. It had been the most marvellous experience of her entire life, and for the first time in her life she felt totally contented and at peace with herself and the world. Idly, her tongue licked his nipple.

'And I thought I was going to bed with an icicle. 'Tis true, what they say.'

She replied without stopping the work of her tongue. She found she liked the salty, sweaty taste and the obvious pleasure it was giving her husband.

'And what do they say?'

He laughed. 'Scratch a Duchess and you'll find a whore.'

She pulled back at that and sat upright, looking at him indignantly. She was not accustomed to such language.

'I am not a whore! You cannot think me so!'

He sat up too and put his arm round her shoulder.

'Of course you're not. You enjoyed it. Whores rarely do.'

She was confused, upset. Surely he had never . . .?

'Richard, you have not been with a whore, have you?'

He laughed. 'What a question for a wife to ask her husband on his wedding night! It matters not what may, or may not, have happened before. Only what happens afterwards.'

He looked down at the stains on the sheet and grinned. 'They'll have a fine time with those in the laundry tomorrow.'

She blushed, not knowing what to say, but he just pulled her closer, saying, 'We might as well give them some more to talk about.'

With that he kissed her as his hands once again explored her body. She responded by reaching for him and felt a strange satisfaction as he grew proud within her grasp. But when she expected him to take her as before he just shook his head, saying, 'Now it is time for you to do the work.'

He pulled her above him, so she knelt with her knees against his thighs, his erection just touching her sex lips. She gradually sank on to him. As she lowered herself, engulfing his manhood until the cheeks of her bottom were bearing hard against his balls, she felt as if the world could not possibly offer greater pleasure. She rode up and down, slowly at first and then ever more rapidly as the heat within her grew fiercer. He just lay back, hands behind his head, watching her breasts rise and fall. Their cries and their climaxes coincided and afterwards she snuggled beside him and drifted into a dreamless sleep of total contentment.

Clarissa slid from between the sheets and, drawing back the curtains, let the early morning sun bathe her body. The memories of the previous night were making her moist and recreating that delicious fluttering deep inside which she had experienced for the first time just a few short hours before. She ran a hand over her breasts, allowing the palm to rotate each nipple in turn as it passed, before gliding on downwards until her fingers brushed the golden thatch and then slid between her legs. In all her eighteen years she had only ever touched herself there when washing. Her nanny had told her it was an offence against God to do anything else. She smiled as she rubbed harder. Her mother and her nanny knew nothing. Such beautiful sensations could never be ungodly.

She heard the bedclothes rustle and the springs creak and then he was standing behind her and she turned, arms wide to embrace him, lips parted to receive his kiss.

Buxton had been awake for several minutes but had stayed silent, content to watch his wife stand at the window playing with herself. She really was very beautiful. Freed from the tight bun in which fashion dictated it be kept, her pale-yellow hair lapped her slim, cream-white shoulders. Her breasts were full and well rounded, and her buttocks were tight globes crowning long, slender legs. He might not have wanted a wife, any wife, but if he had to be married then, he had to admit, he could have fared worse than Clarissa. Given her responses to his advances the night before, perhaps very much worse.

It had not been his intention to be so kind and considerate. That had been a decision taken on whim, and it had proved the correct choice. Angry at being forced to marry, bored by the company of his father and the Earl, he had entered the bedchamber with every intention of venting his feelings on his unwelcome bride. He had intended to make her wedding night an occasion she would remember with pain rather than pleasure. But when he had seen her lying with the sheet pulled to her chin, her body stiff with fear, he had realised that simply to force himself on her as planned would have produced little pleasure. Was there, he had wondered, a fire ready to be kindled, a passion waiting to be released? The real challenge, he had decided, was to discover if there was more to this seemingly innocent and frigid virgin than first appearances suggested.

And so he had decided on the gentle, caring approach, and employed all the techniques acquired over many years in his attempts to melt this ice maiden. And they had worked far better than he could have hoped. Here was someone who, having discovered the delights of sex, would, he was sure, not just develop a taste for them, but an addiction. He would be her teacher and her master and her schooling would start right away.

He stood behind her and she turned, her arms encircling his waist, her mouth moving towards his. He allowed the embrace but avoided her lips. He looked down into her face and smiled as he chided her.

'You were a very naughty girl last night.'

She laughed a high-pitched, carefree laugh. 'Was I?'

He nodded. 'Indeed you were. And do you know what happens to naughty little girls?'

She tried to pull him closer, but he resisted.

'No, husband dear. What does happen to naughty little girls?'

Buxton stepped backwards, breaking her hold, and at the same time he grabbed her wrist and threw her forward to land face down on the bed. Suddenly alarmed, Clarissa tried to rise but his hand pushed into the centre of her back, preventing any movement.

'They get spanked,' he replied, and brought the palm of his free hand smashing down to land with a satisfying thwack in the centre of the globes he had so admired a few minutes before. Clarissa cried out at the unexpected blow, but hardly had she done so before he struck again, then again and again and again, until she began to believe the beating would never end. Tears stung her eyes and she gasped at each smack. She tried to squirm away from him, but he only pushed her further into the quilt, squashing her breasts and making breathing more difficult.

After ten expertly applied smacks, Buxton paused to admire his handiwork. His wife's cheeks, previously so white and spotless, were now inflamed, the impression of his fingers showing clearly against the red blush. He forced his hand between her legs and, without preamble or warning, rammed three fingers into her now dry and tight sex. She screamed at the unexpected violation and the tears began to run unheeded down her face. He withdrew his fingers, but only so that he could spank her again. After a further six, he once again probed her sex. He smiled at what he found. The bitch was beginning to enjoy it. Her body was responding involuntarily to both the pain and pleasure. He delivered several more stinging slaps and then released his hold. Clarissa tried to rise but he simply put his hands beneath her body and flipped her on to her back. Her tear-streaked face was flushed and her nipples stood throbbingly erect. She reached up towards him but he brushed her arms aside. Kneeling, he grasped her long legs, throwing one over each of his shoulders, before bearing down on her, bending her almost double so that her sex pointed at the ceiling. Without a word he drove into her with every ounce of his strength. Clarissa screamed at the pain of his invasion and the discomfort of the position that left her incapable of movement; totally helpless to prevent whatever he might wish to do to her. The gentle, coaxing husband of the previous night had gone. In his place was a dominant, demanding man intent only on his own satisfaction. His actions became quicker and even more forceful before he began spurting inside her, closing his eyes as the pleasure rippled through his body. But, no sooner had he finished than he withdrew, pushed his wife away from him and got off the bed.

'I have decided to tour the estate today,' he told her coldly. 'I do not know when I shall return. Just be sure you are waiting for me when I do.'

So saying, Buxton strode into the adjoining dressing room without a backward glance.

Three

Buxton did not return to the bedroom. As soon as he had washed and dressed he went straight to the stables and ordered his horse saddled. The groom, surprised to see the master of the house abroad at such an early hour, hurried to obey and within a few minutes he was astride Corsair, the proud, high-headed, thoroughbred stallion only he could command.

Soon the wedding party would be rising, and he had no wish to meet them. He found Clarissa's parents supercilious and boring, and he was still angry at his own for forcing him into marriage. Her brother Oliver he regarded contemptuously as just a fat fool of a parson and his own younger brother, Peter, as a poor, spineless excuse for a man because he lived in total awe of their father and seemed to have no thoughts or opinions of his own. The prospect of facing them all around the breakfast table appalled him. He knew that the coaches would be leaving early to take them to the railway station in Colchester for the midday train back to London, and he had no intention of hanging around the house just to stand on the steps and wave them farewell. As far as he was concerned, the sooner all of them were out of his life, the better.

As he walked Corsair down the path from the stables he had a magnificent view of the house and grounds and savoured the realisation that now everything he could see belonged to him. The Hall itself dated from Jacobean times and comprised a three-floor central block flanked at each end by two-storey wings. It was an imposing edifice but much in need of restoration and refurbishment. With his money, he could transform it back into a grand house that would be the envy of all his neighbours. Immediately behind the house was a small area of formal gardens from which the land flowed into a rolling parkscape created by the great Capability Brown himself. Gardens and grounds also needed much attention and he would see that they received the very best. He might only be a Squire, but he intended to live like a Lord. He trotted down the long, narrow, straight driveway beneath the rows of ancient elms, passed through the gates and headed for the village of Castleleigh.

It was a warm June morning and he felt a strange peacefulness, almost contentment, as he followed the twisting cart track of a lane. Perhaps it was the pleasures he had just enjoyed, and the realisations about his wife they had brought, or maybe it was that every field and cottage he passed was his. It was intoxicating to know that he wielded complete power over the lives of those who worked his land and lived in his properties.

As he rode, he considered for the first time how he should conduct himself in his new role of Squire. He thought back over the experiences of the previous night. He had gained more by playing, at least initially, the considerate, loving husband than he would have done by following his natural passions. Perhaps he should adopt the same, thoughtful, approach to being Lord of the Manor. He cared nothing for the villagers and farm-workers with their miserable little lives, but it might be that more could be gained by creating the impression that here was a benefactor rather than an ogre. The velvet glove hiding the fist of steel. It was an idea well worth considering. He would decide after he had seen, at close quarters, what the local yokels were made of.

Castleleigh was a scrawny excuse for a village. It squatted on the summit of a small hill and had only a single main road. On one side of the road was the village green and beyond that the parish church standing in the centre of an unkept churchyard where the rain-smoothed stones tilted like rows of rotten teeth, many barely visible among the jungle of brambles and weeds. The chimneys of the vicarage could just be glimpsed above the pines which lined the driveway behind the church. At each end of the green were rows of dilapidated cottages, while across the road, facing the church, were several larger houses with, in their centre, the Brackenhurst Arms, the village's only inn. From the main road several narrow lanes meandered between terraces of tiny cottages before petering out into the encircling fields.

Buxton reined in his horse on the corner of the green and looked around. Castleleigh seemed deserted. The farm-workers would already be at their labours, their wives would be attending to their daily chores and the inn would not open before midday. A horse was tethered outside the smithy in the corner of the green. Its impatient snorting, and the rhythmic clanging of iron on steel which rang from the darkness within, were the only evidence of life.

Realising that there was little profit in viewing Castleleigh that morning, Buxton decided to tour the estate itself and see how his tenants reacted to the unannounced appearance of their new master.

He had only arrived at The Hall two days before, so the terrain was new to him, but he had taken the opportunity to study some maps of the estate and so gained a fair knowledge of where his properties lay. He decided to head first for the largest of these, Home Farm.

Home Farm comprised some one hundred acres adjoining the grounds of The Hall. Buxton trotted the half-mile from the village but slowed Corsair to a walk as he turned into the track leading to the farmhouse. Cornfields stretched away on either side, the crop almost ready for harvesting. Half a dozen men were working in the fields and stopped to watch him pass. An unseen dog barked as he entered the farmyard in front of a modest two-storey stone house. No one arrived to greet him. Buxton tethered his horse to a ring in the farmyard wall and walked towards the cluster of barns some fifty yards behind the house. He was barely a pace from the door of the largest of these when he heard the girl's mocking laugh.

'Don't be silly, John. We can't. Not now. Not here.'

The youth's voice was pleading, impatient. 'Why not? No one will know. Your father is in the kitchen, already deep in his cups. The men are all in the fields. Who's going to know?'

'Wouldn't be right. That's all,' came the girl's half-hearted reply.

'I'll show you what's right.' The youth's strong, confident tone brooked no argument.

Treading as softly as he could, Buxton edged along the side of the barn until he reached one of the cracked, grime-curtained windows. Cautiously, he peered inside. The pair were standing not a dozen feet away but, so engrossed with each other and the urgency of their individual emotions, he felt no fear

36

of being discovered. He rested his arms on the window sill and waited for the show to begin.

Both girl and youth were in their late teens: he tall, broad shouldered and blond; she small, stocky and dark. There was no sophistication to their lovemaking, no pleasantries or any pretence at foreplay. Their needs and desires were too all-consuming for such niceties. The girl sank down on to a heap of straw that had been piled to one side of a stall and simply lifted her long, woollen dress high above her waist. She wore no stockings or undergarments and Buxton smiled approvingly at the strong legs, the muscular thighs and the uncombed, untrimmed black tangle which crowned them. Her face was in shadow, but there was no mistaking the swell of her large breasts pushing against the confines of her tightly laced dress.

As the girl spread herself across the straw, her legs wide, the youth struggled with belt and buttons until he was able to push his breeches to his ankles. He almost fell on top of her in his haste to sample the delights so temptingly being offered. She cried out with pleasure and brought up her knees as he dived straight into her body. Her legs crossed over his buttocks, forcing every inch of him inside her. The youth gasped as he pistoned in and out and the girl panted with every thrust, her fingers tugging at his thick hair as her hips moved to his rapidly quickening tempo.

And then, drowning their cries and gasps, came an angry voice.

'And who in damnation may you be, sir?'

Buxton turned to find a tall, thick-set, red-faced man standing behind him, a heavy cudgel in one hand. Buxton inclined his head in the curtest of bows.

'Richard Buxton of The Hall. And you are?'

'Joshua Dakins, sir,' the man replied, lowering the cudgel. 'This be my farm.'

'Actually, Mr Dakins, I believe it is mine. But, no mind. Come, join me in watching the cabaret.'

Only a few seconds had elapsed but, by the time farmer and Squire had pushed back the door and entered the barn, the girl was already on her feet, frantically trying to smooth down her dress and brush away the tell-tale straw which clung to it. The youth was having much greater difficulty trying to pull up and fasten his trousers. The farmer exploded in rage at the sight and swung his cudgel at the youth's head, but the boy was too quick for him. He ducked under the stick, sidestepped nimbly and, still holding his trousers up with one hand, shoulder charged his would-be assailant. The farmer staggered back against the barn wall and by the time he recovered, the youth was already sprinting away across the fields. Dakins could do nothing but stand in the doorway and hurl threats after the fleeing figure.

'I know you, Billy Jackson! I know you! You ain't heard the last of this. I'll make you pay for it. You see if I don't.'

Dakins turned back and advanced towards the girl, who was standing fearfully with her back pressed against the far corner of the stall.

'And as for you, you cheap little slut. You harlot! You're no better than an animal. But I'll show you. I'll teach you. I'll have the skin off your back before I'm finished.'

Buxton coughed. It was the slightest of sounds, but sufficient to make the irate farmer stop and turn. He looked at the tall, imposing figure of his new Squire and landlord and the sight was enough to momentarily check his rage.

'I'm sorry you should have had to see such a thing, sir. She has brought shame on my house and the

38

name of my family. But, do not worry, I'll see she is properly punished. I promise you that.'

Buxton beckoned the girl forward. Reluctantly she obeyed, stopping in front of him while still keeping as far away from the farmer as possible. It was the first time he had been able to clearly see her face, and he liked what he saw. She had large, deep, dark eyes and her lips were full, with a natural pout. Although she was plainly frightened, she retained an aura of wilfulness which excited him. It would take much to curb her temper and break her spirit. It was a challenge he would relish. He looked from one to the other.

'This, I presume, is your daughter, Mr Dakins.'

'Aye, sir, Rebecca. And a filthy, hot-headed Jezebel she is. But, she'll pay. I'll take my belt to her as soon as you're gone, sir.'

Buxton held the farmer with a fixed, unblinking gaze, until the man could bear it no longer and had to look away.

'Personally, Mr Dakins, I always believe punishment should be applied as soon after the crime as possible. There is never any time like the present. Pray, do not let my presence disturb or detain you.'

The farmer looked from his Squire to his daughter and nodded as he slowly removed the thick leather belt from his trousers and started to curl one end round the knuckles of his right hand.

'Perhaps you is right, sir. No time like now. And she's more likely to remember her punishment if 'tis carried out before her betters.'

The girl searched desperately for an escape route, but the door was the only entrance and exit and Buxton and her father would make sure she never reached it. She began to back away, but her father took two quick paces forward and grabbed the neck

39

of her dress. As she fell forward, he spun her round by her shoulders and pushed her against the wall of the barn. Her dress was fastened at the back by criss-crossed laces, but they were no barrier. Dakins took a penknife from his pocket and slit the cords.

'Father, don't. Please, don't,' the girl cried, as two strong hands tore at the dress. But Dakins was not listening. He wanted to vent his rage and vent his rage he would.

The girl tried to clutch the material as it was roughly torn from her shoulders, but her father held her wrists and the dress slid down to land in crumpled folds around her ankles.

Buxton leaned against the end of a stall, folded his arms and prepared to watch the show. This morning really was turning out better than he could have dared hope. He had a clear view of the girl's rear and admired the power of her back and shoulder muscles, no doubt developed and honed during years of hard toil on the farm. She would be able to take a great deal of punishment, so much more satisfying than so many of the willow-like, fragile town women he had previously enjoyed.

Dakins grabbed a handful of baling twine and roughly tied her hands to one of the pillars supporting the roof. He stepped back and, as he did so, raised the belt and sent the broad, thick leather biting into the girl's back from shoulder to hip. She cried out for him to stop, but his rage made him deaf to any entreaties. He brought the belt down again, this time leaving a wide red band across both her buttocks. Repeatedly he lashed at shoulder, back and buttocks in turn, while the girl writhed and screamed and begged for forgiveness.

Buxton strolled over to a donkey cart in the far corner of the barn, removed the long, supple lash from its holder and presented it to the farmer.

'This may prove more effective,' he suggested. 'And do not forget the seat of lust which caused such disgrace upon yourself and the good name of your family.'

Dakins understood the meaning behind Buxton's words. He untied his daughter from the post, but her freedom was short-lived. He forced her raw back against the pole and this time tied her arms behind it. The girl hung her head and looked away, her tears running like salt streams down her face, unable to hide any part of her body from the unblinking gaze of her father and the Squire.

Buxton had been attracted by the prettiness of her face. He had admired her strong legs and powerful thighs. He had approved of her muscular back and nicely rounded buttocks. Now he was able to appreciate her heavy, but firm, breasts and pert, dark-ringed nipples. All in all, he decided, she had far too much potential for pleasure than could ever be realised on the farm, however many young men from the village she might have. She deserved more sophisticated and experienced tuition. As Squire, it was almost his duty to see that she received it.

Dakins flicked the lash and the girl screamed as it cut into her ample breasts. The next blow landed across the top of her thighs and the third slashed across her stomach just above the tangle of pubic hair which Buxton found so inviting.

Mentally, he could have watched the girl's performance all day. Physically, that was rapidly becoming impossible. His riding breeches were tight and there was an unequal struggle taking place between the natural inclination of a continually hardening cock to expand outwards and the resistance of the perfectly tailored fit of heavy twill. The contest was making him ache and he knew

41

he must act immediately. There was no way he could have the girl. Even her poor excuse for a father would not, whatever his rank, approve of anything so blatant. Which left only one alternative.

'I believe your daughter has been sufficiently chastised and understands what will happen to her should she sin again,' he told Dakins, who was now breathing heavily from his exertions. He dropped the lash and his daughter sighed with relief as her father began to untie her.

'I have urgent business to attend to elsewhere, Mr Dakins. But I shall renew our acquaintance before very long. You may be sure of that.'

'Yes, sir. Thank you, sir. I shall look forward to that, sir.'

Buxton left the barn and walked back to his horse as quickly as the restrictions of his trousers would allow. He winced as he climbed into the saddle. Someone would have to pay for his discomfort. He spurred Corsair to the gallop, not bothering with the lane and the drive but cutting across the fields straight for The Hall. Corsair took ditch and fence in his stride and within a few minutes, Buxton was sliding from the horse's back. He tossed the reins to a gardener tending the lawn and took the steps two at a time.

Buxton burst into the house, startling a maid who was polishing one of the side tables. The maid curtsied and, at any other time, he might have paused to appraise her. But not now. Not when his blood felt on fire.

'Where can I find your mistress?' he demanded.

'I . . . I . . . I do not know, sir,' the maid stammered, frightened by the urgency in his voice.

At that moment, Buxton saw Lucy standing on the landing at the turn of the grand staircase. He leaped up the first flight and grabbed his wife's maid by the shoulders.

'Where is your mistress?' he repeated.

'Why, sir, in bed, sir,' Lucy answered.

'Bed? At this hour?'

'She said she was tired, sir, and was not to be disturbed till luncheon.'

I'll disturb her well enough, Buxton thought as he strode towards the master bedroom, ever conscious of the compelling ache in his groin.

Clarissa lay naked on the bed, her head resting on a pillow, but she was neither asleep nor motionless. The fingers of one hand were busy playing with each nipple in turn, while those of the other probed the outer entrance to her sex or gently massaged that strange, throbbing button which seemed to be the source of all delight.

Last night, Richard had been loving and caring; that morning he had been brutal and dominant. Strangely, she found she loved both Richards, the kind and the cruel. When he had first started to spank her she had been surprised, then indignant and then angry. But when he had started playing with her, however roughly, and alternating pain and pleasure, each strike of his hand had triggered new feelings which had merged with the more familiar fires inside her. In the end she had found she did not want him to stop and had lain in eager anticipation of each succeeding blow.

She started as the door crashed open and Buxton stormed into the room. She stopped playing with herself and looked up at her husband standing beside the bed. His faced was flushed and he was shaking. His tone was cold and sneering.

'What's this? Still abed? Don't you understand you have a house to run? Staff to organise? Bills to check?

Letters to write? Or do you expect me to do everything for you?'

Clarissa was surprised by his aggression, but then thought this might be just the start of another delicious game he was intent on playing. She looked down in mock contriteness.

'If I have done anything wrong then I am truly sorry. I have been naughty, and I know naughty girls have to be punished.'

So saying, she rolled over and drew herself up on all fours. She wiggled her bottom provocatively. She was expecting a slap. No, not merely expecting, but looking forward to it. Just the anticipation was beginning to make her wet.

Clarissa screamed as the riding crop smashed into the tender skin of her upper thighs. The pain was worse than anything she had ever experienced, but she was too hurt, and too surprised, to move. She heard the swish as the crop flashed through the air, a split second before it sent a bolt of agony coursing across her buttocks. The scream took all her breath, leaving her none with which to form words of protest or pleas for mercy. She tried to roll over, away from the next blow, but it proved an ill-advised move. The whip was already descending as she turned. It had been aimed at her shoulders but, as she twisted, it landed straight across the ends of her breasts, slicing into the nipples she had just been teasing and making so tender and sensitive.

'Stay where you are. When I want you to move, I'll tell you to move.'

Clarissa trembled at the anger in his voice, but did as she was told. She closed her eyes and gripped the bedclothes as the crop repeatedly cut into her breasts, stomach and thighs.

'Open your legs.'

Clarissa opened her legs and, almost immediately, the crop swished down again, cutting exactly between her sex lips, making her entire body convulse from the shock of the searing pain.

She waited, eyes tight shut, for the next blow, but it did not come. When she dared open her eyes, her husband was naked. Her eyes fixed on his pulsating erection; surely it had not been so large or so powerful before.

Buxton just looked at her before snapping, 'All fours. Now!'

Her body aching with every move, she rolled on to her stomach and then pulled herself up into the required position. She felt her husband climb on to the bed, positioning himself between her wide-spread legs.

Surely he was not going to take her like this, like an animal? He rubbed the tip of his manhood along and around the bruised entry to her body. And, as he did so, she found herself responding uncontrollably. In spite of the pain that racked her body, the juices started to flow and her nerves began to tingle. Despite the beating, she still desired him. She wanted him inside her so that he could uncap the fountain of pleasure which was beginning to bubble within. The urgent need for release and relief was all she could think of. Finally, when the liquid began to trickle down her thighs, he entered. But only to thrust forcefully several times before withdrawing. Clarissa moaned in disappointment at the sudden, unexpected pause. She felt the tip of that magnificent instrument move upwards until it parted the cheeks of her bottom. Too late, she realised what was about to happen. The shout of protest turned into a scream of pain as the throbbing cock was forced into her anus, tearing at the tight bands of muscles which were designed to expel, not receive.

Clarissa buried her head in the pillow and sobbed at the pain as he bored ever deeper into her. At last he ceased trying to penetrate any further and began to move in and out. But, whereas a few moments before, every such movement had been an exquisite pleasure, now they only brought a deep feeling of humiliation. Yet, even as she cried and her body shook as her husband rocked backwards and forwards totally oblivious to her distress, she felt the increasing wetness between her legs.

Unable to contain herself any longer, she shifted so that one forearm kept her in the position demanded, freeing her other hand. She rubbed vigorously along the entire length of her mound, her fingers reaching down far enough to actually touch her husband's member as it slid, with increasing ferocity, in and out of her. And then she had three fingers inside her, rotating, pumping, doing everything she could think of to to increase the flow of her cream and juices until they would become powerful enough to burst the floodgates. Her husband's rapid movements no longer hurt her. The only thing she was intent upon was the ultimate experience. And when it arrived she pushed backwards, ramming him even further inside her. Her first climax had barely subsided when she felt him spurt repeatedly into her and she came again and again, oblivious to everything but the wonderful, exultant, primeval joys of lust.

Four

Buxton withdrew from his wife, knelt behind her while he regained his breath, and then climbed off the bed. He stood for a few moments regarding Clarissa and smiling. Clarissa stayed where she was, still resting on elbows and knees, her breasts swaying as she panted in time with the final climactic spasms racking her body.

While he was impressed with the speed at which the iceberg had melted, he also felt slightly cheated. As an expert in such matters, he had not expected so much progress so quickly.

'Just another bitch on heat,' he sneered contemptuously, as he pulled on his clothes.

He looked from the riding crop to his wife and considered administering further discipline, but dismissed the thought. Let her wait for it. That in itself was punishment.

'I am going out again,' he informed the still kneeling figure. 'When I return I expect you to be up and dressed and about your duties as mistress of this household. Do you understand?'

Clarissa merely nodded. The fires inside her had cooled to embers, but their heat still robbed her of speech.

As Buxton left the room he almost cannoned into the hunched form of Miss Trubshaw. Dressed in black from neck to ankles and bowed by age, she reminded him of nothing so much as a shrivelled, emaciated crow.

'Well, what is it?' he demanded curtly.

Miss Trubshaw visibly shook at the authority in his voice.

'Please, sir, I wondered if the mistress was ready to consider the menu for dinner tonight. I should have given the cook her instructions an hour since.'

Buxton glanced at the slip of paper clutched between the crone's gnarled fingers.

'Your mistress is currently indisposed,' he informed the cowering woman. 'I am sure whatever you were going to suggest will be quite acceptable.'

With a quivering 'Thank you, sir,' she turned away, but Buxton called her back.

'How long have you worked here?'

'Fifty years, sir.'

'And as housekeeper?'

'Best part of thirty, sir.'

'A responsible and tiring job for someone of your years, Miss Trubshaw,' Buxton observed thoughtfully.

Buxton spotted the spark of alarm in her pin-prick black eyes.

'I hope my service is satisfactory, sir. I may not be as quick as I was, but I know this house, and those who work here, better than any.'

Buxton gave her a reassuring smile. 'I am sure you do, Miss Trubshaw. I am sure you do. I was just concerned that, at your age, you might be finding your tasks increasingly exhausting.'

The woman shook her head vigorously. 'Not at all, sir, not at all.'

'Glad to hear it, Miss Trubshaw. Glad to hear it. Now, about your duties, if you please.'

'Yes, sir. Very good, sir.'

Thoughtfully, Buxton watched her scuttle away down the corridor. The seed of an idea was beginning to germinate in his mind; an idea which would solve many of his concerns.

By the time Buxton had had Corsair resaddled and ridden him leisurely into the village, the idea had grown into a plan; a plan which became increasingly attractive and tempting the more he considered it.

As soon as he reined to a stop outside the Brackenhurst Arms, a grimy-faced, raggedly dressed boy ran towards him.

'Look after your horse, sir?'

Buxton slid from the saddle and tethered Corsair to a post.

'All he needs is some water.'

'Yes, sir. Right away, sir.'

Buxton took the first coin he found in his pocket and tossed it to the boy. The urchin gazed at the shilling in wonder. He would have worked all day for such payment, not just fetched a bucket of water for a thirsty horse. He pulled at the peak of his thread-bare cap.

'Thank you, sir. Thank you.'

Buxton sauntered into the inn. It was a long, single-storey building with small leaded windows between its criss-cross black beams. The door was so low he had to bend his head to enter and the smell which greeted him was a heady mixture of stale ale and tobacco. The public area comprised a single room, long and narrow and cast into a permanent twilight because of the meagre sunlight the dirt-caked windows allowed to enter. The only patrons of the Brackenhurst Arms that afternoon were half a dozen men seated round a table in a far corner, one of whom was Joshua Dakins.

The group went quiet as he entered and Buxton was fully aware that all eyes followed him as he walked up to the bar. The landlord, a small, fat, florid-faced man, hastily put down the tankard he had been polishing and wiped his hands across his filthy apron. Buxton appreciated that this was an establishment that was unaccustomed to accommodating the gentry and found the realisation amusing. What would they have made of him had they known that his own grandfather had been a pot-man in a tavern far worse than the Brackenhurst Arms?

'A pint of your finest ale, please, landlord.'

The innkeeper could not keep the surprise from his voice.

'Ale, sir?'

Buxton nodded. 'Indeed, sir.'

The landlord gave the tankard he had been cleaning a final polish with the hem of his apron and, turning to the barrels racked behind the bar, began to do as he had been asked. Buxton paid no attention to him, but plenty to the girl who had just entered the serving area from the kitchen.

He estimated she was about eighteen years old, though her lithe figure and short-cropped flaxen hair made her look, at first glance, much younger. But her childlike appearance was belied by the knowing twinkle in her bright, blue eyes and the coquettish twist to her lips. The vision before him was, Buxton instantly understood, neither innocent nor a child. He bestowed upon her his most charming and disarming smile.

'Good day.'

The girl gave him a half curtsey, which she somehow contrived to include a provocative sway of her hips. 'Good day, sir.'

Buxton did not take his eyes off her as he accepted the tankard from the landlord and pushed a handful of coppers across the bar in payment. And she returned and held his gaze as he raised it to his lips and gulped the thick, strong liquid. It tasted foul, but he had not come to criticise and, instead of discarding it, raised the tankard and complimented the inn-keeper.

'A fine brew, landlord. Your own, perhaps?'

The man beamed and nodded.

'It is that, sir. Finest you'll find in the county of Essex, even if it is myself as says it.'

'I do not doubt you are correct there,' rejoined Buxton, taking another pull and trying not to grimace.

'I am Richard Buxton, from The Hall. And you, sir?'

'Thomas Craddock, sir. Landlord here for nigh on twenty years.'

Buxton nodded towards the girl.

'My daughter Alice, sir.'

'Charmed to meet you, Alice.'

'Pleasure, sir.'

Alice performed another bobbing curtsey, this time leaning forward as she did so and allowing her breasts to swing out and push against the confines of her blouse. Knowing that he had noticed, she smiled at Buxton who, for his part, was beginning to feel a very familiar stirring. Yes, he decided, Alice would certainly be a pleasure.

'I wonder,' Buxton mused, as he once again sipped his drink, 'why we do not have a stock of your ale at The Hall.'

The landlord shrugged. 'That's easy to answer, sir. His Lordship did not believe in strong drink. Wouldn't have a drop in the place. He even discouraged his tenants and staff from coming here. Not that they took much mind to that.'

'Well,' Buxton declared, 'times are changing in Castleleigh. And one of the first things to change will be that you shall deliver four barrels of ale to The Hall every week. Would tomorrow afternoon be too soon for you make your first delivery?'

The landlord's eyes opened almost as wide as his mouth.

'No, sir. Not at all, sir. That would be fine, sir.'

Buxton grinned. 'Excellent. Excellent. Send your daughter here up with the first batch and I will ensure your bill is paid immediately.'

'It will be exactly as you say, sir,' replied the landlord, almost unable to believe his good fortune.

Buxton raised his tankard in salute to the girl.

'I look forward to seeing you then, Alice.'

'It will be my pleasure, sir.'

I hope it will be pleasurable for both us, Buxton thought as he turned away from the bar and headed for the group in the corner.

'Good afternoon, Mr Dakins. I am surprised to see you again so soon. Have you no work to do on your farm?'

The farmer's voice was slurred and his hand trembled as he put down his tankard.

'I have men to do most of it, sir. Anyway, after what happened this morning, a father needs a drink to help him recover. I have never been so ashamed, and that is the God's truth.'

'Mr Dakins, perhaps your friends would allow us a short talk in private.'

It was a polite way of telling the yokels to leave. They needed no further urging to get up and find other places near the bar counter where they were out of earshot. It was unheard of for the Squire to enter the inn, let alone drink with the villagers. They felt uncomfortable in such company and glad to be out of it. Buxton sat on the stool facing the farmer.

Dakins's tankard was nearly empty. Buxton topped it up with the contents of his own, glad for any excuse not to have to consume any more of the evil-tasting brew. Dakins nodded his thanks and downed half the liquid in one gulp. He wiped flecks of foam from his lips with the back of his hand.

'I've been thinking, Mr Dakins,' Buxton told him. 'I've been thinking about your daughter Rebecca and what happened in the barn this morning. It was disgraceful, Mr Dakins. Quite disgraceful.'

The farmer stared contritely at the table top.

'I agrees, sir. That girl is the bane of my life. She's wilful and headstrong. She has the Devil in her, that's what she has. Lust, sir. It's one of the deadliest of sins, that it is. But, I can't control her. Her mother could, but she's been dead these three years past. I'm at the end of my tether with her, and that's the truth.'

Buxton nodded understandingly.

'I don't doubt that you are a good man and you try to be a good father, Mr Dakins,' he said consolingly. 'And I appreciate that you have a farm to run as well as a daughter to provide for. That is why I have a proposition which may interest you and solve some of your problems. The girl needs a strong hand; that is obvious.'

'Strong hand, you say. I've beaten her till my arm ached, but what good has it done, sir? None, that's what.'

Maybe because she did not find it quite so unenjoyable as you imagined, thought Buxton, but he kept his thoughts to himself.

'One of the problems must be that you cannot keep your eye on her all the time,' he pointed out. 'That is why I am prepared to offer her a place in service at

The Hall. She will rarely be on her own, she will have to obey the rules of the house and she will only be allowed out one afternoon each week. And, of course, I will ensure that her wages are paid direct to you. If you believe that may be a solution to your problems, I am only too happy to be of assistance.'

Dakins's eyes gleamed at the idea of not only getting rid of his daughter, but also being paid for it.

'That is very kind of you, sir. That is very kind of you indeed. I shall miss her, of course, for she does cook and wash for me now that my wife is gone. But, if it is to be for her own good then who am I to object?'

Buxton smiled and held out his hand. Two sovereigns glinted in his palm.

'On account for her first few months' wages, Mr Dakins. I shall expect to hear that she has arrived at The Hall by seven in the morning.'

The coins were transferred from Buxton's palm to Dakins's waistcoat pocket with lightning speed.

'She'll be there, sir. Oh, she'll be there all right, even if I has to drag her there myself. You can rely on that.'

Buxton left the half-drunken oaf to gloat over his new-found wealth and continue draining his cups. Outside, he paused to savour the fresh, clean country air and let it take away the fetid smell and sour taste of the bar room.

'She's well watered, sir. And I brushed her down 'cause she was sweating up a bit.'

Buxton turned to see the village boy stroking the length of Corsair's muzzle and running his fingers through the horse's mane. He was impressed. Corsair's fiery temperament was legendary. Clearly, the lad had a natural gift as far as horses were concerned.

'What's your name, boy?' Buxton asked.

54

'Tom, sir. Tom Cuttock.'

'And what do you do, Tom?'

'Do, sir? Why, whatever earns me some pennies, sir.'

'Like horses, do you, Tom?'

'Yes, sir. Always have. Like to work with 'em, but there ain't no jobs going. Not round here there ain't.'

Buxton smiled at the youth. 'There is now, Tom. Report to the head groom at The Hall tomorrow. Tell him I said to take you on as a trainee stable lad.'

The boy's face was a portrait of delight. 'Me, sir? Yes, sir. Thank you, sir.'

'I can see you have a talent for horsecraft. I can usc that. I have a string of racers at Newmarket. Who knows, we may even make a jockey out of you. You have the build for it. Now, keep on looking after Corsair while I go to the vicarage.'

'If you're seeking Mr Pimms, sir, I saw him go into the church a few minutes ago.'

'Thank you, Tom. Observant too. I think you'll be a credit to The Hall.'

Buxton felt in remarkably good humour as he strolled across the green towards the church. It had been a highly entertaining and enjoyable day, and it was far from over. Giving extra business to the local publican and employment to Dakins's daughter and the young lad would raise the villagers' opinion of him. That, at some future time, might be useful, for people are more willing to believe rumours about those they dislike than those they approve of. But Buxton was no philanthropist and never undertook any action unless he could clearly see the eventual advantage to himself. Instinct told him that the landlord's daughter would provide excellent sport. Once confined within the walls of The Hall, Dakins's young trollop would find life far more disciplined than she could ever have imagined. And, as for the new stable lad, while he held no personal attraction for Buxton, he could foresee uses for such a strapping youth which had nothing whatsoever to do with horses.

For a community of barely three hundred souls, the Church of St Michael and St George appeared disproportionately large. The main body of the building was of flint beneath a high slate roof with, at one end, a tall castellated tower. Buxton walked between the rows of yews to the imposing, iron-studded main door. He turned the heavy ring and pushed. But the door did not open. He tried again, but still it refused to yield.

Odd, thought Buxton; a church was rarely locked, and never during the day. The lad had said he had watched the vicar enter the church and he certainly could not have left without also being seen. So why would he want to lock himself in?

Buxton walked slowly along the wall to the tower and tried its door, but that too was shut fast. Continuing, he followed the wall round and, at the far end, found the Devil's Door, the small side entrance through which, superstition said, Satan would make his exit whenever a man of God entered. The handle was rusted, but Buxton had the strength to turn it, and his shoulder was powerful enough to force it open just sufficiently to allow him to slip sideways into the building.

He found himself standing behind the choir stalls, between pulpit and altar. No candles had been lit and the shafts of sunlight which speared through the high arched windows and made patterns on the flagstoned floor did little to lift the gloom. Buxton was about to call out and try to trace the elusive clergyman when two sounds, both of which he immediately recognised, stopped him. One was that of a man simultaneously shouting and panting. The other was the swish of a birch. The noises were coming from the tower and, careful to tread as lightly as possible, Buxton approached and peered round the edge of the half-closed door. He had to compress his lips to suppress the laughter which involuntarily rose within him as he took in the scene.

The Reverend Matthew Pimms, his cassock round his ankles, was leaning against a wooden post in the centre of the room. Standing behind him was a small, plump woman in a voluminous black dress. The vicar was resting his head on the back of his left hand while his right vigorously pumped his penis. As he masturbated he shouted, and every time he shouted the woman applied the birch to his lower back, buttocks and thighs.

'Harder, woman. Harder, you whore of Babylon.'

As instructed, the woman increased the force of her blows. She looked extremely bored.

'You must beat the Devil from me. Scourge me of my evil thoughts. Make me truly repent of my sins.'

The woman carried on with her task of turning the parson's fat and hairy arse a brilliant shade of crimson.

'The Devil is coming,' yelled the excited cleric. 'I feel he is about to leave me. Yes! Yes! He is coming!'

But it wasn't Beelzebub which fled. It was jet after jet of come, which splashed against the wooden post and on to the floor. The woman continued the beating until the vicar released his now drooping member and, without turning, motioned for her to leave. The woman propped the birch neatly in the corner and gathered up the pile of silver coins from on the table.

Anxious not to be seen, Buxton moved quickly to the font and knelt behind it. The woman left the room, walked briskly to the door, released the bolt and left. Buxton returned to the tower and pushed the door wide. The vicar was still leaning against the post, breathing heavily.

'Well, what is it? Is there not enough there?'

'The lady seemed satisfied. As indeed do you,' Buxton remarked drily.

The vicar turned so quickly at the sound of Buxton's voice that his cassock twisted round his ankles and he had to clutch desperately at the edge of the table to prevent himself falling. He stared in dismay at his unexpected and unwanted guest.

Buxton bowed his head politely. 'Good afternoon, Mr Pimms. I thought I would pay my respects as we had so little time to talk at the wedding yesterday and it was not possible to invite you to The Hall afterwards.'

The look of dismay turned to one of horror as the vicar recognised his visitor and realised that not only his reputation, but also his livelihood, was in danger. One word from the Squire to the Bishop and he would not only be dismissed from the parish, but defrocked as well. Hastily, he pulled on his cassock, his nervous fingers twitching as he tried to fasten the buttons. Once dressed, he felt slightly less embarrassed, but no more confident.

'I hope that you have not misinterpreted what I was doing,' he finally managed to stammer. 'Pain is good for the soul. Flagellation in order to rid the mind and the body of evil spirits is a time-honoured practice among the truly devout.'

Buxton looked from the stain on the post to the white puddle on the floor. 'Well, you certainly seem to have expelled quite a few of the little demons,' he observed. 'My knowledge of the scriptures is limited, I confess, but is it not a sin to spill one's seed upon the ground? Genesis, if I remember rightly.'

The vicar's face turned even redder.

'An unfortunate side effect. The body responds, but the mind remains pure. Even so, I shall be punished for it.'

Buxton smiled. 'Mr Pimms, I make no judgement on your actions. Personally, I firmly believe that in such matters it is better to give than to receive. My purpose in coming here was not to disturb your devotions but to invite you to dinner, so that you can get to know myself and my wife.'

The vicar looked relieved and his fears eased. 'Dinner? That is very kind of you, Mr Buxton. Of course, I shall be delighted. I trust that what you witnessed can remain a confidence between ourselves?'

'Naturally, Mr Pimms, naturally,' replied Buxton in his most reassuring voice.

'Now, if you will excuse me, I too should like some time in your beautiful church to attend to my own devotions. I will send word regarding a suitable date for dinner.'

Eager to be out in the fresh air and sunlight, the vicar simply muttered 'Of course, of course,' and almost ran from the church. As soon as the door closed behind him, Buxton shot home the bolt.

Alice was on her knees in the middle of the front pew, her hands together in prayer and her eyes fixed on the altar cross. Buxton sat next to her, but she ignored him. She continued to pretend to be ignorant of his presence even when he started unhooking her dress. It was only when he slid the cloth from her shoulders and began gently massaging her neck and shoulders that she responded with a shiver of pleasure and a deep sigh. Buxton's hands found her breasts and he felt the nipples grow hard beneath his fingers. She was encircled by his powerful arms and her half-hearted attempt to pull away was useless.

'Not here, sir,' she whispered urgently. 'It ain't right.'

'The door is bolted. There is no one to see,' Buxton reassured her, but she shook her head towards the stained-glass window above the altar.

'He sees.'

'But He sees everything, everywhere,' mocked Buxton. 'We're just giving Him a better view, that's all. But, if you prefer . . .'

With that, he pulled her to her feet, swept one arm under her knees and carried her down the aisle to the room at the base of the tower, not releasing her until they were standing in the centre and the door had been kicked shut behind them.

The moment he released his grip, Alice let her dress fall to the ground and threw her arms around his neck, pressing her naked body against him. Feverishly, she began kissing him, sliding her tongue between his lips.

Her passion did not surprise him. Buxton knew that she must have followed him from the inn and slipped into the church while he had been making his acquaintance with the vicar. From the instant he had spotted her, kneeling devoutly in the pew, he knew she had not come to worship.

Buxton ran his hands down her back and cupped the slim, firm orbs of her buttocks. He pulled his face away from hers and transferred his lips to her breasts, gently nipping at the swollen nipples for a while before stepping back and undressing as quickly as he could. While she watched impatiently, Alice replaced his hands with hers, kneading her breasts and rubbing her thighs together. The girl gasped as the size and strength of his erection was revealed and immediately sank to her knees and began frantically licking its length. Buxton toyed with her hair as she sucked the

60

tip of his cock and then turned her attention to his balls, taking each in turn into her mouth, while her finger found the ultra sensitive spot between his balls and anus.

Now it was his turn to moan with delight. She was good, he decided; very good indeed. Where she had learned such skills so young, he could only guess. But, whoever had taught her had done their job extremely well. So well, in fact, that if he allowed her to continue it would be over soon, and he wanted to prolong the pleasure.

Buxton pushed her head away and sat on a tall-backed, armless chair, his legs straight out. Alice needed no instructions as to what to do next. She placed one leg either side of his and slowly lowered herself on to the shaft throbbing upwards to welcome her. In one fierce downward thrust she impaled herself upon him, grinding her sex into his pubic hair and crushing his balls. She kissed him passionately, drawing his tongue into her mouth as she rocked backwards and forwards. Every movement sent tremors of delight coursing through his body and he closed his eyes to better concentrate on the thrills she inspired.

Slowly, inch by inch, Alice lifted herself until only the very tip of his cock remained inside her. Then, instead of rocking she clenched him tightly between the walls of her cunt and began to frantically swivel her hips.

Buxton had known very many women, of all sizes and colours and ages, but never had even he experienced such art in one so young. His whole being began to quiver as the inevitable climax started to surge through him. Alice read the warning signals and began to ride him as fast and as hard as she could. Her timing was perfection and, as he gushed into her, so she too cried out and her body began shaking violently and uncontrollably. They clung together as the spasms racked them and, when at last they subsided, still stayed locked together for a while, as each relished the calm after the storm.

Finally, Alice stood up. As her sex cleared his cock, she put her hand between her legs and caught his spunk as it trickled out of her. When she had gathered all she could, she put her cupped palm to her lips and licked up its contents, purring like a cat with a bowl of cream.

The sight was so erotic that Buxton felt himself begin to harden again. The girl noticed the stirrings too and began to move towards him. Buxton raised his hand and stopped her.

'Alice, you are quite extraordinary. But, I think the time has come for us to make a move. It would never do to be discovered pleasuring ourselves in the House of God, now would it?'

Alice gave him an impish smile and began once again to play with her breasts. 'Like you said, sir. He sees everything, don't matter where you are. And He knows what goes on in our hearts and our minds.'

Buxton laughed as he dressed. 'Yes, He does. But the rest of the village does not.'

He scooped up the girl's dress and tossed it to her. 'Now, make yourself decent before we are discovered.'

'Don't think I could ever be decent.' Alice grinned as she pulled on the dress.

'No, Alice, I too fear that that is the truth,' agreed Buxton. 'But, I am certain that there will be many, many more times when we can be indecent together. After all, the first delivery of beer is only tomorrow. Why not make it about three.'

When they had reached the main door and Buxton was drawing the bolt, the sound of footsteps approaching along the path reached them. Buxton pointed to the other end of the church.

'Better go by the north door. Quickly.'

He finished unlocking the door as Alice disappeared behind the pulpit. Opening it, he found the Reverend Pimms about to reach for the handle.

'I forgot my notes for Sunday's sermon,' the vicar explained.

'And on what subject shall we be instructed this week?' enquired Buxton, still blocking the clergyman's path in order to ensure Alice had time to leave the church and skirt the churchyard unseen.

'It is on resisting temptation,' the vicar replied, somewhat sheepishly.

'I shall look forward to it,' Buxton told him, as he finally stepped aside. 'Tell me, Mr Pimms, this physical driving out of the Devil and his demons – you have it done to you, but would you be prepared to do it to others?'

The vicar avoided Buxton's penetrating gaze as he answered. 'Of course, it would be a trial to beat another person, but if it would help save their soul, it would be my duty.'

'Even if that person was a woman?' Buxton persisted. 'A young, attractive woman?'

The vicar nodded. 'Young or old, man or boy, woman or girl – all are sinners.'

'I shall look forward to our next meeting, Mr Pimms,' Buxton told the flustered parson. 'I have a feeling that it is going to be quite uncommonly entertaining.'

Five

How long she stayed in the same position, kneeling on the bed with her head buried in the pillow, Clarissa could not tell. Gradually, her heart stopped drumming and her breathing slowed to its normal rate. She shifted only slightly to ease the ache in her forearms and shoulders and to rub her forehead against the coolness of the satin pillow. She could feel her husband's come sliding slowly from her and trickling down the insides of her thighs to merge with her own, still seeping, juices.

Clarissa heard the clock chime two and closed her eyes in disbelief. Was it really only twenty-four hours since she had walked down the aisle, her arm interlocked with that of a man she hardly knew and whose very presence terrified her? Since she had been a naive virgin, fearful of what was to happen to her? It was just one day, but to Clarissa it seemed like a lifetime. This strange, powerful, dominant man had changed her and, she knew, she would never, could never, be the same again.

She realised she loved Richard with every fibre of her body and soul. He had been kind and he had been hurtful; he had been gentle and he had been brutal. But now, Clarissa acknowledged that she loved and worshipped every facet of his nature, every contradiction. She would do anything for him and let him do anything to her. If it pleased him then it would please her. And she wanted to be pleased. To please and be pleased was, she now understood, all she desired in life.

Clarissa turned over and lay on her back, legs apart, staring unseeingly at the ceiling as she tried to analyse her emotions and to understand the messages they were sending her. Feelings had been aroused within her that were so powerful, so all-pervading that, once released, they could never be chained again. She could only accept them and live with them. They were all she wanted, all she needed. Nothing mattered any more but satiating the urgent cravings within. She could think of nothing else except the delicious prospect of repeating, over and over again, the actions which created such all-consuming ecstasy. She had experienced the heat and now all she desired was to live and die within the furnace.

Clarissa shook herself. This would not do. She had a house to run and a position to maintain. That she was still abed at such an hour would be the talk of the household. Reluctantly, she slid off the bed and stood up. She regarded herself in the dressing table mirror and realised what a mess she was. The riding crop had left a legacy of vivid streaks across her stomach and breasts. She turned so that, by looking over her shoulder, she could see her back. The whip had scourged long lines from shoulders to thighs and her buttocks were a flaming red lattice. She took the towel from its rack beside the washstand and dabbed one end in the cold water. She washed the stickiness from between her legs but, even as she did so, could not resist letting her fingers linger on her mound. The cotton of the towel was rough against the sensitive skin and she shuddered as she sensed the emotions she loved so much once more starting to grow.

Quickly, she withdrew her hand, used the other end of the towel to dry herself and pulled on a simple white cotton shift. She was sitting in front of the mirror tugging a brush through her sweat-matted hair when there was a rap on the door and Lucy entered.

The maid stood demurely in the centre of the room, but though her outward manner was all it should have been, her eyes glinted and she could not keep the mocking lilt from her voice.

'Is there anything I can do for you, Madam? Only, I was wondering at you not being up and about yet.'

Clarissa held out the brush. 'Attend to my hair.'

'Of course, Madam.'

Lucy took the brush and began drawing it through her mistress's long, yellow locks.

In the mirror Clarissa could see Lucy's eyes widen when she noticed the red lines across the top of her breasts. Clarissa regretted for only an instant that she had not put on her dressing gown and completely cloaked herself. What did it matter what this girl thought? She was just a maid. A servant, nothing more. She, and her opinions, simply had no value.

'Is Madam in need of anything?' Lucy enquired as she straightened the tangles in her mistress's hair.

Clarissa was surprised by the question. 'In need of anything? What do you mean, Lucy?'

Lucy grinned slyly, and her voice was low and confidential, as if she were exchanging a gossip with one of her below-stairs friends.

'Well, Madam, it is just that, after the first night, some ladies require a soothing cream or even a poultice. I mean, well, after all, the master is a big, powerful man.'

Lucy had been her personal maid for three years. During all that time, Clarissa had never even scolded the girl, let alone raised a hand to her. But, in the space of just a night and a day, Clarissa had changed. Lucy's mistake was not realising the fact. Clarissa leaped to her feet, one hand knocking the hairbrush flying from Lucy's grip, the other landing flat across her cheek. The force of the blow sent Lucy reeling backwards and tumbling over a stool. For an instant she lay staring up at her mistress, her expression a blend of fear and surprise. Clarissa stood over her, shaking with emotion.

'How dare you be so familiar with me? How dare you?'

Lucy made to rise but Clarissa, with a strength and forcefulness she had never realised she possessed, bent and grabbed her by the hair, pulling her upright. Lucy cried out at the pain but Clarissa paid no attention as she half-pulled, half-dragged the girl across the room and sent her sprawling on to the chaise longue. Clarissa retained her grip on the girl's hair while her knee pressed into the small of Lucy's back, forcing the air from her lungs.

'I know you and the other servants laugh at me. I know it!' she shouted. 'But not any more, do you hear me? Not any more. You think you're special. You are not. You are nothing. Just a common little servant. There are thousands out there just like you. But they know their place. You have forgotten yours. So I am going to teach you.'

Clarissa looked round and saw the riding whip lying on the floor where Richard had flung it. She released the shaking maid, but Lucy's hopes that her ordeal was over lasted only for the moment it took her mistress to pick up the crop.

'Get up.'

Lucy obeyed. Her eyes flickered from the whip to her mistress's face. She had never seen her mistress so angry. For the first time in her life Lucy, who had always relied on her sharp wits and quick tongue to avoid trouble, understood what it was like to experience real fear.

'I . . . I . . . I am truly sorry, Madam,' she began to stutter, but Clarissa shouted her down.

'Sorry! You will be sorry. I am going to give you the beating you have deserved these many months. Take off your clothes.'

Lucy looked stunned. 'Take off my clothes?'

Clarissa slashed the side of her face with the whip. Not a cutting blow, but strong enough to make her cry out and cower away.

Clarissa felt herself trembling, no longer with anger but from the feeling of being in control. Total control. All her life she had done as others told her. She had never questioned, always obeyed. Now, she was in absolute control; she had the power, and the sensation was exhilarating. She raised the whip again. 'Well?'

Lucy's hesitation lasted barely a heartbeat before she began to unbutton her blouse. When that was removed she hastily unbuckled her belt and let her skirt slip to the floor. She stood shivering with trepidation, not sure what to do next.

Clarissa looked at her maid and her lips curled in a cruel smile. She understood the girl's fear and uncertainty. She had to admit that Lucy was a pretty young thing. Her eighteen summers, and all the good food she had enjoyed at her mistress's expense, had given her a figure that was well rounded but firm. The tightly laced corset compressed her breasts and the ankle-length petticoat shielded her from waist to ankle.

'Are you deaf as well as impudent? I told you to undress.' To emphasise her instruction, Clarissa swished the whip against the hapless maid's arm, just below the shoulder.

Lucy winced and immediately began tugging at the laces down the front of her corset. As the last was undone her breasts were freed from their restraint and pushed outwards, wobbling slightly as she slid the garment from her shoulders and let it fall. Her waist was as slim as Clarissa had expected, but the size of the girl's breasts surprised her. They had been so tightly constrained to achieve the flatness which fashion dictated that Clarissa had had no idea they were so large. No idea? Why, she realised, she had never before even considered the subject of the fullness of her maid's breasts. Now, she found them fascinating. Something new was stirring inside her as she gazed upon them and used the crop to motion the girl to continue.

Lucy eased her petticoat down and stepped out of it, hanging her head in shame and blushing as the whole of her body was revealed to the cold, piercing gaze of her mistress. The ankle boots and knee-length black stockings which remained gave her no solace. If anything, their presence only added to her feeling of abject humiliation. Pathetically, she tried to place one arm across her breasts and the other across her thighs, but Clarissa simply rapped the crop across the knuckles of the hand covering her trim black triangle. Her voice was razor sharp.

'By your sides. Stand up straight. Look at me when I am talking to you.'

Lucy wanted to resist, to refuse. Most of all she wanted to turn and run from the room and never return. But she knew that resistance and protest would be futile. And where could she run to? The only paths she would be able to follow would lead her to either the gutter, the workhouse or the whorehouse. Obediently, she did as she was told.

Clarissa felt intoxicated, drunk with the power she had over the girl. Her eyes roamed over Lucy's body. She had never seen another woman naked before. It had never occurred to her to even wonder what other women might look like when undressed. Now, she found the sight strangely stimulating. She was aware of a growing wetness between her thighs and the pit of her stomach was beginning to flutter with the same sensations Richard had so dramatically aroused in her.

'Turn round.'

Lucy turned, thankful to no longer have to look at her mistress; grateful that the most secret parts of her body were obscured. Her relief was short-lived. Lucy screamed as the leather of the crop cut into the soft flesh of her buttocks. She staggered forward but had not even time to regain her faltering balance before the second blow landed and she toppled across the arm of the chaise longue. The third slashed at her shoulders and the fourth bit into her legs just above the knees.

Clarissa shook with excitement. She paused for a moment to regain a semblance of composure before bringing the crop down again and again. She was no longer aiming her blows. She did not care where they landed, as long as she felt the jolt along her arm as they struck and heard the satisfying screams they forced from the writhing, helpless girl in front of her. As she struck, her free hand pressed against the thin cotton of her shift, violently squeezing and kneading the now sopping mound below. Her whole body seemed to be pulsing from the intensity of the feelings surging through it.

Clarissa paused again, this time long enough to allow Lucy to stagger to her feet. Thinking her beating over, the girl turned to face her mistress. She was no longer concerned about her nakedness, just eager to gather her clothes and escape. As she did so, Clarissa lashed out once more. This time she had a target to aim for and Lucy's breasts absorbed the full impact. The pain was more severe than anything Lucy had so far had to endure. She let out a high-pitched scream as she criss-crossed her arms over her chest and instinctively bent double to protect herself from further attacks.

Clarissa looked at the sobbing, trembling figure and was about to raise the whip again when the small section of her brain which could still think rationally told her that enough was enough.

Panting from the exertion, and the emotions it had produced, she pointed the crop not at the girl's body, but at the clothes scattered around her feet.

'Get dressed and get out.'

Lucy had never got dressed so quickly. Within a minute she was at the door, then Clarissa called, 'Wait!' Fearfully, the girl turned.

'I want a bath,' Clarissa told her sharply. 'And I want it in ten minutes. Ten minutes, understand?'

'Yes, Madam. Ten minutes, Madam,' agreed Lucy as she bobbed a curtsey and fled the room.

Clarissa sat on the edge of the bed and pushed her lank hair back over her shoulders. Her body was damp with sweat. Her pussy was still oozing juices. Physically, she felt tired. Mentally, she had never felt so alive. She began to try to rationalise her feelings but soon dismissed the effort as a useless exercise. Not understanding what was happening to her, what she was becoming, was unimportant and irrelevant. All that truly mattered was that it was happening and that she not only welcomed it, but revelled in it.

She heard the sound of footsteps in the adjoining room and knew that Lucy and other servants were busy filling the bath from pitchers of hot water carefully carried from the kitchens below. She waited until the noises ceased and a nervous Lucy stood in the doorway and announced that her bath was ready.

Clarissa rose and followed Lucy into the small chamber which served as her bathroom.

'Is everything to your satisfaction, Madam?' enquired Lucy, clearly worried about what would happen to her if it was not.

Clarissa ran her hand along the top of the water and nodded.

Relieved, Lucy asked, 'May I go now, Madam?'

Clarissa looked at the girl and shook her head, but did not immediately answer the maid's question.

'Lucy, do you think you deserved your punishment?'

Lucy lowered her eyes and mumbled, 'Yes, Madam,' because she knew that was the answer expected of her.

'You know, Lucy, that if you are impudent or overfamiliar with me again, you will receive the same treatment?'

Still averting her gaze, Lucy nodded before repeating her request to leave. Clarissa pretended to be shocked at the suggestion.

'Go, Lucy? Do you expect me to bath myself?' Clarissa asked as she slid the shift from her shoulders and stood naked beside the long enamel-coated iron bath.

Lucy's voice showed her confusion. 'Madam?'

Clarissa merely lowered herself into the tub, wincing slightly as the hot water made contact with the ravaged skin of her back and buttocks. 'Wash me.'

Hesitantly, Lucy picked the soap and sponge from the washstand and advanced towards her mistress. Clarissa lifted one leg high above the water. Lucy rubbed soap on the sponge, producing a thick, creamy lather, and gingerly began to wash her mistress's foot and then soap the length of her leg from ankle to knee. She squeezed the soap from the sponge and rinsed off the suds. Clarissa raised her other leg and Lucy repeated the process.

Clarissa felt wonderfully relaxed as the warm water eased the stiffness that Richard's beatings had caused and washed the perspiration from her body. She could sense Lucy's unease and smiled. When the maid had finished, instead of simply lowering her leg into the water, Clarissa let it fall with a splash. The spray hit Lucy, soaking the front of her blouse and skirt. Clarissa shook her head as she looked at the damp stains on the girl's clothes.

'Lucy, we cannot have you walking round the house with wet clothes. Take them off and hang them by the window to dry.'

Lucy hesitated. 'Oh, they'll soon dry, Madam.'

'They will dry much quicker by an open window,' Clarissa told her in a tone which brooked no dissent. 'Are you daring to question me?'

There was no alternative. Lucy removed her blouse and skirt and laid them on the window sill. Clarissa laughed.

'Lucy, what is the point of taking off your outer garments if those beneath will only get wet as well? Remove them.'

For the second time in less than an hour, Lucy unfastened her corset and pushed down her petticoat. She stood beside the bath in just her stockings and shoes and waited meekly for her next instruction. It was not long in coming. Clarissa rolled over and knelt, offering her thighs, buttocks and back to the girl. She heard Lucy gasp at the marks on her mistress's body.

'When we do something wrong, Lucy, when we break the rules, we must all be punished,' Clarissa told her. 'From the highest to the lowest, everyone must understand their place. Be very careful that your touch is gentle.'

Once again, Lucy did as she was told. She dabbed lightly at the tender skin, squeezing the foaming liquid from the sponge. Broad streams of warm, soapy water slid down Clarissa's back to merge at the base of her spine and form a river flooding through the canyon between her buttocks.

Clarissa sighed with pleasure. She wallowed not only in the feeling of being clean again but, just as much, in the sensuousness of the situation. She turned her head so that she could see her maid as well as feel her ministrations. To perform her task, Lucy had to stand right beside the bath and bend over, bringing Clarissa's face just a few inches from both her breasts and pubic triangle. Clarissa suddenly felt an urgent desire to lick Lucy's swaying orbs and reach out a hand and grasp the secret area between the girl's thighs. Like all the many strange feelings she had so recently experienced, it was an emotion which initially appalled her but which, as the sensations inside began to stir, she instinctively knew she would enjoy. Clarissa shook herself, as if the sudden action could drive the thoughts from her mind. This would not do. This girl was a servant. A nothing. To beat her was one thing; to touch her in such a way was totally unacceptable. But if she could not do such a thing to a servant, that did not mean the servant could not do such a thing to her. Clarissa turned and knelt upright, so that the front of her body was exposed to her maid. Once again, Lucy hovered uncertainly.

'Well, carry on, girl. Do I even have to instruct you on how to wash?' Clarissa chided her.

Tentatively Lucy began stroking the sponge from shoulder to shoulder and then rinsing off the soap with clear water, sending a cascade flowing down Clarissa's breasts and stomach. Nervously, she started rubbing the sponge around the top of her mistress's breasts, but Clarissa soon stopped her.

'That is far too rough. Use your hands.'

'My hands, Madam?'

Clarissa gave the girl a withering look and simply snapped, 'Get on with it.'

Lucy put down the sponge and rubbed the soap between her hands until they were gloved in a rich lather. Reaching out, she began to massage the thick, scented foam into her mistress's right breast. Clarissa closed her eyes to help her savour as deeply as possible the tingling feeling created by every touch of the girl's fingers. She shuddered at the spasm which shot through her as Lucy began to wash her nipples. She felt them stiffening and growing as the maid's palms rubbed against them. She realised that Lucy must know her mistress was being aroused by her work, but Clarissa had long since ceased caring what the girl thought.

Lucy rinsed away the soap and began to walk round to attend to her mistress's other breast, but Clarissa stopped her. 'You can do that just as well from where you are.'

It was true, Lucy could do it just as well from where she stood, but only if she got even closer and leaned across her mistress. It was an action which brought the girl's breasts bobbing against Clarissa's side, their faces only a fraction away from each other. Clarissa shivered at the touch of skin on skin. As Lucy washed her left side, so the girl's breasts pushed against her right. The smell of the maid's cheap scent filled Clarissa's nostrils and when she opened her eyes their lips were almost touching.

Maid and mistress's eyes met and locked. No words passed between them. There was no need, for each intuitively understood the needs of the other. Without being told, Lucy slid her hand down Clarissa's stomach. Clarissa parted her legs as far as the confines of the bath allowed. Lucy took the sponge and began to rub it slowly backwards and forwards between her mistress's thighs. The sponge was rough against the tender flesh of her mound and Clarissa moaned with the pleasure the contact brought. Lucy pushed the sponge further so that it covered both entrances to her mistress's body and then began to push her fingers into it as her palm squeezed it. Clarissa gasped as she felt the pressure of Lucy's fingers alternating between the two holes, while at the same time the top of the sponge planed against her clit.

Lucy adjusted her stance. Instead of standing slightly in front of Clarissa, she knelt by the side of the bath. With the sponge now in her left hand she continued to rub it vigorously down the divide between her mistress's cheeks and push it upwards against her anus. It was a stimulating motion which produced a spreading warm glow deep inside Clarissa. But that was nothing in comparison to the volcano-like explosion being primed by Lucy's activities a few inches further along.

Lucy's long, supple fingers squeezed the lips of her mistress's cunt and then roughly parted them. Clarissa cried out with pleasure as the girl thrust first one, then another into her. Lucy pushed her fingers inside as far as they would reach, while, at the same time, her thumb massaged her mistress's gorged and throbbing button. Clarissa, her eyes closed, panted and swayed, as Lucy increased the speed and power of her pistoning fingers. When the maid leaned over unexpectedly and began to suck on the nearest nipple, the volcano finally erupted. Clarissa came screaming. Her orgasm seemed to last for ever as shock wave after shock wave ripped through her. Lucy continued fingering and sucking until she was certain that there was no more pleasure available.

Lucy moved away and held up a large towel. Still breathless and shaking, Clarissa stepped from the bath and Lucy wrapped it around her. Clarissa sat on a stool while Lucy dried her. Neither spoke. Clarissa would not have been able to form the words to describe how she had felt when Lucy had touched her. Richard had done similar things and aroused similar sensations, but none quite as powerful as those Lucy had summoned. Perhaps only a woman really knows how to please a woman, Clarissa thought.

Clarissa looked down as Lucy began drying her feet. Lucy looked up and smiled. She pressed her thumbs into the sole of Clarissa's foot, lowered her head and began to suck each toe in turn. By that one gesture, mistress and servant each defined their status. From now on, Clarissa knew, Lucy would do whatever she was instructed to. Not because she was afraid, but because she wanted to.

Clarissa rose and stood facing her maid. She reached out and this time succumbed to the urge to touch her. Lucy parted her legs as Clarissa's hand reached her. Clarissa pressed against the girl's mound and then withdrew her hand and looked at the glistening palm.

'This is not bathwater, Lucy.'

'No, Madam'.

'I think it is time that we were both dressed.'

'Yes, Madam.'

Lucy pulled on her own clothes and then helped her mistress into her petticoats, corset and a thin cotton day-dress which, while plain and practical, still managed to accentuate her curves.

The sound of a horseman coming up the drive made Clarissa look out of the window. She beckoned Lucy to join her.

'It seems we have a visitor.'

'That's Colonel Markham, Madam. Lives at The Grange.'

'Go and tell Robert to show the Colonel into the morning room. I shall be down shortly.'

Lucy bobbed. 'Yes, Madam.'

'Oh, and Lucy –'

'Yes, Madam.'

'I do believe cleanliness is so important. Therefore, I shall be taking a bath daily from now on. See that it is organised, will you?'

Lucy smiled. 'Of course, Madam. My pleasure, Madam.'

Six

Richard Buxton leaned on the churchyard wall surveying the scene before him. The mid-afternoon sun softened the contours of the old cottages, the even more ancient inn and the long, low smithy. Whereas that morning he had thought of the village as pathetic, he now found it quaint and picturesque. To his great surprise he realised he was enjoying being the new master of Castleleigh. Already, the memories and allure of the London clubs, theatres and bars, which he had always thought of as essential to his life, were beginning to fade. The city now only held one attraction and, if his plan succeeded, that need not be denied him for very much longer. He saw Tom, still patiently standing outside the inn beside Corsair, and waved him over. Tom sprinted across the green to answer the summons of his new employer.

'Is my horse all right?' Buxton asked as soon as the boy reached him.

'Fine, sir,' Tom replied. 'I've given him a handful of oats and topped up his water.'

'Good. Now, Tom, you can do me a further service. Please go and enquire of master Craddock whether he would be kind enough to favour me with the loan of some paper and a pencil.'

The lad returned within a few minutes and Buxton settled himself on a bench at the edge of the green and began to draw. The casual observer would have assumed he was sketching the rural scene. Buxton, however, had little time for landscapes. His illustrations were of a far more technical nature. When he had finished he considered his work and was pleased with what he saw. He was no Brunel, and certainly no Turner, but they would suffice. Slipping the sheets into his pocket, he headed across the green to the smithy.

The sign over the door proclaimed: JACOB HICK-SWORTH. BLACKSMITH, FARRIER AND WHEELWRIGHT.

'Mr Hicksworth, I presume.'

The smith stopped pumping the bellows and turned at the sound of his name. He was a heavy, powerfully built man with a shock of unruly, curly black hair. He was stripped to the waist and his torso rippled with perfectly honed muscles.

'That's me, sir. And what may I do for you?'

'My name is Richard Buxton and, as you may have heard, I recently took up residence at The Hall.'

The smith nodded. 'Yes, sir, I had heard. It don't take long to hear such news in this village.'

Buxton stepped further into the dim interior of the smithy. 'Do you do work for The Hall, Master Hicksworth?'

'Aye, sir, but there has been precious little of it these three years past. His Lordship did not visit very often you see, so there was no need to keep the stables full. In my father's time, there was always upwards of thirty horses there, but them days is long gone.'

Buxton smiled. 'They are about to return. I intend bringing over some of my racers from Newmarket and I shall need some good, strong mounts for when I join the local hunt.'

'There always used to be a Christmas meet up at The Hall,' the blacksmith informed him. 'I'm sure Colonel Markham will be pleased to see it back there again.'

'Colonel Markham?'

'Master of the Dillsbury Hunt, sir. He lives over at The Grange, just outside Dillsbury on the Colchester road.'

'I look forward to making his acquaintance,' said Buxton. 'In the meantime, I have some work I hope you will be able to undertake for me.'

The blacksmith grinned at the prospect of extra business. If the new Squire was going to restock the stables at The Hall, there would certainly be more food on the table this winter than last. 'I will do my best, sir. What do you require?'

'I have some drawings here, only rough sketches, but they show what I have in mind. Perhaps, if we step into the sunlight you will see them better.'

Outside, Buxton handed the two sheets of paper to the blacksmith, whose brows furrowed with concentration as he studied them. Finally, he asked, 'Are these for a pony, sir?'

'You could say that,' Buxton replied, trying hard not to smile. 'The important thing is that they must be as light as possible.'

'And, these here, sir?' enquired the clearly confused blacksmith. 'I never seen bridle, bit nor harness like these before.'

'An experimental design of my own,' Buxton told him. 'Can you make them?'

'Oh yes, sir. I can make them right enough. No doubt about that.'

'I shall require them by the end of next week,' Buxton told him.

The smith looked doubtful. 'Not much time, sir. I shall have to order the leather and steel, and them small wheels will take some making.'

Buxton produced a guinea and handed it to him. 'On account, Mr Hicksworth. Full payment on delivery to The Hall, providing they are there by next Friday.'

The smith quickly slipped the coin into the pocket of his leather apron. 'They'll be there, sir. But I can't tell you here and now what they will cost.'

Buxton waved his hand dismissively. 'I'm sure your prices will be reasonable, Mr Hicksworth. Ensure you do not compromise on quality. Only the best materials and the finest workmanship will suffice. Now, I will bid you good day and look forward to seeing you again next week.'

A few minutes later, Buxton was sitting astride Corsair and trotting away from the village. He would not, he decided, return immediately to The Hall, but instead go for a gallop across the meadows and work up an appetite for dinner. He felt supremely pleased with the events of the morning and afternoon and there was still the evening to look forward to. The Richard Buxton who turned Corsair off the road and kicked him to a canter was, at that moment, the happiest man in the county of Essex.

At the same time as her husband was sketching on the village green, Clarissa was standing at the foot of the main staircase perusing the card Robert the footman had handed her. It stated simply: Colonel H. T. Markham, The Grange, Dillsbury, Essex.

'The Colonel is awaiting you in the morning room, as you requested, Madam,' the footman informed her stiffly.

Clarissa nodded. 'Thank you, Robert. Please bring us some tea.'

The servant bowed. 'At once, Madam.'

The Colonel rose to greet her as she entered the room. The sight of him almost stopped Clarissa in her tracks. The man was huge, virtually a giant.

At six foot six inches tall, Colonel Markham towered over her. His shoulders seemed as wide as a farm gate and his arms and legs reminded her of oak boughs. The tight-fitting hacking jacket and riding breeches accentuated the aura of strength and power he radiated. Clarissa judged him to be in his mid-forties. His face, ruddied by country life rather than tanned by the sun, was ruggedly handsome. His dark hair was clipped severely short. In every respect, this was clearly not a man to be trifled with or lightly ignored.

Colonel Markham bowed with stiff formality and held out a hand the size of a dinner plate. 'Colonel Markham, ma'am. Charmed to make your acquaintance.'

Clarissa's hand was dwarfed by the Colonel's and, though she knew he could have crushed every bone in it with a single squeeze, his handshake was surprisingly warm and welcoming.

'So pleased to meet you, Colonel,' Clarissa told him. 'Please be seated. We are neighbours I believe.'

The Colonel wedged his massive frame into the confines of the armchair. 'That is correct, ma'am. I live at The Grange; it's just outside the next village, about four miles by road, but only a couple across the fields. I heard that you had taken up residence and, as I was out riding in the vicinity, thought I would pay my compliments. I trust I have not inconvenienced you by my uninvited arrival.'

'Not at all, Colonel,' Clarissa reassured him. 'I am delighted to meet a neighbour so soon, for I know no one in this area. I only visited Castleleigh a few times when I was a girl and the area and its people are therefore new to me. I want to get to know both as soon as I can.'

The footman entered and the conversation paused while he placed a tray on the small table between host and guest.

'Thank you, Robert. We shall serve ourselves,' Clarissa told him. She watched him leave the room, her eyes following the slight swaying of his buttocks as he walked. Really, she told herself, she must stop looking at servants in such a manner. She turned her attention back to her visitor.

'From your title, I take it you are a military man.'

The Colonel nodded. 'Hussars, 18th/21st, for the best part of thirty years. But retired now, though I'm still in charge of the local yeomanry. That's not proper soldiering though. They're a ragtaggle lot, competent enough to deal with the odd riot, but they wouldn't last half an hour in a real battle.'

'Have you seen many real battles?' Clarissa asked as she sipped her tea.

'Enough, ma'am. Enough. Alma, Balaclava, Sebastopol. Came through without a scratch, thank God.'

'If you don't mind me saying, you seem too young to be retired,' Clarissa observed.

'I retired meself, ma'am. My next posting would have been India and I did not like that idea. No real battles to fight there now the mutiny is over and I don't particularly care for heat and flies. Give me the snow of the Crimea any day to the sun of the Punjab.'

Colonel Markham smiled to himself. It was a reasonable enough answer to an obvious question. No point in mentioning the General's daughter.

'There is no need to address me as ma'am, Colonel,' Clarissa told him with a smile. 'My name is Clarissa, Clarissa Buxton.'

'And my friends, among whom I very much hope I may count your good self, call me Harry.'

'And, now you are retired from the army, how do you occupy your time? In addition to leading the local militia that is.'

'I breed horses. Got one of the finest breeding stables in the county. And I hunt of course. I am Master of Foxhounds hereabouts.'

'I have not hunted for years,' Clarissa told him.

'Our next meet is in three weeks and, of course, we would be delighted if you would join us.'

'I shall look forward to it. Though I shall need some practice. I have lived in London these past two years and a canter in The Row hardly prepares one for the hunting field.'

'And does your husband hunt?' the Colonel asked.

'Actually, I do not know. Though he is a very fine rider. I am sure he would be pleased to be given the opportunity.'

'Consider it done,' the Colonel told her.

'Does your wife hunt?'

The Colonel shook his head. 'I am afraid my wife is prone to the ague which comes off the marshes hereabouts. She is rarely strong enough to leave the house.'

'I must call and pay her my respects,' said Clarissa as she watched her guest drink his tea. His frame was huge and she could not stop herself wondering if other parts of his anatomy were in proportion. The thought sparked a tingle between her thighs.

'The stables here have been allowed to fall into a terrible state of disrepair in recent years. I know my husband intends to rebuild and restock them and I am sure he would welcome any advice from an expert such as yourself.'

'You are very kind, Clarissa, to refer to me as an expert. Though, I suppose that is what I am. Of course, I shall be delighted to give your husband all the help I can.'

The itching between her thighs was becoming more insistent. Clarissa considered making an excuse to

85

leave the room and find somewhere private where she could relieve it, but dismissed the notion as being too impolite. Instead she said, 'It is such a lovely afternoon and I have not been in the fresh air all day. Perhaps, Harry, you would care to accompany me to the stables now so that you can judge the task before us.'

The Colonel rose. 'A pleasure, ma'am. I mean, Clarissa.'

They walked side by side around the house and along the overgrown track leading to the stables. Clarissa was very aware that the Colonel's eyes were upon her and that he was appraising her. The shyness and reserve, which had marked her all her life, had evaporated in a matter of hours. She knew he liked what he saw, and could almost read his thoughts. She also knew that, being a gentleman, her companion would restrain himself. If any moves were to be made, she would have to make the first one but, to retain her own propriety, it dare not be too obvious.

Her opportunity came halfway along the path when she spied a stone sticking up from the sun-baked clay. Her toe struck against it and, arms outstretched to save herself, she pitched forward. Instantly the Colonel reacted. His powerful arm streaked out and encircled her, preventing her falling and pulling her upright. He could have grasped her by the shoulders or round the waist. Instead, his arm wrapped round her body and his hand clasped her breasts, where it lingered for longer than safety demanded. The feeling of his strong arm around her and his hand clutching her breast re-awakened the earlier tingling. She looked up at him.

'Thank you. I shall see this path is attended to.'

The Colonel withdrew his arm, sliding his hand across her breast as he did so. 'Glad to be of service. That could have been a nasty fall.'

86

No more was said about the incident because no more had to be. They walked on in silence. By the time they reached the stables the air between them was charged with the anticipation of unasked questions.

The stables of The Hall were a hundred yards behind the house. They consisted of four two-storey, red-bricked blocks built around a spacious, stone-flagged courtyard which was reached by passing through an imposing arched gateway on top of which was a four-sided clock.

From a distance they looked impressive. But the nearer Clarissa and the Colonel came, the more their dilapidated state became apparent. The clock had clearly not ticked for years and half the hands were missing. Broad patches of plaster had fallen from the arch, exposing the brickwork beneath. Moss filled the cracks in the walls and scores of tiles had long since slid from the roofs. Most of the windows were either cracked or missing altogether. Inside, weeds pushed their way through broken, uneven stones and there were piles of rusting harnesses and other litter in every corner. A donkey cart, missing one wheel, leaned drunkenly against a wall.

As they passed through the arch, Samuel, the head groom, ran to meet them. Samuel touched the peak of his cap in respect. 'Is there anything I can do for you, Madam?'

Clarissa paused barely a moment before replying. 'Yes, there is. The Colonel's horse is tethered at the house. Please go and ensure that it is being properly cared for and remain with it until we return.'

'Yes, Madam.'

The groom set off at a brisk pace down the path back towards the house. Clarissa and the Colonel watched until he was well out of earshot.

The Colonel's tone was low and conspiratorial. 'So, we will not be disturbed during our inspection.'

Clarissa merely smiled sweetly up at him, but the look in her eyes told him that that was exactly what she had planned. She gestured towards the buildings which surrounded them. 'Well, as you can see, we have a lot of work to do.'

'A Herculean task, if I may say so,' the Colonel replied. 'Quite frankly, Clarissa, I would not allow my servants to live in such conditions. Certainly not my horses.'

'You mean your horses live better than your servants?'

'Of course,' replied the Colonel as if the question surprised him. 'I breed horses and they earn me money. Servants only cost me money. Servants are ten a penny, but a good horse is worth thousands of pounds. So, my dear, who should I treat the best?'

'You prefer horses to people, then?'

'In my experience there is little difference between them,' the Colonel replied. 'It is all a question of breeding. Two carthorses will produce another carthorse. Two servants will produce children who in turn will become servants. Two thoroughbreds will produce another thoroughbred. A gentleman and a lady will produce children who will become gentlemen and ladies in their turn. It is the way of the world. Always has been and always will be.'

'And I can tell that you have an eye for thoroughbreds, Harry,' Clarissa commented as they entered the first of the stable blocks.

The Colonel laughed. 'Indeed I do. Particularly fillies. I am especially good at spotting the potential of young fillies.'

'Does that also apply to people as well as horses?' Clarissa asked.

'Of course. It is all a matter of breaking and schooling. Once they are trained, they are yours for life.'

The stables they now stood in were the best kept of the entire block. The bedding was fresh and the floor swept, but of the ten stalls only two were occupied. The Colonel looked the bay gelding and the grey mare up and down and shook his head.

'If I may say so, Clarissa. These are not even fit for dog meat and wood glue.'

'They were here when we came,' Clarissa explained. 'That stall there is Corsair's. He is my husband's horse and as fine a stallion as you will see anywhere.'

'And, if I may ask, where is your husband at the moment?'

It was a perfectly natural question to ask, but both understood the importance of the answer.

'I believe he is touring the estate,' Clarissa replied. 'I do not expect him to return until dinner.'

Clarissa pointed towards the hayloft above the stalls. 'Do you think that wood is rotten? If so, we shall have to pull it down and replace it. I would not want there to be any accidents.'

'Where?' the Colonel asked as his eyes followed the line of her upstretched arm, providing Clarissa with the opportunity she required. She took his hand and raised his arm so as to better point out the problem. At the same time, her other arm curved round the small of his back. The Colonel lowered his arm without allowing her to release his hand and faced her. Clarissa, in turn, lowered her embrace so that her hand rested on the seat of his breeches. 'I think, Clarissa, that you are far more dangerous than that hayloft will ever be.'

They looked into each other's eyes and both understood that the time for innuendoes had passed.

The Colonel put his arms round her in a bearlike grip which forced the air from her. His lips pressed hard on hers and her mouth opened to receive his tongue. Clarissa squeezed his buttocks and then managed to push the lower half of her body away from his just far enough to allow her to slip her hand round to the front of his breeches and rub the swelling mound within.

Without a word, the Colonel released her and began tearing off his clothes. Hacking jacket and cravat were tossed into a corner of the nearest stall, quickly followed by his shirt. Clarissa, herself eagerly unbuttoning and discarding her dress, gasped at the sight before her. His barrel-sized chest, and most of his stomach, was a jungle of coarse, curly black hair. Clarissa pushed down her petticoat and kicked it away. She pulled at the laces of her corset until sufficient had been unfastened to allow her breasts to swing free.

'Damn these things,' cursed the Colonel as he balanced on one leg, attempting to pull off his knee-high riding boots.

'Forget your boots,' Clarissa told him breathlessly as she clawed at the buttons on the side of his breeches, virtually tearing them off in her haste. Her fingers closed over the waist band and she pulled them down to the top of his boots.

Clarissa gasped at the sight which confronted her. The Colonel was massive. Before Richard, she had not even known what a cock looked like. She had thought him big. But if her husband was well endowed, the Colonel was virtually deformed. It was already fully ten inches long and still growing. She put her hand round it and thumb and forefinger did not even meet. Clarissa grabbed his hand and fell back on to the straw, pulling him down beside her.

As they kissed, her breasts squashed against his chest. The coarse, matted hair grated like wire as it rubbed against the soft skin and her nipples felt as if they would burst as the friction made them swell and harden. She reached down and grabbed the Colonel's throbbing erection. She ran her hand slowly upwards and it seemed she would never reach the tip. When she eventually did so, she found her fingers stroking metal as well as skin. Astonished, Clarissa pulled away from his embrace and looked down. Shining at the edge of his foreskin was a small golden ring.

The Colonel laughed. 'I suppose you have never seen one before. They used to be essential in the army. The breeches were so tight that, if you had anything downstairs, you got yourself pierced, put a chain round your waist and another down your arse and pulled it backwards. It keeps the front smooth, don't you see? Fine for the mess, but damned uncomfortable at the gallop.'

'Now! Take me now!' panted Clarissa.

The Colonel started to clamber on top of her, but she stopped him. 'This is a stables. Have me like a horse. You'll be my stallion and I'll be your mare.' So saying, she rolled over, placing her head on the straw, drawing up her knees and pushing her buttocks towards him. The Colonel needed no further urging. He knelt between her legs and began to push his way into her.

Clarissa's channel had never been so lubricated, but still the lips of her hole tried to resist entry to the massive invader. As he forced his way into her, Clarissa feared she would be split in twain by the sheer size of the thing. At first, she winced with the pain but, as the monster bore ever further inside her, inch by wonderful inch, stretching her to the very limit, she no longer felt any pain, just a swirling sensation in her brain that made her nearly swoon, and the most amazing shuddering in her loins. Just as she thought he would never stop, she finally felt his balls pressing hard against her mound.

The Colonel rode her just as she had requested: like a rampant stallion. He withdrew almost to the limit before ramming into her again. Clarissa cried out with the intoxicating mixture of pain and pleasure and buried her face further into the straw. The feel of the little gold ring inside her, scraping against the walls of her passage, heightened her arousal. The Colonel's cock was like a battering ram, mercilessly pounding into her. She heard his gasp, and when he came it was like a battery of cannon all firing inside her at the same time. The feeling of spurt after spurt of warm spunk exploding from him triggered her own climax, and she screamed and bit into the straw, as the dam burst and she too ejaculated.

Clarissa felt the huge shaft slowly slide from her body. She rolled over and lay back on the straw looking up at the massive figure kneeling beside her. Although beginning to wilt, the Colonel's cock was still massively impressive. Clarissa reached out and squeezed its helmet, coaxing the last small droplets of come from it. She put her hand to her mouth and licked her palm clean, savouring the delicious salty taste of his cream.

The Colonel laughed and shook his head in wonder at the woman who smiled up at him. It was not the first time he had been seduced, hopefully it would not be the last, but it had certainly been the most unexpected. 'You are astonishing, my dear Clarissa, quite, quite astonishing,' he told her as he rose and pulled up his jodhpurs.

Clarissa watched him dress. She agreed with him. She was astonishing. Certainly, she was astonished by her own actions. She had always believed adultery to be a mortal sin. That was what the Church and Society had always taught her and never in her life before had she questioned the instructions of either. Now, before the flowers of her bouquet had even begun to fade, she had allowed another man to take her. No, not allowed, enticed. And she had enjoyed every second of their lovemaking. Lovemaking? No, there had been no love involved. It had been passion, it had been desire; but it certainly had had nothing to do with love.

'Clarissa, may I suggest that you too get dressed,' the Colonel advised as he buttoned his jacket. 'There is always the possibility of someone discovering us, and the fact that we are here alone will anyway cause talk among the servants.'

Reluctantly, Clarissa followed his advice. She would quite happily and contentedly have lain for much longer on the soft straw, feeling the warm come drip from her body, but his words made sense. There were appearances to be maintained.

'So, tell me, Colonel, how did you find your new mare?' Clarissa asked as they walked side by side down the path back towards the house.

The Colonel made a pretence of considering the question seriously. 'A filly, I think, rather than a fullblooded mare. She has superb potential, but perhaps she still requires a great deal more schooling.'

'I fully agree with you, but it is all a matter of opportunity,' Clarissa told him.

'In my experience, most of the opportunities we have in life, we make ourselves. Take tomorrow, for instance.'

'Tomorrow, Harry? What is happening tomorrow?'

'There is a lodge on my estate I use as a base for shooting parties. I have one such party arranged for next week. Therefore, I must be at the lodge tomorrow at midday to ensure that all is in order for their arrival. Were you to be there then I would be able to fulfil my promise to help you with your riding.'

'Horses?' asked Clarissa with feigned naivety.

The Colonel's laugh was loud and hearty. 'Those too, Clarissa. Those too.'

'And where exactly is this lodge of yours, Harry?'

'Just follow the bridlepath to Manor Farm. Once you have rounded the copse beyond the cornfields you are on my land. You can see the lodge from there. It is white with a round tower, set among a plantation of pines. You cannot miss it.'

'Unless my husband requires me for other duties, I shall be there. I look foward to your further tuition,' Clarissa assured him as they reached the house, where the groom waited patiently beside the Colonel's horse.

Clarissa stood and watched as the Colonel mounted and rode away, not down the drive this time, but across the field and along the track which she knew led to Manor Farm. The sound of hoofbeats and her husband's voice shook her from her thoughts.

'And who might that be?'

Clarissa turned. 'Oh, hello, Richard. His name is Colonel Harry Markham, one of our neighbours and master of the local hunt. He has been paying his respects.'

'I have been hearing about the Colonel in the village. I am sorry to have missed him.' Buxton leaned down and pulled a piece of straw from his wife's hair. 'Clarissa, you look as if you have been rolling in a haystack.'

'I was showing Colonel Markham the stables, Richard. He is an authority on horses and horse breeding.'

'Then our stables and our horses would hardly have impressed him,' Buxton commented wryly as he slid from the saddle and handed the reins to the groom. 'I have business to attend to now, Clarissa. I shall see you at dinner.'

Buxton found Robert the footman in the hall and summoned him into the library.

'Robert, I heard some very disturbing news in the village today. It appears his Lordship did not keep a cellar.'

'There was a very well-stocked cellar here at one time, sir,' the servant explained, 'but his Lordship sold all its contents some two years ago.'

Buxton sighed, 'Damn the man. So, I cannot even have a glass of wine with my dinner tonight?'

'I think that will be possible, sir,' replied the footman. 'You see, unfortunately, when the carriers came to collect the wine for the auction, they overlooked two cases of a rather fine 48 Burgundy. I do not know how it happened.'

Buxton laughed. 'No, Robert, I am sure you do not. And how many bottles of this rather fine Burgundy remain?'

'I am afraid that all the bottles in one of the cases were broken, sir. But the other remains intact.'

'Then ensure one is served at dinner tonight.'

The footman bowed his acquiescence. 'Very good, sir.'

'I presume his Lordship sold his port and spirits as well?'

'The port, yes, sir. His Lordship always kept very little spirits in the house. However, when he was ill last year he did instruct me to obtain some brandy for medicinal purposes.'

Buxton grimaced. 'Medicinal brandy, you say? I think I can do without that rot-gut stuff.'

95

The footman allowed himself a half smile. 'Actually, sir, his Lordship did not state the type of brandy he wanted me to purchase. I therefore acquired two cases of Napoleon Cognac.'

Buxton leaned back in his chair, put his hands behind his head and laughed.

'Robert, you are going up in my estimation with every word you speak. What exactly is the staffing here?'

'There is the housekeeper, Miss Trubshaw, Mrs Paton, the cook, her husband Charles, who is the gardener, two maids of all work and myself. His Lordship rarely visited, therefore he saw no need for more.'

'Well, I do,' Buxton told him. 'I intend to entertain frequently – and well. I intend to put The Hall at the centre of local society. I have already appointed two new servants. They are Rebecca, the daughter of farmer Dakins at Home Farm, who will be coming here tomorrow to start as a maid, and a young lad named Tom, who will work in the stables.'

Buxton saw the footman's eyes widen at the mention of Rebecca Dakins.

'You know this Dakins girl, Robert?'

'I do believe that nearly everyone hereabouts knows Rebecca Dakins, sir,' the footman replied stonefaced.

Oh, I'm sure they do or have done, Buxton thought, but he decided not to enquire further just then.

'We shall require more staff and, of course, a butler. I believe I have found someone to be butler.'

The footman stiffened slightly at the news and requested formally, 'And may I know who that is to be, sir?'

'You, Robert. I think you will fill the post exceptionally well. As from this moment, you are my butler.'

Robert bowed. 'Thank you, sir. It is a great honour and I will do everything possible to be of service to you in my new position.'

'I'm sure you will, Robert. I'm sure you will. Another change I intend to make is to pension off Miss Trubshaw. I think she has served The Hall well but is now too old to undertake the additional responsibilities which will be required of her in the future. I have another in mind for the position. Someone with very special qualifications which will be of great help to me in my plans for the house and the estate. Now, Robert, I have work to do. Please bring me a glass of this so-called medicinal brandy.'

Once the footman had left, Buxton sat at the broad, leather-topped desk in the window bay and began to put pen to paper and write the letter he had been composing in his mind for most of the afternoon.

'*My Very Dearest Maxine . . .*'

Seven

The man was securely restrained. His body was incapable of any movement except the merest swaying forwards or backwards in an involuntary response to the blows cutting into him from every angle. His arms were raised high and wide and almost all his considerable bodyweight was supported by his wrists which were tightly strapped to a roof joist. His legs were spread as far as the joints would allow. His feet were locked in iron clamps which bit into the flesh of his ankles like mantraps. Every bone, muscle and tendon was stretched to its ultimate limit and flaming arrows of pain shot through his limbs with every minute reaction to the whip. He was tall and powerful, and his many years in the outer regions of the Empire had tanned his skin a light mahogany. The only part of him which was not impressive for its size and strength was his penis, which was small and flaccid and only stirred into a semblance of life when the cat-o'-nine-tails tore across his back.

Maxine applied the nine-thonged instrument with all her considerable power, till his legs, thighs, buttocks and back were a crimson battlefield. When there was little unmarked space left there, she began subjecting chest, stomach and genitals to the same expertly calculated punishment. The man was blindfolded and quivered with the delightful anticipation of not knowing when, or where, the next blow would land. Whenever the whip found its target, the sound which escaped his lips was not a scream, but a high-pitched sigh of perfect contentment.

Maxine did her job with patient professionalism. Even after so many years, so many men with so many different demands, she usually still enjoyed her work. Dominating a man might not be as enjoyable, nor as rewarding, as training a girl but it could still rouse her and, more importantly, provided the means to maintain her extremely comfortable lifestyle. But that night she felt bored with the whole business; not only tired of it all, but also resentful and lonely.

Finally, she threw down the whip and pulled the sash beside the door. Within a few seconds Violet was standing before her, head bowed and eyes fixed on the floor. She wore only a tightly laced black corset which, instead of cupping and covering her breasts, dug into the skin below them, leaving them totally exposed while at the same time forcing them upwards and outwards. From the waist down she was completely naked. Around her neck she wore a black leather slave collar, while a thin gold chain joined her ankles so that she hobbled rather than walked. Maxine pointed to the floor in front of the man.

'Keep him aroused, but do not let him spend.'

Eyes still downcast, Violet tottered to the place her mistress had indicated. She knew exactly what to do. She knelt and took the man's limp member in her hand, rubbing it gently while her tongue flicked around its helmet. Eventually it began to respond to her manipulations, but even then it was so small she found she could insert the entire length into her mouth without gagging, to the extent that her top teeth became entangled in his thick pubic hair and her bottom teeth rasped against his balls. Rhythmically she rocked her head and sucked, ever alert for the first pulsation which would warn her that he was about to spurt and ready to stop instantly when she felt it. The punishment her mistress would inflict on her should her charge succeed in satisfying himself while she was absent made the girl tremble with that strange mixture of fear and longing which she had come not just to accept, but to continually yearn for.

Maxine did not wait to see how well Violet performed the task she had been set. If she failed she would be severely punished, but Maxine doubted that she would. In recent weeks, Violet had adopted the role of slave with an eagerness and passion which she had at first found gratifying, but now found almost tedious. She knew there was little more she could teach the girl and, when that stage was reached, she always started to lose interest. That night, in particular, she quite simply did not care.

Maxine walked down the narrow spiral staircase from the attic room which she had long since converted into a chamber housing such a diverse and ingenious collection of instruments of pain and punishment that they would have been the envy of any medieval inquisitor. She found the person she sought in one of the bedrooms on the second floor.

Latricia was standing totally naked with her back to a roaring fire looking down disdainfully at the woman who grovelled at her feet. The two women were opposites in every way: Latricia, tall and slender with small, firm breasts and flowing light brown hair framing a beautiful and proud face; the woman, small and obese with massive pendulous breasts which flopped against her rolls of stomach fat. Her huge buttocks wobbled grotesquely every time she moved and her thighs were tree trunk-sized hams of loose flesh. Her features were piglike and crowned by close-cropped, dyed blonde hair which contrasted starkly with the matted black thatch between her thighs.

Maxine leaned against the wall and watched the performance, assessing the skills of her prodigy. Latricia, knowing she was being judged, responded by putting even more energy and enthusiasm into her work.

Since meeting Maxine she had discovered a natural affinity for her new profession and not only enjoyed, but revelled in, the power she could wield. The woman, who was now licking her feet, was the wife of a successful grocer who owned three shops in the area. Once, when she was a child, Latricia had begged her for stale bread to help feed her starving brothers and sisters and had been sent away not just empty-handed but also with her ears stinging from the cuff they had received. Tonight, this same woman would soon be pleading to lick her arse.

Latricia bent down and grabbed the woman's hair. The woman cried out as her head was roughly jerked upright and she was forced to her knees so that her eyes were level with Latricia's shaven mound. The woman put out her tongue in readiness to obey what she anticipated would be her mistress's next command, but Latricia yanked her head backwards.

'I did not tell you to do that. You do nothing, remember nothing, until you are instructed. How many times must I tell you that?'

The woman shuddered at the pitiless anger in Latricia's voice. She opened her mouth to reply, then quickly closed it. To speak out of turn would, she knew, only compound her crime and increase the severity of her punishment.

Latricia turned and bent forward. She put her hands behind her and pulled apart the cheeks of her buttocks, exposing her anus.

'Now, you may lick.'

The woman buried her face in Latricia's buttocks and began to slaver along the divide.

Latricia's scornful tone quickly stopped her. 'Not like that, you stupid cow. Do you think I want your spit all over me? I want to feel your tongue inside me. Right inside me. I want you to taste my shit.'

The woman obeyed instantly. She began by rotating the tip of her tongue around the entrance to Latricia's opening before gradually easing it inside and wiggling it from side to side and up and down as fast as she could.

Latricia felt herself becoming aroused, but not from the woman's ministrations themselves. It was the sense of supreme power that was the catalyst of the reactions which were beginning within her. Surely, there could be no work more enjoyable or rewarding than this. She allowed herself the pleasure of savouring the situation for a while and then, without warning, raised her right leg and kicked viciously. The sole of her foot landed between the woman's breasts, sending her crashing backwards. Latricia turned and stood over the prostrate form. The woman looked up at her but did not move.

'Stand.'

The woman stood, head bowed, arms at her sides. Latricia slowly circled her.

'You are fat. You are ugly. You are stupid and you are common. What are you?'

The woman hesitated for only a moment, but it was all the excuse Latricia needed. She reached forward and clamped the woman's left nipple between thumb and index finger, pulling and turning as she did so. The woman shrieked with the sudden, unexpected pain. Latricia merely squeezed and pulled harder.

'What are you?'

'I am fat. I am ugly. I am –'

'Louder!' Latricia snarled as she reached for the woman's other breast and captured the nipple between her long fingernails.

The woman squealed again as Latricia's talon-sharp nails dug into her skin and this time shouted her response.

'I am fat. I am ugly. I am stupid. I am common.'

Latricia could feel the woman's nipples becoming ever firmer between her fingers. So the old sow was enjoying it, was she? It was time to see how much she would revel in the next stage of her ordeal.

Latricia released her grip and selected three thin leather belts from a collection of instruments laid out in readiness on a nearby table. Quickly and expertly she used one to bind the woman's arms behind her back. With the next, she encircled one of the woman's massive breasts and pulled it so tight that it lifted and the veins pulsated and stood out like lines on a map. She continued until the tit looked like an overfilled balloon about to burst. The woman squirmed and her face distorted with the pain, but she made no sound and offered no protest.

Latricia took the third strip of leather and wrapped it once around her hand. She raised her arm and swung the belt at her helpless victim with all her strength. The brass buckle tore into the woman's engorged breast and she screamed. Again and again Latricia wielded the belt, and each time the woman's high-pitched scream echoed round the chamber as metal and leather found their mark, but she made no plea for clemency. She was paying for this service and she could always bring it to an end if she so desired. But then, she knew, she would never be allowed to return and the thought of never more being able to see or serve her new mistress was worse than any amount of humiliation and pain. And, slowly, her body was beginning to shake, not with pain, but the bubbling sensation that began in the pit of her stomach and then spread like a fire through every inch of her body; a sensation which she had never known before discovering this house and which she was now completely addicted to experiencing over and over again.

After twelve strokes Latricia tossed the belt aside, but made no move to release the woman. Instead, she selected a broad leather paddle. Slowly at first, and then with increasing momentum, she stroked the thick, round handle between the woman's legs. When at last she withdrew it, the shaft was wet and sticky. Latricia looked from it to the woman, her face a portrait of disgust.

'You filthy old slut. How dare you enjoy yourself? Clean it!'

Latricia held the handle towards her and the woman leaned forward and licked her own juices from it.

'Stand against the wall. Over there.'

The woman shuffled over to where her mistress indicated and stood in front of a full-length mirror.

Latricia was about to start beating the woman's huge, sagging buttocks when Maxine interrupted.

'Enough for now.'

Latricia lowered the paddle and looked questioningly at her.

'I have other work for you this evening, Latricia,' Maxine explained. 'Untie her.'

Latricia freed her captive, but the woman was far from happy at being released so early. Hands on hips, she squared up to Maxine.

'I haven't paid good money to be sent packing before I'm ready,' she complained. 'And I ain't ready yet. Not by a long chalk I ain't.'

It would have been a mistake to address Maxine in such terms at any time. That evening, the woman could not have chosen a worse moment to confront her.

Maxine's voice quivered with barely controlled rage.

'You dare to question me, do you? Well, perhaps you have a point. After all, we do not want a dissatisfied client, now do we?'

Maxine ignored the canes, belts, tawses and paddles laid out on the table and instead opened a cupboard beside the fireplace. When she turned back to face the woman, she was holding a fearsome bull whip in her hand.

'So you like pain, do you?' she sneered. 'You actually think what you experienced tonight was real pain? Well, if that is the case, you have never known real pain. Let me introduce you.'

And with that Maxine cracked the whip. She merely moved her forearm and flicked her wrist, but it was enough to send the six feet of supple leather, with its sharpened bevelled edges, scything across the room.

The woman was too stout and too slow to move away in time. The whip sliced into the rolls of stomach fat and she screamed as she had never screamed before. Maxine struck again, this time wrapping the leather round her legs and yanking her off her feet with the expertise of a cowboy roping a steer.

The fall knocked the breath from the woman's body. She lay, unable to move and aware that the delicious stirrings of arousal of a few minutes before were gone. Now all she felt was fear and the white-hot pain that seared through her stomach. She began to cry, a convulsive sobbing that racked her body.

Maxine jerked the whip free and was about to strike again when the woman cried out, the words tripping over themselves in her haste to make amends.

'I'm sorry. Truly sorry. Please forgive me. Of course I will leave. I will do anything you ask of me. Forgive me, Mistress. I did not mean to offend.'

Maxine withheld the blow but did not discard the whip.

'Get dressed and get out. I may allow you to return in the future, or I may not. We shall see.'

Hastily, the woman rose and began pulling on the clothes that were piled on the bed. Neither Maxine nor Latricia spoke until she had scurried from the room.

'I hope you will allow her back, Maxine,' said Latricia as the door closed behind the terrified woman. 'I have a particular interest in working on that one.'

Maxine shrugged as she put the bull whip back in the cupboard.

'She can come back if she wants to and you can do what you like with her. I really have no interest in the matter.'

Latricia drew a thick velvet cloak around her shoulders.

'And what is this other work you have for me this evening?'

'The General needs finishing off. He's in the attic. I feel very tired tonight and, quite honestly, I just can't be bothered.'

Latricia smiled. 'It will be a pleasure. There is something about that man I truly dislike.'

'He is a complete bastard,' Maxine told her. 'When he was in India he was known as Flogging Freddy. Apparently, he had the men beaten for the most minor of offences. What they couldn't know, of course, was that it wasn't them he wanted on the frame, but himself. The person who introduced him told me that during the Mutiny he had mutineers strapped to cannon barrels and actually laughed as they were blown to bits.'

'I think I shall enjoy looking after him tonight,' Latricia observed.

'Violet is, shall we say, keeping his pecker up till you get there. What there is of it.'

Latricia half smiled at the name. 'The inviolate Violet. How charming.'

Maxine knew of the nickname the other girls had given Violet, but no one had ever spoken it in her presence before. She had kept Violet totally for herself, and the other residents of the house had known better than to interfere with her. But now, perhaps, the time had arrived to broaden Violet's experience.

'When you have finished with the General, Latricia, you can do what you like with Violet. You can give me all the details tomorrow. Tonight I am going to my room and I do not want to be disturbed until morning.'

Leaving a surprised, and very pleased, Latricia behind her, Maxine did as she had said and went to her room. She took off her clothes and lay on the bed. The room was warm, but the pink satin sheets were soothingly cool against her skin. She stared at her reflection in the mirror above the bed and thought about her life.

She was rich and she was powerful. Not simply powerful in the sexual and physical sense; the sort of power which allowed her to dominate men or women as her whim dictated. No, she held very tangible and positive power. Should she ever publish her diaries she would cause havoc across the country and threaten the very fabric and structure of Society. From Royal Dukes to bankrupt Barons, from Cabinet Ministers to top civil servants, from members of the Imperial General Staff to lowly subalterns, from captains of industry to merchant bankers – she had known them all and catered for their desires, however degraded and perverse they might have been.

She had done well. She had had to. Almost from the time she could first walk and talk, she had understood that she had but two assets, her body and her mind. She could die young as a pox-ravaged, gin-soaked whore in the East End gutters, or she could make a future for herself by combining the allure of her physical charms with the power of her intellect. Before she had reached her thirteenth birthday, she had realised that selling her own body was short change. How much better to sit safe by a roaring fire, secure in the knowledge that others were out there in the cold dark streets, earning the pennies to pay for the coal that was keeping her warm. And so her career had progressed. No one had cared for her and she had cared for no one. Then Richard Buxton had entered her life and nothing had ever been the same since.

She had known very many men in her thirty-three years, but none had ever made her feel the way he had. Strangely though, she had not liked him very much on their first meeting. He had arrived three-quarters drunk in the company of the Honourable Archie Limpster, a chinless wonder of the type she instinctively despised. They had selected a couple of girls and rogered them as much as the copious amounts of alcohol they had consumed allowed. They had not asked for, and so not received, the attentions which were the speciality of the house. The pair had been loud and brash, but otherwise unremarkable. They had paid their money and gone on their way and she had thought no more about either of them.

A week later Richard had returned alone, sober and eager to demonstrate that his manners could be impeccable. She had invited him into her salon and they had talked about his family and how, despite his wealth, he felt not just an outsider but almost unwanted within the prim and proper social circles he was required to move in. She had found him witty and intelligent, not at all the drunken oaf she had first thought. That had been three years ago, and on that night, just as she had four weeks before, she had suggested a diversion to take his mind off his troubles. Then too, she had drawn back the curtain to reveal the activities in the room beyond the mirror. Maxine recalled the scene as though it had only happened the previous day.

Her name had been Annie. She had had long fair hair and a wonderfully innocent, elfin face. She was small and slim, but with breasts that were totally out of proportion to the rest of her body. Maxine smiled as she remembered the look on Richard's face as he watched them bounce up and down just a few inches from the other side of the mirror. That they were bouncing so vigorously had not been surprising for Annie's wrists had been strapped to each of the brass bedposts and her bottom was writhing under the fierce and continuous application of a thin willow cane. Maxine could not recall who had been wielding the cane, but she did remember that he had certainly been enthusiastic about his work.

Richard had drunk in the scene, that endearing half smile curling the corner of his lips. Maxine had glanced down and seen the growing bulge in his tight, fashionable trousers. Her hand had glided over it and then round to the buttons at the side. One by one she had released them until the front flapped down and she could slide her hand inside and begin massaging him. He had said nothing while her expert fingers gently squeezed and stroked. He had not even looked at her, but instead kept his eyes fixed on Annie's gyrating breasts. She had pulled at his trousers, tugging them down to his knees, and then knelt in front of him and begun to lick and suck. After many minutes, he had finally pulled away and she had stood up. He had put his arms round her waist and kissed her passionately before whispering in her ear, 'I want to explode, but I want to explode inside you, not over you.'

In seconds they had both torn off their clothes and were lying on the rug in front of the fire. His lovemaking had been forceful, but not brutal, and she had responded with the same energy and enthusiasm. For the first time in many years she had enjoyed sex with a man and, when it arrived, her climax had been the most powerful she had ever experienced with either man or woman.

They had spent the night together, and the next day she had shown him around the house and revealed all its secrets. He had met the girls and even enjoyed himself with Annie while she had watched. He had taken to the cane and the whip as a bee to a honeysuckle. In the two days he had spent at her house, Richard Buxton had discovered within himself a desire and a need which only she, and the very special services she could provide, were able to satisfy.

As she thought back over that first night they had spent together, and the countless others that had followed, Maxine's hand reached down and her fingers caressed her slit and gently rubbed her clit. She spread her legs and pushed two fingers into herself, then a third, while the fingers of her other hand clawed at the swollen, throbbing button. It had been a long time since she had satisfied herself in that way, for she always had so many others, men or girls, it did not always matter, who could do the work for her. But now she was panting and writhing like a teenager desperate for her first orgasm. And, when the climax came, she found herself shouting one word over and over again.

'*Richard! Richard! Richard!*'

Eight

Clarissa was still sleeping and Buxton saw no reason to wake her. He had planned his programme for the day ahead and Clarissa had no role in it. His hand was on the door handle when her voice stopped him and made him turn.

'Richard?'

'Yes?'

'You do still love me?'

'Love you?'

'Want me. You do still want me, don't you?'

'When I want you, Clarissa, I'll have you,' he told her coldly. 'Now, if you will excuse me, what I want at this moment is my breakfast. Will you be joining me?'

'I have a slight headache. Would you mind asking Lucy to bring me a tray?'

'Of course,' Buxton replied and left the bedroom before his wife could make any more requests and delay him still further.

In the breakfast room, Robert was standing beside the massive mahogany sideboard on which were arrayed a selection of silver tureens and salvers. He drew a chair from the head of the table and stood behind it, waiting for his master to sit. Buxton waved him aside.

'That is quite all right, Robert. I will see to myself,' Buxton told him. 'My wife is feeling a little under the

112

weather this morning. Please find Lucy and tell her to take her mistress's breakfast to her room.'

When the butler had left, Buxton helped himself to poached eggs and rashers of ham and poured himself a cup of strong, black coffee. He rounded the meal off with several slices of thickly buttered toast. He usually ate sparingly in the morning, but if the day went as he hoped, then he would need the energy a full stomach would provide.

He felt fit and refreshed after a night's untroubled slumber. He had told the truth when he had explained to Clarissa that he was tired. But that was not the reason he had rejected her advances. If she was to fully appreciate her place in his life then she had to understand that she could make no demands upon him. Overnight, the repressed virginal girl had turned into a sex-hungry, wanton woman. By treating her coldly, and denying her what she so ardently craved, he could stoke the fires of desire he had kindled inside her to a blazing inferno of lust. By so doing, be could be sure of stamping his authority on their relationship.

He finished his second cup of coffee and pulled the bell sash. Robert answered the summons in seconds.

'Has the Dakins girl arrived yet?'

'Yes, sir. I have put her to work cleaning the grates in the library.'

Buxton nodded. 'Thank you, Robert. That will be all.'

Rebecca Dakins was kneeling in front of the huge stone fireplace at the far end of the library, shovelling ash and clinker into a bucket. She did not hear Buxton enter and it was not until he tapped the toe of his boot against her bottom that she was aware of his presence. She looked round and glared up at him. Her apron was blackened by ash and soot, her hands were grimy and there were black smears across her forehead where she had tried to keep her fringe out of her eyes. She looked a sorry sight, but she still looked very pretty, and the ill-made, coarse cotton dress could not totally obscure the enticing curves of her figure.

Buxton told her sharply, 'Don't you know you are supposed to stand when your betters enter a room?'

Without apology, and with the surliest of demeanours, Rebecca stood up and faced him. She eyed him defiantly.

'Well, you young slut,' Buxton demanded, 'what have you to say for yourself?'

There was true hatred in the girl's eyes as she glared at her new employer and muttered, 'Beg pardon?'

The back of Buxton's hand smashed into her cheek, sending her reeling back against the mantelpiece. 'Beg pardon, what?'

'Beg pardon, sir.' The girl responded grudgingly.

Buxton knew the blow must have stung, but there were no tears in her eyes.

'That's better, Rebecca. You are a dirty little slut of very little consequence. I have promised your father I will teach you obedience, and I shall fulfil that promise. Do you understand?'

Just as Buxton had hoped, his words succeeded in igniting the girl's temper.

'I ain't no slut, and you ain't got no right nor cause to call me such,' she flared. 'I never asked to come here. This ain't no work for the likes of me. I'm a farm girl, I am. I work in the open, not indoors. And, as for my father, he ain't nothing but a drunken old sot who sold me to you for the price of a few quarts of ale.'

Buxton admired her spirit just as much as he looked forward to the pleasure of breaking it. 'You need to be taught your manners, Rebecca. And there is no better time than the present.'

So saying, he took one step forward, grabbed her by the hair and threw her face down across the desk. The impact knocked the wind from her and, before she could even try to rise, his left forearm was pinioning her in place while his right hand was pulling up her skirt. She wore no undergarments and her long, shapely legs, and the tight pink mounds of her buttocks, were soon exposed. Without warning, and with all his considerable strength, Buxton brought the flat of his hand down on the inviting orbs. The girl stiffened at the impact but made no sound. From what he had witnessed in the barn the previous day, Buxton had not expected her to. It would take far more than a mere spanking to make this one cower; but it would suffice as a preliminary. He was raising his hand to deliver the seventh blow on the rapidly reddening cheeks when he heard the library door open.

Robert coughed apologetically and made to leave the room. 'I am sorry sir. I did not realise that you were not alone.'

Still maintaining his grip on the girl, Buxton called him back.

'Don't leave, Robert. As butler you should know the nature of the staff you will be responsible for. This wretch has been surly and insolent and she is being punished for it. I will not tolerate such attitudes from my servants.'

Robert joined them and stared at Rebecca's inflamed arse.

'From what you were saying yesterday, Robert, I believe you know this trollop. Is that so?' Buxton asked.

Robert nodded. 'I know her, sir. So does nearly every other man in Castleleigh. She is just a piece of

115

filth, sir. She might be called a whore, 'cept she don't take no money for it. She is known as the village carrier 'cause most people have ridden her at some time.'

Rebecca squirmed and glared round at the butler. 'Most people, Robert Flaxman, perhaps, but not you. Thought you were so superior, didn't you? Just because you lived at The Hall and wore a fancy uniform. But you ain't half what the village lads are.'

The girl wriggled her naked bottom and laughed. 'Take a good look, Robert Flaxman. Take a very good look. I never let you see this before, even though you begged me so often, and you ain't ever going to see it again.'

Buxton looked at his new butler. The man was seething with suppressed rage.

'Robert, this impudent doxy clearly needs much more severe chastisement. She simply cannot be allowed to address a man in your position this way. But, I fear, this is not the place to administer it. We need somewhere where we can be certain of not being disturbed.'

The butler thought for a moment before suggesting, 'We could always use the chapel, sir.'

Buxton was surprised. 'The chapel, Robert?'

'Well, sir, it has not actually been a chapel these fifty years past. It is used as a storeroom now; no one ever goes there.'

'And where is this chapel?' Buxton asked.

'Directly below here, sir.'

Buxton considered the idea but promptly dismissed it. 'The problem, Robert, is that we can hardly take her there without other staff seeing us, and how should we explain that?'

'We can reach it without being seen, sir. If you will allow me?'

Without waiting for his master's approval, the butler walked to the bookcase built into the wall beside the fire and took down several heavy, leather-bound volumes to reveal a handle set into the masonry. He pushed the lever up and then, using both hands, pulled at the shelves. With a protesting creak of unoiled hinges a whole section of the bookcase swung back into the room, exposing a stone staircase.

'During the Civil War,' Robert explained, 'the Brackenhursts were Royalists, but the country here-abouts rose for Parliament. The third Earl had this stairway built so that, if Roundheads were sighted, he and the family could escape to the chapel. There is an even older tunnel which leads from there to the stables. By these means they could be away before Cromwell's men even got near the house.'

'The third Earl be praised,' laughed Buxton. 'Well, Robert, let us inspect this chapel and see if it is suitable for our purposes.'

The butler lit an oil lamp and led the way into the darkness beyond the doorway. Buxton pushed the girl in front of him and brought up the rear. The stone steps were narrow and corkscrewed steeply downwards. The air was thick and stale and cobwebs brushed their faces as they descended. At last they reached the bottom and Robert held up the lamp to illuminate a small door secured by a single heavy oak beam.

'If you would hold this for a moment please, sir?'

Buxton took the lamp. The butler grasped the beam with both hands and lifted it clear of the brackets set in the wall on either side. He turned the metal ring and, throwing his whole weight against it, managed to force open the door just far enough to allow them through.

The chapel turned out to be a small, high-ceilinged rectangular room. The white plastered walls were broken by regularly spaced, arched stained-glass windows along one side with a much larger one at the far end before which an altar must once have stood. The floor was of red tiles and there was a door set in the wall opposite the windows which, Buxton presumed, led to a corridor linking the chapel to the main part of the house. Except for some narrow wooden benches stacked in a corner, it was empty. Buxton approved of what he saw.

'Capital, Robert. I think this will suit our intentions perfectly.'

'This is the east wing, sir. It has not been used for many years. No one ever comes here.'

'Then there is no danger of us being disturbed?'

The butler grinned. 'None at all, sir.'

'Better and better,' Buxton mused as he looked at the benches and then up at the stout wooden beams running from wall to wall above their heads. 'We shall need rope, Robert, and a whip. Go at once, and if you think of anything else which might assist us in our work, bring that too. But be quick. I will guard this wretch until you return.'

Once the butler had disappeared back up the stairs to carry out his master's instructions, Buxton turned his attention to the girl. Rebecca was standing in the centre of the room, clearly nervous of her new surroundings and frightened of what was about to befall her, but still defiant. She turned on her employer.

'Ain't nothing you can do to me what ain't been done before. I been beaten before. 'Tain't nothing new to me.'

Buxton sighed. 'Oh, Rebecca, you really do have so much to learn about discipline and obedience. That I

118

am the best person to instruct you in these matters is your misfortune, though perhaps it may just prove to be your salvation.'

The girl spat on the tiles at Buxton's feet. 'You do your worst. I ain't scared of you, nor no man.'

Buxton picked up a pine bench and placed it in the centre of the room beneath one of the beams. Once it may have provided seating for the devout during Sunday service; now it could be used for a much different, and far more entertaining, purpose.

'Take your dress off, Rebecca.'

The girl barely hesitated. She knew any protest would be pointless. She untied her apron and threw it aside before unfastening the row of buttons down the front of her dress. It tumbled round her ankles and she stepped out of it.

'And your shoes.'

Rebecca kicked off her shoes and stood completely naked before him. Many men had seen her like this. This so-called gentleman was just one more. She was pretty, she knew that. She knew too that she had a body men yearned to touch and craved to enter.

'Lie on your back on the bench, Rebecca,' Buxton commanded and she complied without a word.

'Legs either side.'

Again she did as she was told. She showed no shame at assuming such a position. Buxton looked down into her eyes and realised that, far from being embarrassed, she was actually enjoying displaying her body to him. Robert seemed to be taking an inordinately long time carrying out his tasks. Buxton unbuckled his belt and pulled it free of the loops.

'Play with yourself.'

For a moment the girl's composure faltered. 'What you say?'

Buxton brought the buckle end of the belt swishing down across the top of her thighs. 'I do not repeat orders.'

Rebecca began to massage her breasts. Again, Buxton lashed her, this time at an angle so that the heavy brass buckle struck between her legs. 'Not there, here.'

The girl raised herself from the bench just far enough so that she could reach her hand down between her thighs. She ran her fingers through her pubic hair until they reached her mound and then began to rub them along the slit.

'Make yourself wet, Rebecca,' Buxton told her. 'Make yourself very wet. If I do not think you have made yourself wet enough, I will double your punishment.'

In response, Rebecca rubbed harder. With one hand she pulled aside her cunt lips and with the thumb and index finger of the other she squeezed and massaged her button. Her face flushed, her stomach fluttered and her thighs twitched slightly as her breathing quickened.

'Inside.'

Still tweaking and rubbing her clit with one hand, Rebecca plunged two fingers of the other into her pussy and began to vibrate them as fast as she could. Her eyes half closed and she spread her legs as far apart as possible as her hips jerked in response to the rapidly increasing momentum of her actions.

Buxton watched her approvingly as he removed his jacket and shirt, which were quickly followed by his trousers and shoes. He leaned naked against the wall, using two fingers to slowly rub the length of his erection.

The girl was everything he had hoped, and expected, her to be. As soon as he had seen her in the barn the previous day, he had sensed that she was a slave to her passions; and that when aroused those passions would become uncontrollable. Her half-drunken father had not noticed the tell-tale signs, but he had. The way she had almost flaunted her body before him and, most particularly, the way she had moved in response to the belt and the lash. She had cried out, certainly, but long experience had taught him that the pitch of those cries owed as much to pleasure as to pain.

The sight which greeted the butler on his return was one he had never expected to see anywhere, least of all inside The Hall. It stopped him in his tracks and he stood dumbstruck in the doorway, rope in one hand, riding crop and a long, brass-studded dog leash in the other, goggling at the scene. Buxton smiled at him and beckoned him forward.

'Well, Robert, what do you think of her now?'

The butler looked from the panting, writhing girl to his master. 'Like I said, sir, a dirty little slut. No more, no less. She deserves all she gets. That's what I think.'

'Quite right, Robert,' Buxton agreed. 'And we must make sure she gets it all.'

So saying, he walked over to the girl, grabbed her by the arm and pulled her off the bench.

'You were enjoying it far too much, Rebecca. We can't have that, can we? You are not here to enjoy yourself,' he told her sternly. 'You are here to be taught obedience. Obedience means doing what you are told, when you are told. I have not told you to come, Rebecca. You will come when I tell you to come. Not before and not after. Do you understand?'

The girl's eyes were glazed as she looked at him and nodded her assent. Her breasts heaved and her legs quivered from the sensations still rippling through her body.

Buxton stood on the bench and threw the rope over the beam above. He tied one end round the girl's wrists and pulled on the other so that only the very tips of her toes still touched the floor. He looked at the butler.

'Robert, as she has so grossly insulted you, you may be the first to chastise her. Do you prefer the crop or the leash?'

The butler gulped. Never in his wildest imaginings, even when he had lain in bed fantasising about farmer Dakins's daughter and vowing revenge for the way she had treated him, had he ever conjured such a scene.

'The leash, sir,' he replied at last.

'Then please begin, Robert. And don't spare the rod on this already spoilt child.'

The butler needed no second invitation. Positioning himself behind her, he swung the dog leash against Rebecca's back with every ounce of his strength. The high-pitched scream it produced was music to the ears of both men. Once more he drew his arm back and sent the thick leather, with its row of metal studs, slicing into her skin just below her buttocks. Rebecca screamed again and her taut frame shuddered as it absorbed the blow.

As the beating continued, with Robert striking repeatedly at every area of her back, buttocks and legs, Buxton held the rope in one hand, occasionally pulling it to lift her just clear of the ground and increase the pain in her arms, while he gently and slowly masturbated with the other.

Rebecca Dakins's body was streaming with sweat and her breath came in harsh, rasping gasps as she writhed under the pain of the leash. But Buxton could see into her eyes. The half-glazed expression he had noticed as she had lain on the bench and approached her climax had returned all too soon. He held up his hand.

'Enough, Robert. At least for the moment.'

Reluctantly, the butler lowered the leash. Buxton let go of the rope, allowing the girl to relieve the strain on her shoulders and arms and place her feet flat on the floor. The flogging he had just witnessed, together with his own actions, had brought him to a situation that could have only one outcome.

'Back on the bench, Rebecca,' he ordered, and the girl obeyed instantly. She lay on her back and again spread her legs.

Buxton straddled her and then lowered himself so that his cock was thrust between her breasts.

'Push them together. Tight together,' he commanded.

Rebecca squeezed her breasts together, trapping his manhood in her cleavage. Buxton moved rapidly back and forth, savouring the exquisite feeling of his cock rubbing against the girl's soft, tender skin. His climax was not long in arriving, and when it did so it was with a power which surprised even him. A long jet of spunk flew from the tip of his cock and splattered against Rebecca's chin before dripping down her neck and forming a white sticky pool in the hollow of her throat. It was followed by another and then another. Buxton lifted himself a few inches clear of her body and allowed the final spurts to splash over her heaving tits. He stood up and looked down at the come-stained body below for a few moments before turning to the butler.

'Your turn now, Robert. How would you like her?'

The butler had watched the performance wide eyed, still not quite able to fully believe the sights he was witnessing. He was all too well aware of the throbbing inside his trousers and the urgent need to relieve it.

'Like the bitch she is, sir,' he replied as he unfastened his trousers and kicked off his shoes.

Once again, Buxton yanked the girl upright before positioning her so that she was kneeling on the floor, her forearms resting on the bench, her arse in the air.

Without further invitation, Robert knelt behind her, pushed apart her thighs and rammed into her. Rebecca's whole body jerked from the force of the invasion. A long, deep sigh escaped her lips before she instinctively began to respond. As he thrust forward, she pushed herself back against him, until they were moving in ever quickening unison. Buxton sensed that for both of them the end was very near.

'You may come now, Rebecca.'

The words had hardly left his lips when both servants cried out their pleasure. Robert's final backward movement was so violent that his cock was freed from the constraints of the girl's passage just as he came, spraying his cream over her buttocks from where it seeped down the cleft to merge with her own juices.

Finally, when he had spent all he had to spend, the butler stood up and looked sheepishly at his master. Buxton clapped him on the shoulder.

'Capital, Robert. Capital. A fine performance. Now, I suggest we get dressed and go about our respective business.'

Rebecca made to rise, but Buxton placed his foot on her buttocks and stopped her.

'Not you, Rebecca. Not you. I have not finished with you yet. As you will discover all too soon.'

Buxton took the spare end of the rope and tied it securely round the bench, so that the girl had no alternative but to remain in the same position. Taking a handkerchief from his pocket he forced it between her lips and knotted it tight at the back of her head. He turned to the butler.

'That should keep her quiet and out of trouble for the next few hours.'

Without a backward glance at the hapless servant, the two men climbed back up the staircase to the library.

Buxton seated himself at the desk, leaned back in his chair and smiled at the butler.

'A fine way to start the day, Robert. Nothing like some early morning exercise, what?'

The butler returned his smile. 'Undoubtedly, sir,' he agreed.

'Robert, I want you to get a message to the Reverend Pimms. Tell him that I have a matter of the utmost urgency to discuss with him and would be very grateful if he would favour me with his presence at luncheon.'

'Certainly, sir. I shall deliver it myself. And if Mr Pimms should ask what this urgent matter is?'

Buxton laughed. 'Just tell him it concerns the subject we debated yesterday. I am sure he will understand. And I am also certain that he will not be late for lunch.'

Nine

The door slammed behind her husband and Clarissa was left alone with her thoughts and fears. She cast her mind back over the events of the previous night and tried to work out what she had done to make Richard so cold towards her.

He had been very quiet at dinner, answering her questions wherever possible with single words or just grunts and shrugs. He had told her that he had visited Castleleigh, talked with some of the villagers and hired some extra servants. He had also informed her that he intended to replace Miss Trubshaw with a new housekeeper who would be better able to assist her with her day-to-day duties, and that he had promoted Robert from footman to butler. As soon as the meal was over, he had gone to the library, saying he had to check the estate's accounts. She had gone to bed and lain there waiting for him for over two hours. When he had eventually joined her, his breath had been heavy with brandy and he had just undressed, got into bed, rolled over on his side and ignored her. She had snuggled up behind him, pressing her breasts against his back and looping one leg over his. She had run her fingers soothingly along his shoulders and down his arm before reaching for his cock, but her fingers never made contact with their objective. He had roughly gripped her hand and pushed it away, telling her, 'Clarissa, I am tired tonight. I wish to sleep.'

For a few moments she had accepted the rebuff, but her loins were aching with the need she felt for him and so she had tried a different approach to arouse his interest.

'Richard, I have been very naughty today, very, very naughty, and I do understand what happens to naughty girls.'

He had merely shrugged his shoulders and told her, 'Then you should be ashamed of yourself. It's your business, not mine. I am going to sleep. Goodnight, Clarissa.'

Within minutes she had heard his rhythmic breathing and realised that he had already slipped into sleep. She had felt cheated and abandoned. She had lain on her side, legs drawn up, looking into the darkness and feeling sorry for herself. It was not right that he should treat her with such indifference. She had needs as much as he and, as her husband, it was his responsibility to fulfil them. Her mind had wandered from him to the Colonel. The remembrance of the passion and urgency of their encounter in the stables rekindled the tingling inside her. And, as she had recalled every detail of their coupling, she had begun to sweat and, without thinking, her hand had slipped between her legs. She had closed her eyes, the better to concentrate on the mental images which were so strongly stimulating the rest of her body. Her fingers had moved with the speed of arrows as she had sent them flying in and out of her hole. When she climaxed she had had to bite into the pillow to stifle her cries and make her body go rigid to prevent disturbing the sleeping man beside her. But there had been nothing she could do to stop the stream of warm liquid which had spurted from her when the ultimate moment arrived. Satisfied at last, she had drifted into unconsciousness and her sleeping hours had been filled with strange, erotic dreams of Richard and the Colonel and young Lucy.

Now, Richard was dressed and gone and the memory of the dreams was fading rapidly, but she still felt the same urgings as the previous night. If her husband did not want her, then there were others who did. She had been uncertain about accepting the Colonel's invitation to a tryst, but Richard's coldness had dispelled her anxieties. She would go to the hunting lodge. Just the first thought of the Colonel's massive member, and the power with which he had ravaged her body, made her start to moisten, and it was only a sharp rap on the bedroom door which brought her back to the reality.

Lucy entered, almost bowed double by the large wooden tray she was carrying.

'I did not know what you would like, so I brought something of everything,' she explained as she pulled out the four small feet from beneath the tray and positioned it across Clarissa's legs.

Clarissa sat up. She wore no nightdress and the movement made her breasts bounce as they cleared the sheets and counterpane. She considered the selection on the tray before declaring, 'I think some toast and honey to start with, please, Lucy.'

The maid spread butter generously across a piece of toast, spooned copious amounts of thin honey on top and handed it to her mistress. 'Here we are, Madam.'

Clarissa held the slice by one corner and raised it to her lips. As she did so it tilted and a large blob of warm butter and honey dropped into her cleavage. She reached for the napkin to wipe it away, but Lucy had other ideas.

128

'I'll see to that, Madam,' she said quickly and, before Clarissa could protest, she bent her head and began hungrily licking up the spillage.

The feel of Lucy's head between her breasts, and the tickling of her tongue along the divide between them, made Clarissa's stomach shiver with pleasure. Clarissa let go of the whole slice. It landed at the base of her neck and Lucy merely took it and drew it downwards, coating each orb in turn with the warm, sticky mixture. Having transferred all she could from bread to breasts, the maid tossed the slice aside and returned to her work. Clarissa leaned back against the propped-up pillow and revelled in the sensation.

Lucy's tongue ran the entire length of Clarissa's breasts as it lapped up the worst of the mess, before sliding down to concentrate on her nipples. Lucy sucked the sweet substances from them in turn, careful to ensure that each was thoroughly licked clean. Clarissa moaned as she ran her fingers through her maid's hair, pressing the girl's face ever closer against her skin. At last, Lucy straightened and asked in the most innocent of tones, as if what had just happened was the most normal of events, 'And what would you like to follow, Madam?'

Clarissa looked at her and smiled. 'Whatever you suggest, Lucy. I leave the choice to you.'

Lucy regarded each of the various dishes on the tray in turn. 'I can recommend the sausages, Madam.'

So saying, Lucy removed the tray and placed it on the table by the bed. She selected a long, fat sausage and without asking permission, drew back the bed-clothes, totally exposing her mistress's nakedness. Lucy perched herself on the side of the bed and began rubbing the length of the sausage through Clarissa's tuft of hair and gliding it up and down the entrance to her sex.

The feel of the warm meat against the most sensitive part of her body made Clarissa shudder. She drew up her knees and widened her legs to allow easier access. Tantalisingly, Lucy rotated the sausage slowly around the opening. The thin film of fat on the meat merged with the juices now freely flowing from her mistress and it slid easily inside.

Clarissa sighed and her hands clutched at the pillow as Lucy pushed the sausage inside her. Unlike with Richard or the Colonel, it was not the length nor the circumference which excited her; it was the bizarreness and wantonness of the whole situation. Her maid was fucking her with a breakfast sausage! Clarissa would have laughed had it not been for the tightness in her chest caused by the adrenaline pumping into her body. Instead, she could only gasp at the delirious sensations washing over her. Just as she reached the brink of orgasm, Lucy withdrew the tube of meat and held it up for Clarissa to see. It was wet and shiny with her moisture. Holding it as she would a man's prick, Lucy licked it and pretended to suck, before putting it into her mouth and biting it in two. She giggled. 'I've always wanted to do that to a man.'

Having been so suddenly deprived of her climax, Clarissa was in no state to appreciate her maid's comments. Her tone was urgent and imperative.

'Don't stop, Lucy. Please, please don't stop.'

Lucy threw the other end of the sausage on to the tray and looked round the room. She spied what she wanted on the dressing table and was there and back within a couple of heartbeats.

Clarissa moaned the instant she felt the rough bristles of the hairbrush jab like needles against the swollen, ultra sensitive skin between her swollen cunt lips. Using her free hand, Lucy parted the lips as far as they would go, before energetically rubbing the head of the brush between them. Clarissa began to shake with increasing violence as the scores of stiff hairs made contact with her clit. Judging the moment to perfection, Lucy turned the brush and, without any warning or preamble, plunged the thick, wooden handle up to its hilt in her mistress's cunt.

Clarissa's whole body convulsed at the sudden, aggressive penetration, making her sit up and jerk forward. Once again, Lucy rammed the handle inside her. Clarissa clutched at the girl's hair, pulling Lucy's face down on to her belly, quivering and shouting uncontrollably as climax after climax set every nerve vibrating.

Lucy pulled herself free from Clarissa's hold. She withdrew the brush and replaced it with her face. Her teeth gnawed at the most tender spot of her mistress's body and then her mouth was over the hole and she was ravenously gulping down the pungent fluids as they flowed free.

Finally, totally spent, Clarissa collapsed back on to the bed. Lucy stood up and used the napkin to wipe up the liquid smeared across her mouth and chin. She smiled.

'Was breakfast entirely to your satisfaction, Madam?'

Clarissa could only shut her eyes and nod assent. It was several minutes before she gathered sufficient breath to speak.

'Lucy, that was wonderful. Absolutely, completely wonderful.'

'Happy to be of service, my Lady,' Lucy replied in her best maid's voice. 'Would Madam like to take her bath now?'

Clarissa, the sweat and stickiness washed from her body by Lucy's soap-covered hands, her hair caught into a functional tight bun, and dressed in a full-length maroon riding dress, looked at herself in the full-length mirror and liked what she saw. There was a glow to her normally pale cheeks and a dancing sparkle in her deep-blue eyes. As well as the reflection of herself, she could see that of Lucy standing behind her. The maid was completely naked, this time not having waited until her dress was wet before removing it and the rest of her clothes. Clarissa turned and placed her hand on the girl's shoulder, drawing her nearer. Clarissa's tongue drew a line across the centre of her maid's forehead before she tilted her head and kissed her full on the lips as her hand reached between her legs and its palm pressed hard against her mound. But the embrace lasted only a few seconds. Clarissa removed both lips and hand the instant she sensed Lucy was beginning to respond to them. She stroked the girl's hair as she spoke soothingly to her.

'Sometime, Lucy. But not now. When I am ready. Not before. Now, get dressed or I may have to whip you again for the presumption you showed at breakfast.'

Lucy was crestfallen at the sudden end to her expected pleasures, but did as she was bid.

'Make sure the bedroom and bathroom are thoroughly cleaned before I return,' Clarissa instructed as she left the room. 'Oh, and fresh sheets on the bed for tonight.'

She found her husband in the library poring over ledgers and account books. He hardly spared her a glance as she entered.

'Feeling better now? Headache gone has it?' he enquired without looking up.

'Yes, thank you, Richard,' she replied. 'In fact, I feel so well that I intend going for a ride across the estate. Unless, that is, you have any other duties for me to perform.'

Buxton shook his head and spoke without looking up from the column of figures he was calculating.

'Do what you will. I am sure that a ride in the fresh air will do you the world of good. There is no need to hurry back for luncheon. I am expecting the vicar. We have many parochial matters to discuss. They will only bore you.'

'Very good, Richard,' said Clarissa meekly. 'Doubtless, I will see you at dinner.'

'Doubtless,' agreed her husband in a tone which made it clear he was not particularly looking forward to the occasion.

Once outside the library door, Clarissa heaved a deep sigh of relief. Richard's day would be spent with his books and the vicar. She was free to do as she wished, and she knew exactly what she wished to do.

A young lad she did not recognise met her at the entrance to the stables. She looked questioningly at him. 'Who are you?'

The youth touched his cap in the customary mark of respect. 'Tom Cuttock, my Lady. I only started here this morning.'

'Saddle my horse. It's the grey mare, in case no one has told you. And be quick about it.'

The lad ran to do as he was told and Clarissa followed him into the stable. Corsair was snorting and stamping in his stall, angry at his enforced idleness. Clarissa looked at the pile of straw in the corner and smiled at the memory of what had happened on top of it the day before. She was confident the Colonel's hunting lodge would offer more comforts than a heap of straw, and just as much fun.

The stable lad finished tacking up and led her horse towards her. Clarissa held up her hand and stopped him. She pointed at the saddle. 'Did I ask for that?'

Tom looked perplexed. 'It's a side-saddle, my Lady.'

'I know what it is, you fool,' Clarissa snapped. 'I also know its damned uncomfortable. I am going for a cross-country hack, not a dressage parade. Put on a proper saddle.'

Masking his surprise, the boy was quick to obey and soon mistress, lad and horse were standing outside in the courtyard.

'Would you like the mounting block, my Lady?' Tom enquired, but his question earned him only a withering look.

'What I would like, you impudent pup, is for you to find some useful work to do instead of bothering me.'

Clarissa pointed to the furthest block of stables. 'Those have not been cleaned properly in years. By the time I return, I want them swept and all the old straw burnt. Understand?'

'Yes, my Lady. Right away, my Lady.'

Tom hurried off across the courtyard and Clarissa watched him until he disappeared into the gloomy interior of the old stables. As soon as she was sure she could not be seen, she put one foot in the stirrup and swung herself into the saddle.

The long, full riding habit had, indeed, been designed for side-saddle riding and, as a result, she found herself sitting uncomfortably on yards of material, while the sides of her dress were forced up, blatantly displaying her lower legs. After taking a final look around, Clarissa stood in the stirrups and pulled her dress up to the top of her thighs, so that when she sat back in the saddle, it spread around but not under her. She wore no undergarments. She had reasoned that if the day turned out as she very much hoped it would, they would be superfluous. Now, there was an added delight. The leather was hard and cool against her skin as she pushed herself down on to it and guided her mount out of the stable yard and on to the bridlepath which would eventually lead her to Manor Farm and the hunting lodge beyond.

For half a mile, until the land dipped into a shallow meadow, she was content to walk the horse. As soon as she crossed over the lip of land and started heading down the slope, secure in the knowledge that no one in house or stable could see her, Clarissa kicked it into a trot. She moved perfectly in rhythm with the gait of the horse, raising and lowering herself in tempo with it. The feeling of her bare legs wrapped round the animal's sweating flanks, and her sex slapping repeatedly down on to the saddle, was exhilarating. Within just a few hundred yards, both she and the leather beneath her were wet and she was breathing far harder than the mare.

When she reached the bottom of the meadow, she pushed the horse to a canter. As it increased speed, she sat firm in the saddle, leaning forward so that every vibration of the animal's movement shot up into her. The canter speeded into a full gallop and Clarissa shouted her excitement. She gripped the reins tightly and her knees pressed hard into the horse's sides as she finally succumbed to her climax.

Reluctantly, she slowed back to a walk in order to regain her composure. It would not be seemly to arrive at the lodge hot and flustered. She must retain at least a semblance of dignity.

When she reached the shallow stream bordering the field beyond the meadow, Clarissa dismounted. While her horse drank she knelt and splashed handfuls of the cool, clear water over her face. The position of the sun told her it must be nearly noon, but Clarissa was in no hurry. She judged the lodge to be less than a mile away and she knew Harry Markham would wait for her. She took her handkerchief and dipped it in the stream. Squeezing the cloth almost dry, she raised her dress and washed away the worst of the stickiness between her legs. Her improvised toilet completed, Clarissa lay on her back beside the stream, skirts pulled high around her waist, and waited contentedly for the sun to dry her face and limbs.

Half an hour later, she spotted the tower of the hunting lodge rising beyond the pines, just as the Colonel had described it. A few minutes more, and she was walking the horse sedately up a winding, rutted path towards the door, outside which Markham was sitting, tilted back in his chair, feet resting on the rim of a stone water trough.

The lodge was a two-storey, white stone house that looked as if it might once have been a church. The windows were tall and arched and a cross had been cut into the stonework above the door. At one end there rose a round tower with narrow, arrow-slit-like windows.

The Colonel rose as she approached and he held the reins while she dismounted.

'Riding straddle, I see,' he observed. 'Not very ladylike, Clarissa.'

Clarissa smiled. 'Perhaps not, Harry. But very enjoyable.'

The Colonel laughed and led the way into the hunting lodge. Clarissa found herself in a long, high-ceilinged room. The white stone walls were festooned with trophies from field and river. Wherever she looked, the cold, beady eyes of long dead stags and foxes glinted down at her. In a glass case above the massive inglenook fireplace was suspended the biggest pike she had ever seen. Between the trophies, the walls were decorated with rifles, rods and swords and framed prints of hunting scenes. A glass-fronted cabinet against one wall housed a collection of stuffed pheasants, partridges, grouse and other fowl. Most of the rugs which covered the flagstoned floor were made from the skins of lions, tigers, zebras and other exotic animals from far-off lands. The ceiling might originally have been white, but had long since been tanned a deep brown from the smoke of the countless cigars which had been smoked by the men who had relaxed in the leather armchairs and chesterfields which dotted the room. She appreciated immediately that this was a man's place, where women were talked about but rarely allowed to enter. Being invited into such a totally masculine environment only served to heighten her excitement and her anticipation.

'An impressive display,' Clarissa commented.

'Not all mine own. Though many are,' the Colonel replied.

'Do you mount all your victories?' Clarissa asked innocently.

The Colonel laughed. 'Most, but not all. Unfortunately, the law does not permit one to preserve people in the same way as animals. During a skirmish outside Sebastopol, I took the head clean off a Cossack with a single blow. Big brute he was, with a full beard and moustache. I recall thinking how well he would look stuffed and hanging on the wall.'

Clarissa shivered at the idea. 'Harry, you are not being serious. That is too barbaric to even contemplate.'

The Colonel shrugged. 'All men are barbarians at heart. It is just that we are forced to wear the cloak of civilisation.'

Clarissa decided that the time for pleasantries and small talk was past. She had come with only one objective in mind and she saw no point in delaying its attainment. She turned and put her arms round him. 'Harry, you may be as barbarous with me as you like. In here, this is your kingdom and I am merely a subject.'

The Colonel bent and kissed her hard, pressing her body against his as his hands clasped her bottom. His tongue slid through her open lips, tickling the roof of her mouth. Clarissa ran her hand up and down his thigh. She could feel the steadily growing bulge in the front of his breeches as she pushed herself against him and her nipples stiffening as her breasts were squashed by their embrace.

Without warning, the Colonel slipped one arm round her back and the other behind her knees and lifted her clear off the floor as if she weighed no more than a baby. Clarissa lay limp in his powerful arms as he carried her effortlessly through the door at the far end of the room, up a twisting flight of wooden stairs and into the master bedroom above. The room was sparsely furnished with only a wardrobe, a chest and the biggest bed Clarissa had ever seen. It must have been eight feet wide and almost as long, and it was covered with a deep eiderdown which almost engulfed her when he laid her upon it.

Clarissa rolled over. 'Help me with my dress, please, Harry.'

The Colonel was only too eager to oblige. He sat on the bed and rapidly flicked apart the hooks and eyes. Clarissa pushed the cloth from her shoulders and the Colonel simply grasped the hem and pulled the dress off her, before removing her calf-length riding boots. Clarissa lay on her stomach. The Colonel slid his hand along her back from neck to knees.

'You have been in the wars, I see, Clarissa,' he commented as his fingers glided over the marks caused by her husband's beating of the previous day.

'Richard believes in strict discipline, Harry. And so do I. If we are bad then we deserve to be punished for it.'

'And are you bad, Clarissa?'

Clarissa wriggled her bottom and spread out her arms. 'It would seem so, Harry. But perhaps you can teach me the error of my ways.'

'I can but try, Clarissa. And when I try, I always try very hard.'

Clarissa heard the rustle of clothing and knew he was undressing while he spoke. She tingled with excitement as she waited to feel his flesh against hers and to subject herself once more to that massive instrument. Just the thought of it forcing itself into her tight passage made the cream start to trickle, as her body automatically began to prepare itself for the coming invasion.

The springs groaned as the Colonel climbed on to the bed and lay beside her. She moved to face him, putting one arm round his neck and kissing him hungrily, gnawing at his lips in her passion while her free hand reached down and her fingers encircled his cock. The Colonel's hand pushed her legs apart and roughly grabbed at the softness between; not gently stroking as he had done the day before, but clawing. Clarissa pulled even more vigorously at the pulsating rod, digging her nails into the tight, tender skin. The Colonel removed his hand from between her thighs, but only for a moment. Clarissa started and gasped as the flat of his hand smacked down hard against her mound. Then he was probing her, not with his fingers, but his knuckles, forcing first two, then a third inside her, rotating them like a corkscrew as he did so. Without slackening the frantic momentum of his fingers, he pulled away from her kiss and turned his attention to her breasts, biting savagely at each nipple in turn. Clarissa let go of his member and clutched his balls, squeezing them in her hand while her middle finger traced the rim of his anus. The Colonel's mouth left her breasts and she lost her grip on him as he slid down the bed and buried his face in the wetness between her legs.

Clarissa splayed her legs as far as the joints permitted, at the same time raising her knees and thrusting her sex towards him. She felt delirious from the amazing sequence of sensations she was experiencing. She cared nothing for her family name, her reputation or her husband; only that there should be no end to the wonderful feelings bubbling inside her.

Lucy had used her tongue like a feather, to flick and tickle and tantalise. The Colonel was employing his like glasspaper; rubbing it roughly in and around the opening to her sex. While Lucy had nibbled and kissed the lips and the precious button at their top, the Colonel bit and chewed, causing pain and pleasure in equal measure.

All too aware of the crescendo building inside her, Clarissa grabbed him by the hair and yanked his face away.

'Now, Harry! Now! Take me now!'

The Colonel needed no further encouragement. He rolled on top of her and she cried out as his huge cock bludgeoned its way into her body and began to slide in and out. She wrapped her legs round his back and pushed against him, the better to drive every inch inside. His massive frame squashed her, almost forcing what little breath she had left from her lungs. She felt the wiry hair of his chest grating against her breasts. His breath was hot on her face and his fingers tugged at her hair. They spent together, both coming at precisely the same moment. He with a long sigh; she with a wail. Clarissa closed her eyes as she felt the warm gush of his seed and climax after climax racked her.

It lasted but a few minutes, although it seemed like hours, before she felt him withdraw. He lay on the bed beside her and she clung to him as he cradled her in his arms.

'Clarissa, I said yesterday that you are astonishing. That was a gross understatement. You are absolutely incredible. A true thoroughbred.'

Clarissa kissed him lightly on the lips. 'Perhaps, but I still feel I shall need more schooling in the future.'

The Colonel grinned as he disentangled himself from their embrace and stood up.

'The future is only what happens next. And what happens next is a little surprise I have prepared for you.'

She watched as he opened the door. Standing on the threshold was a young man in the uniform of a Hussar who, Clarissa estimated, was no older than herself. He was tall and strong and the family resemblance was striking.

'Come in, Edward, come in,' invited the Colonel.

The youth stood at the end of the bed, clicked his heels together and bowed.

'Captain Edward Markham. Your servant, ma'am.'

Clarissa giggled as she opened her legs wide and revealed all her charms to the young man's wide-eyed gaze.

'Clarissa Buxton, sir. At your service.'

Ten

The Reverend Matthew Pimms sat on the edge of the sofa in the morning room sipping the small glass of inferior sweet sherry the butler had given him. Nervously, he twiddled the stem of the glass between his fingers as he gazed into the depths of the dark brown liquid. He felt sorry for himself, he felt slighted, but most of all he felt afraid. Until less than twenty-four hours ago his life had been so placid, so smooth, so completely predictable. Now, the even path he had always trodden had suddenly become strewn with sharp rocks, ready to trip and tear him; and the road no longer ran straight and true into the distant horizon of his old age, but ended abruptly at the very lip of a precipice.

The new Squire had said that they must have dinner, but had not specified a date. Then, without warning, he had been tersely summoned – no, not summoned, commanded – to present himself for luncheon forthwith. What did this newcomer really have in store for him? He was all too well aware that the rich and powerful Richard Buxton could do with him as he wished. In civil or ecclesiastical court he would have no defence against the interpretations that would be placed on the scenes the Squire had witnessed the previous day. True, the Squire had said he was not concerned at his actions; but had he changed his mind? Did he now intend to inform the Bishop? If he did then there was no hope and no future. As it was, he could barely live on his stipend and the remains of his great aunt's legacy. His house might be impressive, but he could afford no servants to look after it; just a housekeeper who stayed only for the extra shillings she earned ministering to his special needs. Bereft of parish and an outcast from decent society, he would starve. He thought back to the wedding service conducted by the Squire's new brother-in-law, the unctuous Oliver Fitzhumphreys, who had treated him little better than an altar boy. He already had a parish somewhere in the north, but perhaps he wanted to move nearer London. If so, family ties, even new ones, might prove stronger than any claim he could make to retain his living.

The Reverend Matthew Pimms rose and paced the length of the room; stopping in front of the mirror above the mantelpiece, he saw only a broken man with a desolate, empty future staring back at him. The sudden sound of the door opening made him jump and spill his sherry down the front of his cassock. He was still frantically rubbing at the dark, damp patch as he turned. Richard Buxton stood in the centre of the room, eyeing him with undisguised amusement.

'Good afternoon, Mr Pimms. Pray do not let me disturb you.'

The vicar abruptly stopped rubbing his cassock and blushed. 'You startled me, sir. I am afraid I upset my drink,' he managed to stammer.

'Best thing to do with that stuff, if you ask me,' Buxton told him jovially. 'Not fit to cook with as far as I am concerned, but I have already made restocking the cellar a priority. Come through to luncheon and have a decent drink.'

Without bothering to wait for a response, Buxton led the way across the hall and into the breakfast room. The significance of the location was not lost on the hapless vicar, who meekly trailed in his wake. So, he was to eat in the breakfast room; clearly he was not deemed worthy or important enough to be allocated a place in the main dining room.

'I apologise for keeping you waiting, Mr Pimms,' Buxton told him as they seated themselves either side of the table, along the centre of which were lines of dishes and tureens containing a varied collection of cold meats, pickles, sauces, summer vegetables and fruit. Buxton nodded to the butler standing patiently at the head of the table.

'You may pour the wine, Robert.'

The butler filled both their glasses. Buxton raised his in a mock salute.

'Thank you for coming so quickly, vicar. It is most appreciated, as I am sure you have many parochial duties which require your attention.'

As Buxton spoke, Robert spread slices of ham, chicken and guinea fowl across their plates. Buxton raised his hand as the butler reached for the tureens of vegetables. 'Thank you, Robert. That will be all for the moment. I will ring when I need you again.'

The butler bowed and withdrew. Buxton invited, 'Help yourself to vegetables and condiments, Mr Pimms. We do not stand on ceremony here.'

The vicar needed no second invitation. The fare before him might be merely a light lunch for the Squire of Castleleigh, but it was almost a banquet to the impoverished cleric. He ladled a small mountain of vegetables on to his plate and greedily tucked in, thankful that he would not have to face the usual boiled mutton and overcooked cabbage on his return to the vicarage.

Buxton ate sparingly, just toying with the meat before him, as he watched his guest devour his food with the appetite of a starved cannibal unexpectedly presented with a particularly succulent missionary. As the vicar gulped down his wine, Buxton refreshed his glass. At last, when only the pattern remained on the vicar's plate, Buxton pulled the bell sash. The butler entered carrying a platter of assorted cheeses in one hand and a bowl of fresh strawberries in the other. The Reverend Pimms eyed both longingly, but his host merely waved them away as he pushed his plate into the middle of the table.

'Thank you, Robert, but I feel we have both eaten as much as we require. Have you carried out the tasks I requested?'

'Everything is in order, according to your instructions.'

'Excellent. The vicar and I will retire to the library.'

The butler did not even try to hide his smirk. 'Of course, sir. Very good, sir.'

Buxton turned his attention back to the vicar, who was disappointedly watching the butler carry the cheese and strawberries from the room.

'The reason I asked you to come here today, Mr Pimms, concerns that matter we discussed yesterday. I am sure you recall our conversation.'

The vicar nodded; the food he had so ravenously consumed was suddenly a dead weight at the pit of his stomach. Now he would discover exactly what was in store for him.

'Do you know of a girl named Rebecca Dakins, Mr Pimms?'

The question caught the vicar off guard. 'She is a member of my flock,' he replied carefully. 'Though truth to say I have not seen her in church these many years past.'

'But what do you actually know about her?' Buxton persisted.

'I know, as does all the village, that she is a bad lot, sir. A wanton, Godless fornicator. I wish to speak no evil of anyone, but that is common knowledge.'

'And did you also know that I have given her a position here at The Hall?'

The vicar shook his head. 'No, sir, that I had not heard.'

Buxton sighed dramatically. 'I too had heard of her reputation and thought I might assist her back on to the path of righteousness by providing a more stable and disciplined environment than that which she has been accustomed to. Alas, my good intentions have been ill received. Within a few hours of coming here she had reverted to her former ways, which is why I need your help.'

'My help?'

'Of course,' Buxton replied. 'I have tried to instruct her on the errors of her ways. I have tried to reason with her and appeal to any sense of decency which she may still retain; I have even chastised her but, I regret, all to no avail. Which is why I sent for you.'

'For me?' The vicar was clearly still perplexed but also starting to relax as he gradually realised that the summons he had received had not been an invitation to discuss his own precarious future.

'The girl,' Buxton explained, 'has no respect for my position and mocks any punishment I may care to inflict; but your authority comes from a much higher source. At your hands, she may at last be made to see the error of her ways.'

The vicar drained the dregs from his glass. 'You wish me to counsel her?'

Buxton smiled. 'No, Mr Pimms. I wish you to scourge her. To drive the devils from her and so save her.'

'And where is the miscreant now?'

'She is safely secured. You will understand that I dare not let her wicked ways contaminate my other staff,' Buxton replied. 'I have put her in the old chapel, a fitting place you will agree, for her to be cleansed of her sins. Come, I will show you.'

Without further explanation, Buxton led the vicar to the library. The bookcase had already been swung free and the door opened, with an oil lamp ready lit beside it. Buxton made a mental note to praise Robert for his thoroughness. 'This way' was all he said as he raised the lamp and descended the stairs.Whatever the Reverend Pimms had been expecting, the sight which greeted him when he followed Buxton into the chapel still struck him like lightning.

Rebecca Dakins sat on a bench against the wall. Her arms were stretched wide and her wrists were securely tied to rings hammered into the stonework. Her legs were splayed and fastened by cords to the feet of the bench, so that all her charms were displayed. In addition to the improvised gag, a black cloth now covered her eyes. In the centre of the room had been placed a leather-covered daybed. In the corner stood an old hall stand, but instead of walking sticks and umbrellas, it held a variety of instruments including whips, belts, crops, thin bamboo canes and a newly cut bundle of birch twigs.

Buxton waved his arm in a gesture which encompassed the girl and everything else in the room.

'Here is your sinner. Do whatever you deem necessary to save her from herself and bring her back to the straight and narrow.'

The Reverend Pimms stared wide eyed at the girl, unable to quite believe the opportunity being afforded him. If he noticed the dried stains on her chin, breasts and stomach, he did not enquire as to their origins.

Buxton untied the gag. Immediately, the girl asked, 'Who's there?' He ignored her and, after pulling the birch from the stand, he handed it to the vicar.

'I believe this is your preference.'

Without taking his eyes off the girl, the vicar accepted the bundle of twigs.

Buxton removed the blindfold. The girl glared defiantly at him for a moment before spotting the vicar and laughing.

'Oh, so 'tis you, is it? Old red bum himself. Come to do to me what that crone of a housekeeper does to you, have you? Well come on, get on with it. I ain't afraid of you, nor your god, nor no one.'

The vicar visibly shook with rage at her words. So she knew about his housekeeper's other duties did she? And if she knew, so too did most of the village. How they must be laughing at him behind his back.

Buxton felt like laughing too, but controlled himself and managed to adopt a suitably serious demeanour.

'You see my problem, vicar. Now she adds blasphemy to her catalogue of sins. In what position would you prefer her to receive her cleansing?'

'Across the bench, sir, if you please,' the vicar answered through clenched teeth, making practice swipes of the birch through the air as he spoke.

Buxton untied the girl's wrists and ankles. She did not struggle or protest as he pushed her face down on to the bench and fastened her arms to its sides. He stepped back and leaned against the wall.

'All yours, Mr Pimms.'

The vicar had raised his arm to deliver the first blow when there was a discreet cough from the doorway.

'I am sorry to interrupt you, sir, but we have had a delivery of beer from the local inn. The girl is most insistent that you ordered it and refuses to take it back. In fact, sir, she is demanding to see you personally.'

Buxton laughed. 'I am sorry, Robert; I had quite forgotten. I should have told you. I ordered the ale yesterday when I was in the village and I promised to pay for it as soon as it arrived. The girl is only doing as she was told.'

Buxton turned to the vicar, who still held the birch aloft waiting to strike.

'I am sorry, but I must leave you for a short while. Please carry on, and pray do not let your natural compassion interfere with your duties.'

Buxton found Alice sitting patiently on the seat of a small pony cart round the side of the house outside the tradesmen's entrance. She was wearing a plain blue dress which fitted tight across her breasts and hips, accentuating her figure. Six barrels were stacked in the cart behind her. But it was neither Alice nor the ale which made Buxton pause for a moment as he approached. It was the sight of the other girl. Sitting beside Alice was one of the most charming and instantly desirable creatures he had ever seen. She could not have been warmed by more than sixteen summers. Her flaxen hair hung straight down her back almost to her waist; her eyes were clear blue pools and her lips were full and pink. Three buttons of her blouse were undone, allowing a tantalising glimpse of cleavage, while her skirt reached only to her calves to display perfectly turned, long and slender legs and hint at what might be above them. Alice waved to him as soon as he entered the small gravel yard.

'Good afternoon, Squire. I've brought your delivery as requested.'

'Good afternoon, Alice,' Buxton responded. 'Thank you for being so punctual. However, you did not tell me you would be accompanied.'

'This is my cousin Maria, sir. She lives over Great Roding way but is staying with us for a few weeks.'

Buxton bowed his head in polite acknowledgement. 'Charmed to meet you, Maria.'

The girl smiled. 'Honoured, sir.'

Buxton turned to the butler. 'Robert, see to the unloading, will you? You can put the barrels in the servants' hall for the time being. The ladies will accompany me inside. I promised to pay the landlord on delivery and I would not wish to disappoint him.'

Leaving Robert to his task, Buxton ushered the two girls into the house. He did not speak until they reached the small sitting room adjoining the master bedroom, where he perched on the window ledge and regarded each in turn before addressing Alice.

'While it is, of course, a pleasure to meet your cousin, I had rather thought you would be alone. I will locate my purse and then you may depart.'

Alice giggled. 'Oh, sir, Maria is more than just my cousin; she is my very best friend. Isn't that so, Maria?'

In answer, the girl turned to her companion, placed her arms round her neck and kissed her full on the lips. Alice's hands stroked down along the girl's curves before coming to rest on her buttocks. Maria's tongue lightly traced the lines of Alice's lips as her cousin continued to fondle her bottom with the fingers of one hand while the other undid the buttons of her blouse. Alice pushed the blouse from the girl's shoulders and, bending her head, greedily sucked on each nipple in turn.

'Oh that we should all have such best friends,' observed Buxton softly as he moved to make the twosome a trio.

Positioning himself behind Maria, Buxton removed her blouse and then pushed her skirt to the floor. Her figure was exquisite: slim, but at the same time firmly rounded before and behind, where it mattered. As Alice kissed and licked her nipples, he ran his tongue along the contours of Maria's shoulders and then down her spine until he reached the top of the cleft at its base. Buxton prised the cheeks gently apart, planted a lingering kiss in the centre of each, and then slid his tongue between them. Maria sighed and leaned forward so that with the same motion she was pressing her breasts further forwards, towards Alice's enveloping lips, and her rear further backwards, towards Buxton's exploring tongue.

Without warning, Buxton stopped licking and bit hard into the soft flesh. The girl yelled in surprise but made no move to pull away from him. On the contrary, she thrust even further back, as if inviting more of the same. Buxton did not disappoint her. After several nips, each of which elicited a high-pitched squeak from Maria, he rose and replaced his teeth with his hand. The girl gasped each time his palm crashed across her buttocks, but she made no protest. As Buxton spanked her, so Alice sank to her knees and switched her sucking from Maria's nipples to the ridge of ultra sensitive skin between her legs. Maria clutched her cousin's hair, gripping the tresses tightly as she pulled her face hard against her rapidly saturating mound. Buxton reached round and, while he continued to smack her with one hand, dug the fingers of his other into the tender skin of her left breast. Unable any longer to contain the surge within her belly which hands and lips had created, Maria shouted and came, her body jettisoning her juice in a long thin stream which showered Alice's face and neck.

Buxton and Alice stepped back a pace. Maria stayed where she was, her eyes closed and her body swaying from side to side as her climax gradually subsided.

He smiled at Alice, who had lifted her dress and was using the hem to mop Maria's fluids from her face. 'I think your cousin could benefit from a little lie down, Alice,' he told her as he picked the girl up and carried her through into the bedroom. Buxton tossed her on to the middle of the bed, where she lay, legs apart and arms spread wide, breathing deeply. He heard the rustle of clothing behind him and turned to find Alice standing completely naked beside the same window where just the previous morning Clarissa had bathed in the morning sunlight. But, as far as he was concerned, had they both been standing there at that instant, his choice would still have been the same. He reached for her and she snuggled willingly into his arms, pulling his face down to hers and kissing him fiercely. Maria's voice, though little more than a low whisper, interrupted them.

'Alice, please. Please, Alice,' the girl pleaded, rolling on to her side and stretching out her arms towards her cousin.

'Alice, you must not disappoint your cousin,' Buxton told her, and Alice nodded her agreement. She clambered on to the counterpane and cuddled up to Maria.

Buxton watched Alice cradle the young girl in her arms and gently run her fingers over breasts and stomach while he undressed.

Alice's touch quickly reawakened Maria's passions. Her hand slid between her cousin's legs and three fingers slipped easily inside her. Maria shivered with delight as they penetrated her and immediately began to please Alice in the same manner. Buxton, by now naked and aroused, stood beside the bed drinking in the scene of the two lovelies, lips pressed against lips and nipples squashed against nipples, vigorously fingering each other; both were apparently oblivious to everything else but pleasing themselves by pleasing each other.

It was as erotic a scene as even he had ever witnessed, and the fact that it was taking place on his marital bed only enhanced the excitement he felt. Mentally, he could have happily stayed an observer for a long time; physically, that was not possible. He knelt on the bed and gently prised the two girls apart until they lay side by side on their backs looking up expectantly at him. He took hold of their hands and lingeringly licked the cream from their fingers, savouring the taste of each finger of each girl in turn. As he placed the last of Alice's fingers between his lips, Maria squirmed round so that her legs were against the headboard and her mouth was against his eager erection. With the dexterity of a circus sword swallower she took almost his entire length into her mouth until he could actually feel the tip sliding past her tonsils. The breath which came from her nostrils was hot against his pubic hair as she sucked hard on his cock and he sighed with total pleasure each time the muscles of her throat contracted and closed round the tingling nerve ends of his helmet. Maria did not pause when Alice lifted her rear and slid under her hips, pulling her down and almost suffocating herself beneath her cousin's sopping entrance.

After only a few minutes, Buxton knew he could not last very much longer. It was not a question of when, but where, he should choose to come. Maria settled the matter for him. Just as he had decided to withdraw, she reached between his legs and squeezed his balls in the palm of her hand while her finger drove into his anus. The combination was too great to resist and Buxton lunged forward as spout after spout pumped from him and shot down the girl's throat. Maria, finally unable to breathe, pulled her head back and pulled quick and hard at him so that the last spurts splattered her nose and lips. As Buxton finally subsided, Alice moved to kneel beside her and, while still ramming three fingers into her friend's cunt, she licked away the warm, white dribbles that were trickling down Maria's face.

Buxton lay in the middle of the bed, one arm round each girl's shoulders. Alice softly caressed his cock and fiddled her fingers through his pubic hair. Maria lay on her side, idly licking at his left nipple and allowing her hand to slowly skim his stomach and chest. Buxton wondered if he had ever in his life felt so relaxed and so at peace. The sound of the door in the room beyond opening brought him abruptly back to reality. Putting a finger against his lips to indicate to the girls to keep silent, he hurriedly dragged on his dressing gown and opened the adjoining door.

The butler seemed quite unperturbed by his master's appearance.

'I am sorry to bother you, sir. It is just that I was becoming somewhat concerned about the reverend gentleman and wondered if I should ascertain whether he is all right.'

For a moment Buxton was nonplussed. 'The reverend . . . oh, of course, you mean the vicar. I had quite forgotten about him. No, do not disturb him, Robert; I will see to him.'

'Very good, sir. And the young ladies? The ale has been unloaded now.'

Buxton waved the butler towards the door. 'Do not concern yourself, Robert. I will see to their welfare as well.'

154

The butler bowed. 'As you wish, sir.'

Back in the bedroom, after the butler had left, Buxton looked regretfully at the two naked girls on the bed.

'I am sorry, but duty calls and I have other matters to attend to.'

Alice swung off the bed, walked up to him and put her arms round his neck.

'You telling us we got to go?'

Buxton shrugged. 'I am afraid so, Alice. If I could, I would willingly have stayed here the whole afternoon.'

'Don't seem fair, really,' Alice pouted. 'She gets her fun and you gets yours. But what about me?'

Buxton had to admit that she had a case. Bringing his mouth close to her ear, he whispered, 'Tell Maria to wait in the pony cart and that you will join her later. You may accompany me on the business I have to attend to, though you must tell no one about it.'

As she had been instructed, Alice went straight to the library after she had seen Maria back to the cart. Buxton was standing beside the bookcase waiting for her. As she entered, he pulled the lever and the secret door, its hinges now well oiled, swung silently back to reveal the dark staircase beyond. Alice eyed it suspiciously.

'So what exactly is this business what you got to attend to?' she asked.

'I take it you know Rebecca Dakins?' queried Buxton.

Alice snorted. 'Oh, I knows her all right, and I hates her, the little slut. Thinks she can have any man she wants does that one.'

'And naturally you know the Reverend Pimms.'

'The vicar? 'Course I do.'

'Well, Alice,' Buxton explained as he pointed at the stairs, 'down there Miss Dakins is being punished for being a Godless harlot and the person doing the punishing is none other than our esteemed parson. I thought you might like to watch and, afterwards, I can pay you the compliment I had no time to pay you earlier.'

'You mean he's beating her?' Alice asked in surprise.

'I very much hope so,' Buxton replied as he lit the oil lamp. 'Now, do you wish to accompany me?'

Alice nodded vigorously. 'To see miss high and mighty Rebecca Dakins get her desserts? You bet I do.'

Buxton had expected to hear any number of sounds as he descended the stairs: shouts, screams, pleas, cries of pain or lust. What he had not expected was total silence. The pathetic scene which met his eyes when he entered the old chapel immediately answered his unspoken questions.

Rebecca Dakins was still lashed to the bench as Buxton had left her. The enthusiastic application of the birch had left her back, buttocks and legs a mass of ugly red streaks. The Reverend Pimms was sitting naked, head bowed, on the settle where Rebecca had been chained, the birch lying across his lap and his cock a sorry excuse for manhood. There were no stains on the leather to indicate that it had ever risen to greater heights.

The vicar looked up as he heard Buxton enter and instinctively crossed his legs and placed his hands over his groin as he spotted Alice close behind the Squire. Buxton's tone was as matter of fact as if he were merely enquiring as to the state of a mutual friend's health.

'And how is your charge, Mr Pimms? Chastened in body I see, but how about in spirit?'

A crimson flush of embarrassment covered the poor parson from the top of his head to the middle of his chest. He stared at the smiling girl standing perfectly composed and at ease beside Buxton.

'I . . . I have done my best to prove that sin is painful,' he stammered. 'But, I fear she has not properly heeded my warnings. Is this another for chastisement?'

Buxton laughed. 'Fear not, vicar. Alice's soul is in no peril, for the moment at least. Though she may still be the instrument of divine retribution as far as this trollop is concerned. Oh, and do not fret that young Alice will tell of what she sees here. You are the very soul of discretion, aren't you, Alice?'

'If you means I can keep my mouth shut when it suits me, yes I can,' Alice replied as she stepped forward and grasped Rebecca's hair, pulling her head back so that their eyes met. 'Got your come-uppance at last, have you, Rebecca Dakins? Not so high and mighty now, are you?'

In answer, Rebecca spat full in her face. Alice calmly wiped the spittle from her cheek before swinging the back of her hand hard against the side of Rebecca's face. Rebecca flinched, but her pride refused to allow her to cry out. Alice let go of her hair and pushed her face down on to the bench. She surveyed the tethered girl's richly scored back and buttocks. 'You can take more than that, slut. I knows that. You can take heaps more than just that.'

'I am of the same opinion, Alice,' Buxton agreed. 'But I fear the good Mr Pimms's energies are spent. Also, I am concerned as to the effects of his activities on his own soul.'

The vicar looked puzzled. 'My own soul, sir? How do you mean?'

'You have doubtless driven some of the demons out of this wretch, but what about those still haunting you? Is it not our duty, mine and Alice's, to help you cleanse yourself as you have tried to cleanse another?'

Slowly, realisation dawned on the vicar, helped by the fact that Alice had discarded her dress and was unhurriedly peeling off her black stockings. He looked at Buxton, clearly still uncertain and reluctant to jump to the wrong conclusion.

'You mean that it might be beneficial if I should suffer as you saw me suffer yesterday?'

'Naturally, only if you believe that,' Buxton told him. 'I am sure that Alice's arm is just as strong as that of the lady who usually assists you.'

The vicar looked at the now naked girl who was leaning nonchalantly against the opposite wall running her fingers idly along the length of a thin bamboo cane. He felt a stirring between his legs as he imagined what would happen to him if he agreed. The landlord's daughter had seen him naked and she had witnessed what he had done to the Dakins girl. Whatever he did now, he could neither save himself nor make matters worse, should she decide to gossip. And only he truly understood how badly he craved what was being offered him.

'I believe it would be beneficial,' he agreed as he rose, turned to face the wall and grasped the iron rings set into it, stepping backwards so that his arms were at full stretch and his rear offered an easy and tempting target.

Buxton waved Alice forward. 'Come, Alice. It is your duty to help your vicar.'

Alice stood behind and to one side of the parson. She held the cane, but did not use it straight away. Instead, she lightly and slowly ran the flat of her hand down his spine and over his buttocks. The vicar shivered at her touch and his cock began to grow. Alice reached beneath him and gave it several encouraging rubs. The vicar sighed, 'I am a sinner, do with me as you like.'

Alice answered his request by swinging the cane with a will. The vicar yelled as the thin bamboo cut into him. Again and again, Alice almost buried the cane in the quivering flesh of his buttocks. With each stroke the vicar cried out and his cock grew longer and thicker and throbbed harder. He let go of one of the rings and began to pull vigorously at his increasingly excited member, but Buxton had other ideas.

'I think we can do better than that, vicar,' he told the shaking cleric and, while Alice continued to wield the cane, he untied Rebecca and pushed her to her knees between the vicar and the wall. Rebecca did not need to be told what was expected of her. Her lips closed firmly around the parson's engorged prick and she sucked greedily, while she stroked with one hand and squeezed his balls with the other.

It was the first time any woman had ever serviced him in such a way, and the combination of Rebecca's expert mouth and hands, and the pain which shot through him every time Alice swished the cane, soon brought him to a state bordering on delirium. He shouted at her to hit harder; he cursed his own weaknesses; he called upon the saints to forgive him. And when the inevitable moment arrived he just simply screamed long and loud with pleasure and relief. Rebecca jerked her head back and the first gush of come struck directly between her eyes, the next splattered her cheek and the third her nose and lips, but she kept pulling until she was certain the vicar was completely spent.

Alice put down the cane as Buxton pulled the girl away and sat her on the bench. As he did so, he put a hand between her legs and smiled at the wetness he found. Just as he had thought: for Rebecca Dakins this was not punishment, but pleasure.

It took several minutes for the vicar to compose himself sufficiently to stand upright and turn round.

Now that the excitement was over, and the passion had subsided, acute embarrassment returned. Without a word he hastily pulled on his clothes while Buxton and the two naked girls watched with undisguised amusement.

'Thank you for your efforts this afternoon, vicar. You have been of service to me and I have been able to be of service to you. That is how it should be, I am sure you agree.'

The vicar merely nodded, unable to meet his gaze.

'Now, if you will excuse us, there are other matters which need attending to. I am sure you can find your own way out.'

Once again the vicar just nodded and then he almost ran from the room in his haste to be gone.

Buxton laughed as he looked from Alice to Rebecca. 'And now what's to be done?'

In answer, Rebecca rose and started unfastening his trousers while Alice undid the buttons of his shirt. Neither spoke until he was naked. Then Alice said, 'You did promise.'

She climbed on to the bench and wiggled her bottom invitingly. Buxton straddled the bench and, without any preamble, plunged into her. Not to be outdone, Rebecca slid beneath them and ran her tongue from his balls along his thrusting cock until she reached the top of Alice's love lips. She sucked hard on the pulsating button, bringing cries of joy from the other girl, before repeating the process. Buxton's fingers drove deep into Alice's breasts as the tempo of his movements accelerated. The combination of Alice's tightness and Rebecca's tongue pushed him to a peak of delight he had rarely, if ever, enjoyed. He felt Alice's muscles constricting as her first climax arrived and, in the same instant, he also came. Alice felt the hot cream spurt repeatedly inside her and her whole body shook as a second, even more powerful, climax surged through her.

Panting, Buxton withdrew; but Rebecca had not finished. She reached up and squeezed Alice's cunt lips together. As Alice knelt up she released her hold, allowing Buxton's spunk to drip on to her face while her tongue licked just inside Alice's entrance. The unexpected sensation instantly reawakened Alice's passion and she gasped as she came for a third time and her own juices mingled with Buxton's. Rebecca did not stop until Alice was completely dry.

In the library, ten minutes later, Buxton laid a hand on each girl's shoulder.

'Alice, you must return to your cousin. But do not worry, I think I shall be requiring frequent deliveries of your father's ale. Rebecca, you must return to your duties. But, may I suggest you wash your face before you do so. I understand white make-up is no longer in fashion.'

The girls bobbed curtsies and Alice spoke for them both.

'Yes, sir. At once, sir. We are always happy to do what the Squire wants us to do. You know that, sir.'

Buxton watched them go. Yes, he knew that, and the knowledge made him smile in anticipation.

Eleven

What was it Richard had said? 'Scratch a Duchess and you'll find a whore.' Yes, well, perhaps he had been right; but not in the way he meant. She was a whore, she freely admitted the fact. If the majority of middle- and upper-class English women were truly honest then they too would also agree. They sold themselves, or were sold by their families, either for money or security. Just because they did not stand on street corners, or haunt taverns or work in brothels, it did not mean that they were any better than those who did. In many ways they were worse. At least the prostitute sold her body openly and without hypocrisy, whereas such as herself did so to pay family debts or forge closer bonds with other dynasties or simply because women who did not marry were outcasts, pitied and patronised by Society. She had been simply bartered by her father; his aristocratic connections and influence and her body in return for solvency and estates free from mortgages. So be it. If she was a whore in all but name, she might just as well be a whore in her actions as well. The only difference was that she was enjoying her new position far more than any streetwalker ever did. And her position at that moment gave her very great enjoyment, as she spread her legs even wider and smiled up at the gangling youth who was busy unbuttoning his tunic.

The Colonel smiled at both of them as he sat on the window seat and prepared to watch the show.

'Don't hurry, boy. Take your time,' he advised his son, as the youth pulled frantically at his knee-high riding boots. 'The lovely Clarissa ain't going nowhere, are you, my dear?'

Clarissa did not answer. Instead, she ran her hands over her breasts, massaging them as she pressed them together. Then she licked the ends of her fingers and slowly skimmed them across the tips of her nipples as she began to sensuously gyrate her hips. Leaving one hand coaxing her pink buds to a prominent stiffness, she slid the other between her thighs and toyed languidly with her pubic hair while she watched Edward Markham undress.

The young subaltern gulped and the Colonel laughed.

'Careful, Clarissa,' he warned, 'or the pup will be messing himself before he ever gets free of those damned breeches.'

Clarissa looked at the rapidly growing swelling beneath the young man's trousers.

'I think you may be right, Harry. Perhaps a different view will produce less excitement,' Clarissa agreed as she turned over, presenting her back and bottom for his scrutiny instead. From the corner of her eye she could glimpse the Colonel contemplating the fading marks of Richard's beating the previous day.

'So, Clarissa, this husband of yours is not a gentle person,' he observed thoughtfully.

'He can be, Harry. But I was very naughty, and naughty girls have to be punished, don't they?'

'Indeed they do, Clarissa. Indeed they do. You can't break a horse without using the whip.'

Clarissa sighed. 'The trouble is, Harry, I just do not seem to be able to stop being naughty. So I suppose I shall just have to keep taking my punishment.'

Clarissa felt a hand gently stroke her shoulder and rolled on to her side and looked at the young man who had finally managed to free himself from the constraints of his uniform.

Edward Markham was almost as tall as his father but lacked his bulk. His frame, though solid, was slender in comparison and his chest was as smooth as a baby's. In one important aspect, however, they clearly shared a family trait. Edward Markham's cock jutted straight, long, thick and hard above two enormous balls. The total effect was that of a siege cannon, primed and ready to fire. But any cannon, however big, is only as effective as the gunner behind it.

Edward sat on the edge of the bed, clearly highly nervous and uncertain what to do next. Clarissa appreciated the danger that the cannon might explode before the order to shoot was given. She squirmed further away to allow him more space and, reaching out, took hold of his arm and encouraged him to join her in the centre of the bed. Lying side by side, she ignored the barrel pressed against her stomach, which felt as if it reached from the bottom of her belly to the middle of her ribs, and simply stroked his thick black hair as her tongue slid into his mouth and their lips joined. He responded eagerly to her kiss, forcing his mouth hard against hers, but made no other move. Clarissa realised that she would have to dictate each move. She smiled inwardly at the realisation that the pupil of just a few days before was now the teacher. She dismissed the idea that this was his first time, simply because the other young officers would certainly have, on some occasion, taken him to a house where such pleasures were always on offer; but she doubted that he had ever been with a lady before, and certainly had never suffered the handicap of having to perform in front of his highly accomplished and experienced father.

Clarissa used her arm to guide his so that his hand made contact with her right breast. The young man fondled it clumsily, squeezing harder than was necessary in his excitement but, far from complaining, Clarissa let slip a low moan as encouragement for him to continue. She pulled her lips from his and lay back on the coverlet, so that her entire body could be his playground.

He lowered his head and tentatively sucked at a nipple while his hand continued to squeeze her breast, but he made no move to explore further down to those parts which were aching to be touched. Instead, he suddenly rolled on top of her, almost crushing the air from her body, until he realised his mistake and balanced his weight on his elbows. The cannon barrel still lay along her stomach and the poor boy seemed unsure how to manoeuvre it into position. Clarissa heaved herself further up the bed and raised her hips. Reaching down, she guided the tip between the lips of her sex and, by bringing up her knees and rotating her hips, drew him into the moist passage. She gasped as the size of him stretched her muscles to their limits. Surely, she thought, they could not be pushed wider even when giving birth. But that would be agony, while this was sheer bliss. When, finally, his full length was inside her and his balls were rammed against her, he instinctively began to move, getting faster and fiercer with every thrust. Clarissa clung to him, her nails ripping the skin of his shoulders and back, her lips smothering his eyes and nose and mouth with kisses as her entire frame heaved and shook. She wrapped her long legs around the small of his back, giving even greater momentum to every inward thrust. She felt the massive organ inside her suddenly jerk and explode. No artillery officer could ever have timed his shot more precisely. As the cannon fired, the thin walls that were holding her climax in check disintegrated instantly under the impact. She did not scream; she wailed. A high, piercing cry that took all her breath and left her gulping for air. This was no single roundshot, but canister fire, and she shuddered and shook with every fresh explosion. At last the barrage was over and he withdrew. Clarissa grabbed him and pulled him down next to her, clinging to him until she ceased shaking and could breath normally again.

'Ow!'

Clarissa cried out at the sudden impact of thick leather across the side of her thigh. She released Edward and rolled over to face the source of the unexpected onslaught. As she did so the belt descended again, striking flat across her stomach. Edward was equally surprised and leaped from the bed to confront his father.

'What do you think you are doing?'

Before replying, the Colonel struck once more. This time, the edge of the belt sliced a neat, perfectly straight line, through Clarissa's golden tuft. Clarissa's body jerked with the force of the blow, but she made no attempt to leave the bed and escape any further attack. The Colonel wrapped the buckle end of the belt tighter around his hand as he answered his son.

'What does it look like I am doing, Edward? I am punishing Clarissa because she has been very, very naughty.'

'But, Father, she's a lady. A gentleman never strikes a lady,' Edward protested.

The Colonel guffawed at his son's naivety. 'You have so much to learn, Edward. So very much to learn. And who better to teach you than your father?'

166

He turned to Clarissa. 'And what do you think, Madam? Do you agree you deserve to be punished for your naughtiness?'

Clarissa picked up two pillows, placed one on top of the other in the centre of the bed and lay face down on them so that her arse was invitingly and irresistibly on offer. She giggled as she wiggled her bottom at the two men.

'To err is human, Harry; to forgive, divine. I'll err and you be divine.'

'See what I mean, Edward?' the Colonel asked, sending the belt smacking into Clarissa's buttocks as he spoke. 'Now, go downstairs and bring me the fly rod that's hanging beside the fireplace.'

The youth began to pull on his trousers but his father stopped him.

'No time for that, Edward. No one is going to see you. Now, be quick.'

While his son was carrying out his errand, the Colonel sat beside Clarissa and ran his hands over her tight globes, separating her cheeks with a finger which reached down to tickle the entrance to her back passage.

'Clarissa, my dear, you have a most wondrous arse. One of the finest I have ever seen, and I have seen very many.'

'And it is all for your pleasure, Harry,' Clarissa purred. 'Do with it as you wish.'

The flat of the Colonel's hand made a very satisfying thwacking sound as he responded to her invitation. By the time his son reappeared carrying the fishing rod, he had delivered six hard smacks and Clarissa's bottom was already turning red, the imprint of his fingers standing out clearly against the soft flesh. Clarissa sighed and writhed at every blow, rubbing her thighs together to further stimulate and encourage the delicious moisture beginning to seep down her cunt.

The Colonel rose and took the rod. It was a long, highly supple length of ash. He began to unscrew the top two sections.

'I presume you have never spanked a woman before, Edward. Well, here is your opportunity. Pray continue while I prepare more elaborate methods of punishing young Clarissa here.'

The youth leaned over and tentatively smacked Clarissa's left cheek.

'No, boy, not like that,' his father told him. 'Good God, man, you're not shaking hands with her. Doubt if she even felt it. Like this.'

Using all his strength, the Colonel brought his hand down on to Clarissa's buttocks. Clarissa shivered and a low moan escaped her lips at the severity of the blow. She felt her cream beginning to moisten the insides of her tightly clenched thighs. She opened her legs to allow it free passage and slid a hand beneath her so that the tips of two fingers compressed her clit.

Edward, still slightly bewildered by the events he was being encouraged to participate in, but becoming increasingly aroused by the spectacle before him, copied his father. Every time his hand smashed into her, Clarissa moaned with delight, and with every smack his own manhood became bigger and stiffer.

The Colonel watched approvingly for a few minutes before calling a halt to the proceedings.

'Enough, Edward. She is ready for more.'

He grasped Clarissa's arm and pulled her from the bed, making her stand in the centre of the room. In his right hand he held the bottom section of the fishing rod; five feet of thin, springy wood. In his left was a length of velvet curtain cord.

'Put your hands behind your head, Clarissa,' he commanded and instantly she obeyed.

Expertly the Colonel tied her wrists together behind her neck so that her elbows pointed towards the ceiling, leaving her entire body exposed and completely defenceless. The Colonel prowled round her like a lion gloating over its helpless prey and then, without warning, lashed out. The rod ripped into her diagonally from left shoulder to right buttock. Clarissa screamed and stumbled forward. She had never experienced such agony. Tears filled her eyes and her nerves screamed in protest; but even in the same instant that her back suddenly felt ablaze, so the fluttering in her belly intensified fivefold and the stream between her legs became a river. The Colonel continued to circle her, choosing his target with the cold-blooded concentration of a sniper. He was in no hurry, and the sheer arrogance of her tormentor only served to turn up the heat beneath the cauldron of feelings within Clarissa. The rod whistled through the air to land plumb across her breasts, almost pushing her aching nipples back into her body. Clarissa screamed again. She saw the third blow coming and this time tried to twist away, but only succeeded in receiving it on her left breast and arm instead of her stomach. She staggered and the Colonel laughed.

'That's right, Clarissa. Dance for us. Show us those dainty little steps they taught you.' This time he aimed the rod low and it bit into the back of her legs.

Clarissa began to dance before the two men, moving her feet gracefully in time to an old country folk tune she had heard at a village fête many years before. The rhythm of the music inside her head, the swaying of her body and the feel of her bare feet sliding across the polished floorboards was intoxicating. She closed her eyes as she improvised the steps and the melody only she could hear swelled to blot out every other sound. When the next attack came, and the rod scored her back again, she was so entranced by her own movements, and the rapidly rising crescendo of lust inside her, that she scarcely reacted to it. What should have made her scream in pain merely made her move faster and lighter, like a Dervish dancing himself into a trance.

The Colonel's voice sounded as if it were coming from the end of a long, echoing tunnel.

'Enough for the present, I think, Clarissa. We have other needs you must attend to.'

He untied the cord and freed her hands, but Clarissa continued to dance, oblivious to everything but her secret music. As she moved her hands explored her lithe nakedness, caressing her breasts, sliding down her stomach and thighs and then meeting and lingering between her legs; she slapped her thighs and buttocks to the beat of the silent rhythm as she swayed and bent like a flower before a hurricane.

Only the roughness of the Colonel's hands and his vigorous shaking of her shoulders brought her back to reality. She opened her eyes and stared uncomprehendingly at the two naked men for a moment, and then she laughed. Taking the Colonel's hand in hers, and clutching the arm of his son with the other, she drew them back to the bed.

Lucy kicked at the cat. The cat jumped in time and raced from the room. Lucy picked up a small porcelain vase from the dressing table and hurled it against the wall, smashing it into a thousand fragments. Damn the woman! Why was it that she was always the one who gave but never received? Miss high and mighty Clarissa Buxton did not mind her servant pleasing her, but was she prepared to please her servant in the same way? No, that would never do; that would be below her dignity. She did not consider them woman and woman, only mistress and skivvy. She had served Clarissa for three years. They had grown into womanhood together, but there had never been any closeness between them; the distance which propriety dictated had always been scrupulously maintained. Despite her passion for her mistress, and the power of the fantasies which filled her head when she lay alone in the darkness of her garret bedroom, Lucy had accepted her role; even been grateful for it. But now everything had changed. In just a few short days her mistress had become a totally different person. It was a change which Lucy not only welcomed, but which also fuelled her desire and strengthened her secret love for her mistress. She wanted to give her mistress her body, as well as her adoration, but her mistress had declined the obvious invitation. Her only concern was her own satisfaction and Lucy felt the fierce anger and humiliation of the spurned. She was also frustrated. There was a hunger inside her which she had to feed. She yearned, if not for her mistress's touch then the touch of another – male or female, it did not matter. The longer her craving went unappeased, the more urgent it became.

Lucy slipped off her dress and looked at herself in the mirror. She was attractive, she knew that. Her figure was firm and supple and curved in all the right places. Her hair shone and her eyes sparkled. She had had many men, from farm labourers and servants to a Naval officer; even the Earl himself had once taken her to his bed. But she had never been with a woman. The only woman she had ever desired was her mistress, and her mistress had cruelly rejected her. Tears pricked her eyes as she considered the unfairness of her treatment.

Lucy plucked the candle from its holder on the dressing table, lifted her right leg on to a stool and, still watching herself in the mirror, pushed it up inside her. Slowly she ran its length in and out of her body. She tweaked her nipples before rubbing hard at her clit. But she felt nothing; no growing sensations that would ultimately satisfy her longing. She withdrew the candle and put it back in its holder. It was no good. This time only the real thing would suffice.

Tom sat on the rim of the horse trough in the stable yard and unwrapped the small linen bundle on his lap. Using his pocket knife he hacked the hunk of bread into four thick slices and cut the lump of cheese into squares. Eager to impress on his first day, he had risen at five and had not stopped work since. He had swept the stables, cleared away piles of rubbish and cleaned all the harnesses. He had been so keen that he had worked through his allocated lunch break. Now, he was famished and looking forward to rest and food. The sun was shining, the smell of hay and horses drifted on the breeze, he had a job he had always wanted and a kind and considerate master. At that moment, there was nothing else in life he could think of wishing for. He was raising bread and cheese to his mouth when he heard the girl speak.

'And who might you be then?'

He turned to see Lucy standing behind him.

'Me name's Tom. I'm the new stable lad,' he replied. 'And you are?'

Lucy sat beside him, picked up a piece of cheese and nibbled it. 'My name is Lucy and I am the personal maid to the Lady of the Manor.'

Tom bit into his bread and cheese. 'Sounds a good job that. You been here long?'

'I came here with my mistress a couple of weeks ago. Before that we lived at the Earl's main house in Derbyshire. Much grander and more important than this old place. We had over fifty servants there.'

Tom, who had never seen a house bigger than The Hall, and had never strayed more than ten miles from Castleleigh, was impressed, just as Lucy had intended he should be. He reached down, picked up a small earthenware flagon and offered it to her. 'Fancy some ale?'

The day was hot and, had she been truthful, Lucy did indeed fancy some ale. But she was not prepared to admit it.

'At The Hall all we drink is wine,' she told him haughtily.

Tom swigged from the flagon. 'Funny, I just seen some beer being delivered.'

'That would have been for the servants.'

Tom took another mouthful of his lunch, spluttering bread and cheese as he spoke.

'Well, you're a servant, aren't you?'

Lucy regarded him coldly. 'I am the Honourable Clarissa Buxton's personal maid. I am not just any old servant.'

Tom washed down his food with another draught from the flagon. 'Sorry, I'm sure.'

'You got a girlfriend then, Tom?'

The sudden change in the tack of the conversation caught the lad by surprise.

'No. Well, not just at the moment.'

Lucy smiled mischievously. 'Not just at the moment,' she mimicked. 'Bet you never have had a girl, have you, Tom?'

Tom could feel himself beginning to blush.
' 'Course I have.'

Lucy placed her hand on his knee and began to beat a tantalising tattoo with her fingertips. She moved closer so that their thighs were touching.

'Bit of a lover are you then, Tom?'

'I don't know what you mean,' was all he could think to reply.

Lucy ran her hand a few inches higher and squeezed his thigh.

'What I mean, Tom, is that I bet you never been with a girl. I reckon you wouldn't know what to do with one.'

Tom bridled at the attack on his manliness.

'I been with plenty. Not that it's any of your business.'

Lucy slipped her arm round his waist, slid her hand beneath his leather jerkin and began to massage the small of his back, gently prising his shirt from his trousers as she did so.

'You can make it my business, if you wants, Tom,' she told him in a low, coaxing voice, as her left hand reached the top of his thigh and her right slid down the back of his trousers.

Tom could not control either the blush, which spread across his cheeks and down his neck, or the growing ache in his groin caused by the pressure of flesh against unyielding waxed linen. Lucy's breath was hot on his reddened cheek; she smelled of perfumed soap as her hair brushed his face. He could think of nothing to say, and so he said nothing.

Encouraged by his lack of protest, Lucy pressed her face against his and began to lick the inside of his ear, blowing softly as she did so. Her hand glided over his crotch and she rubbed the ever-rising bulge which lay beneath her fingers. She felt the lad shiver and knew the final outcome was now inevitable.

174

'Let's go somewhere private, Tom,' she urged and, without giving him a chance to object, grabbed his hand and pulled him to his feet.

Lucy led the clearly nervous, but just as obviously excited, lad through the stable yard gate and followed the bridlepath which Clarissa had ridden along two hours before. She walked quickly, clutching Tom's hand in hers in case he changed his mind and, after a couple of minutes, turned off the path on to a grassy track. A quarter of a mile further and they were hidden from sight within a small copse of tall fir trees. In the heart of the wood was a large round pool encircled by lush grass and shaded by the overhanging boughs of the trees. Lucy sank on to the soft green bed and Tom followed her down. The early afternoon sun glinted like a million jewels off the still water; birds called noisily from the branches; the air was thick with the smell of pine resin and wild flowers. It was the perfect time and place for lovers. Ever since Lucy had discovered this secret place she had dreamed of lying on the bank beside her mistress, of loving and being loved, and afterwards both of them swimming naked in the pool. But, at that moment, love had never been further from Lucy's mind. It was passion not poetry, sex not scenery, she needed.

Tom lay beside her, uncertain what to do next; he was still confused by all that was happening to him. Lucy lay on her side, looked at him and smiled. She had guessed that he had never had a girl before, probably never even been kissed. Well, if this was to be his baptism, she would make sure it was a baptism of fire that he would never forget.

Lucy ran her hand through his hair and drew his face close to hers. She leaned over and kissed him with all the passion that had been so long imprisoned

175

inside her. She gnawed at his lips and slid her tongue rapidly in and out of his mouth. Her fingers squeezed his crotch so fiercely that Tom was forced to knock aside her arm for fear that matters would conclude too soon. He reached out tentatively and touched her breasts, but it was too insignificant a gesture for Lucy. She put her hand over his, encouraging him to squeeze them as hard as he could. While he fondled her breasts she undid his shirt and licked the sweat of the morning's labour from around his nipples. Her tongue traced slowly down the centre of his chest and stomach. She kissed and lightly licked his navel while Tom, no longer able to reach her breasts, just lay back on the grass, closed his eyes and sighed with pleasure.

The kissing and licking stopped abruptly and Tom opened his eyes to see Lucy standing over him removing her dress. His eyes feasted on her body as each part was revealed to him. Lucy had only one garment to dispense with, but she shed it with the skill of a striptease artiste. First her shin, then her thighs were bared for his wide-eyed gaze. Half-inch by half-inch, she continued raising the hem until he was goggling at the curly black triangle. Lucy, her dress now up above her hips, rotated on one foot like a slow motion ballet dancer and Tom stared at the perfect curves of her buttocks. And then she was facing him again and the cloth was being slipped above her breasts, which bounced invitingly as they were freed. Lucy pulled the dress over her head and tossed it aside. She kicked off her shoes and stood, completely naked, above him and smiled.

'Your turn now, Tom.'

The youth scrambled to his feet, shrugging off his jerkin and pulling off his shirt even before he was upright. He bent and untied the laces of his boots and yanked them off. He unbuckled his belt and the buttons popped from his trousers as he tore at them in his haste. His trousers fell and he stepped out of them and towards Lucy.

Lucy had watched his clumsy undressing with amusement. There was no finesse about his actions and she knew that, unless she took the initiative, his lovemaking would be equally awkward and gauche. But, overall, she liked what she saw. He might be of only medium height but he was muscular and without a trace of fat. She looked down at the pole which jutted at ninety degrees from a tangled undergrowth of dark-brown hair. It was not the biggest she had ever seen, but it was certainly more than adequate.

She held him close as they kissed, both sets of fingers buried in the crack of his bottom so that his cock was throbbing along the length of her stomach. She transferred her lips from his and instead kissed his neck, then chest, then stomach, gradually sinking down while she continued to clutch the cheeks of his arse. When she was kneeling before him she moved her head back just far enough to release his rod. She started to lick its purple helmet and nibble at the foreskin and Tom shook with the intensity of sensations he had never experienced before. He had always wondered what it would be like; now he knew and it was better than anything he had ever imagined. Lucy stopped licking and nibbling and started sucking and instinctively he moved his hips in time with her bobbing head. Leaving one hand playing with his buttocks, the fingers sliding down and tickling his anus and the underneath of his balls, she used the other to stroke his shaft, leisurely at first and then with increasing momentum as she sensed his climax was near. Tom gasped and grabbed her hair as he came. The shaft jerked crazily inside Lucy's mouth and the back of her throat was splattered with his thick cream, but she carried on sucking and pulling at him until she was gulping down spurt after spurt of the salty fluid. Not until she felt him beginning to wilt did she pull away. She wiped splashes of come from her lips with the back of her hand as she looked up at him and grinned.

'Come here.'

Lucy stretched herself on the grass with Tom beside her. Lucy lay on her back staring at the sky while Tom rested on his side gazing adoringly at her. Lucy had enjoyed playing with the lad and, as always, had been excited by the feel of a swollen cock in her mouth and savoured the taste of his spunk as it had gushed down her throat. But, most of all, she had enjoyed being in total control. She had not intended to suck him; most of all she had wanted to feel him deep inside her belly, but she was experienced enough to know that two or three thrusts would have brought the overexcited novice to completion, and that would have been far too frustrating. The next time he would last longer and, with Tom's youth and strength, the next time was now.

Lucy turned and kissed Tom as she reached for his limp cock. The instant she touched it she felt it stir and half a dozen gentle strokes were all that was required to make it rigid again. She pushed Tom on to his back. She was not in the mood for further foreplay. All she craved was satisfaction. She straddled him and sank straight down, absorbing every inch he had to offer with one urgent movement. She paused for only a moment to enjoy the feel of his balls squashed between his thighs and her anus and then began to ride. There was no subtlety, no finesse, to her actions. She ground down on him, using him like a pestle within her mortar. As she moved, her fingers tore at her clit. As she felt the waters within ready to flood, her speed increased and her muscles contracted tight around him. Tom stretched a hand towards her breasts but she knocked it aside. His fondling would slow her down just when she knew she was on the cliff edge of her climax. She saw the lad constricting his stomach muscles as he tried to hold back, not wishing these new and wonderful feelings to end too soon. But the sight of this beautiful girl sliding up and down on him, clawing at herself, her breasts bouncing with every move, was finally too great. He relaxed and Lucy felt the first jet speed from him. In the same moment, the waters were finally freed and she cried out as climax after climax surged through her with such power that she threw back her head and wailed at the sky as her body trembled out of control.

When the shaking eventually stopped, and the hunger inside her was sated at last, she stood up and, without speaking or looking at Tom, pulled on her dress. Taking his cue from her, the lad clambered to his feet and also dressed. As soon as she had buttoned and smoothed her dress, Lucy turned on her heel and walked away. Tom, with more clothes to contend with, had to run to catch her up, the laces of his boots still untied. He fell into step beside her as they left the shelter of the trees and headed back down the track towards the bridlepath.

'Lucy?' Tom asked hesitantly, clearly not sure how to continue.

'Yes?' Lucy replied, quickening her pace. She wished only to get back to the house and wash; she could guess what he was going to ask and she did not want to hear it.

'Lucy, there's a fair over High Mallen way next Saturday – would you care to go there with me?'

'No, Tom. We cannot walk out together. It would never do. You must realise that you are just a stable lad, while I am personal maid to the lady of the house.'

'She may be the lady of the house, but she certainly ain't no lady,' blurted the lad, and instantly wished he had kept quiet as Lucy stopped and rounded on him.

'What do you mean by that?' she demanded sharply.

'Nothing. I don't mean nothing,' Tom answered, avoiding her piercing gaze.

Lucy grabbed his shoulders, forcing him to look her in the face.

'Yes you did. Tell me what you meant or I'll make such trouble for you, you won't have no job here any more. All I got to do is tell my mistress you attacked me. The Squire is the magistrate, remember. You'll be lucky not to be transported to Australia.'

Tom shifted uneasily at the truth of her threat.

'If I tells you what I know, you promise you won't tell no one else?'

'Just tell me, Tom. Now! Or else.'

'It was this morning. I was exercising one of the horses when I see the mistress lying beside the stream. She had her dress up round her waist and she was . . .' Tom hesitated while he tried to find the right words.

'Doing what, Tom? What was she doing?' Lucy almost shouted the questions at him.

'She was doing to herself what you did to yourself back there. You know.'

'And that was all?'

Tom shook his head.

'No, when she'd finished she rode off towards The Grange and I followed. When she gets to the old hunting lodge there's Colonel Markham waiting for her. He helps her down from her horse and the moment her feet touches the ground they're kissing and cuddling each other. I know I shouldn't have done, but I tethered the horse and crept up to the window and I sees the Colonel pick up the mistress and carry her upstairs. Then the Colonel's son, Master Edward, arrived and I had to run off or he'd have caught me. I hid in the bushes and after a few minutes went back to the window and I sees Master Edward, stark naked, taking a fishing rod from the wall.'

Tom smirked. 'Now, I don't suppose the three of them were discussing fishing, do you? Anyway, like I said, she may be a lady in name, but she ain't no lady in what she does. And her only just wed too.'

Lucy felt as if her stomach had become a hollow pit. How could her mistress have done such a thing? She had felt jealous enough when the engagement had been announced and had sobbed in the lonely darkness of her room on their wedding night as she pictured the new master enjoying her beloved mistress; doing with her so many of the things she had dreamed of them doing to each other. But she could accept her mistress's marriage. Not only was that natural in the course of things, but she knew Clarissa had had no say in the matter. But this? This was totally wrong. Her mistress was giving her body to another man, two other men probably, when she could have, should have, been giving it to her.

Lucy let go of Tom's shoulders and pushed him away.

'I don't believe you, Tom. I won't believe you,' she shrieked at him.

'It's the –' Tom began, but Lucy was no longer listening. She turned and ran down the path, the tears coursing down her cheeks.

Lucy did not stop running until she reached The Hall. There was a girl she did not recognise standing beside a pony cart in the courtyard, but she paid her no mind as she entered the house. All she wanted was the sanctuary of her room where she could be alone with her thoughts.

Half an hour later, her eyes red-rimmed from crying, Lucy was calm again. The feelings of loss, of rejection and of revulsion were still there, but now they had been overshadowed by an even more powerful emotion: hatred. If she could not have her mistress then no other would; not even her husband. Coldly and calculatingly, Lucy began to plot her revenge.

Twelve

Clarissa had been unusually quiet throughout dinner, as if she were nursing a problem which she either could not, or would not, discuss. Whatever the cause of her silence, Buxton was grateful for it. He did not want to have to listen to a catalogue of the trivial events which had probably comprised her day's activities. Perhaps she was not feeling well; certainly he had noted the stiffness with which she had walked into the room, and the way she regularly shifted in her chair as if trying to relieve some discomfort. He did not care in the least about any troubles his wife might be experiencing, except that they provided him with the opportunity he wanted.

'You seem troubled, Clarissa,' he observed as he crumpled his napkin and tossed it on to his empty plate. His activities during the day had made him ravenous and he had eaten everything put in front of him, while his wife had managed only a few mouthfuls.

Clarissa avoided eye contact as she replied, 'I do not feel very well, Richard,' adding untruthfully as an afterthought, 'women's problems.'

Buxton nodded. 'In that case, Clarissa, I think it might be advisable if I were to spend the night in the guest suite. I have to work late on estate matters, ledgers and accounts, that sort of thing. I will not retire until at least midnight and I would not wish to disturb you if you are feeling poorly.'

Clarissa tired to sound grateful, rather than relieved. She would now have at least eight hours' grace in which to try to soothe away the tell-tale marks of the fishing rod. 'That is very considerate of you, Richard, thank you.'

Buxton rose. 'Not at all my dear. It is the least I can do. I think I should start work now, so I will see you at breakfast. Goodnight.'

Buxton had hardly had time to settle himself in his favourite chair in the library window bay and pour himself a large Cognac before Robert entered.

'Excuse me for disturbing you, sir, but madam's maid, Lucy, asks if she can have a word with you.'

'About what, Robert?' Buxton asked, reluctant to be drawn into any tedious servant problems.

'I am afraid she refuses to say, sir. She is just insisting that she must talk to you, and only you.'

Buxton sighed. 'Very well, Robert. I suppose I had better see the wretched girl. Send her in.'

The butler ushered Lucy into the room and left her standing in front of Buxton. The girl was obviously nervous and seemed tongue-tied by her surroundings and the importance of the man before her.

'Well, Lucy, what is it that you want to tell me? Just speak out, there's no need to be frightened,' Buxton told her encouragingly.

'It's about the mistress, sir,' Lucy began. 'I been fretting all evening about whether I should tell you what I know. I do not want to seem disloyal, sir. I've never been one for telling tales or gossip. But, in the end, I knew it was my duty to tell you.'

'Tell me what, Lucy?' asked Buxton, becoming exasperated at the maid's reluctance to come to the point. 'Speak up, girl. Just spit it out.'

'It's about my Lady and Colonel Markham, sir.'

Buxton sighed impatiently. 'What about my wife and Colonel Markham, Lucy? For goodness' sake just say what you came to say, or we'll be here all night.'

'They're lovers, sir. The mistress has been with the Colonel, and his son Edward, all afternoon in the hunting lodge on the Colonel's estate.'

Buxton sipped the fiery liquid in his glass while he assimilated Lucy's words. Another man might have been shocked by such news, or flared into a rage, but Buxton was not as other men. In truth, the prime emotion he felt was amusement. So, he thought, while I was seeing to Rebecca and rogering Alice, Clarissa was tumbling with the Markhams. He was surprised, but not angry. Richard Buxton might have been many things, good and bad, but one thing he certainly was not was a hypocrite. However, for the sake of propriety, he must at least appear to play the role such a revelation demanded of him. He looked coldly at the maid.

'That is a very serious allegation, Lucy. Very serious indeed. How do you know this?'

'From Tom, the stable lad, sir. He saw them, sir. Through the window, sir.' The words gushed from the maid as she lowered her head and fixed her eyes on the carpet, unable to bear Buxton's piercing stare.

Buxton pondered the importance of the maid's words. If two servants knew already then, probably before morning, it would be common knowledge below stairs. He cared nothing about his wife's infidelity, but he was most certainly concerned about his own standing in the eyes of the servants, and the villagers as well for that matter, for certainly the gossip would spread through Castleleigh faster than the plague.

'And who else have you told about this, Lucy?' he demanded.

'No one, sir. No one at all. But, I thought I had to tell you, sir. I could see it was my duty, sir,' Lucy replied hastily.

'I would have thought your first duty was to the mistress you have served for so long,' Buxton told her sternly. 'I can see how your loyalties have been divided, but I find that a poor excuse for not keeping faith with your mistress. I am disappointed in you, Lucy. Very disappointed indeed.'

Lucy looked up in surprise, shocked by his words. She had not expected to be thanked for bringing such bad news, but she had not expected to be rebuked either.

Buxton put down his glass and stood up. Lucy shifted uneasily from foot to foot and once again cast her eyes downwards. Suddenly she felt her hair grabbed as Buxton pulled her head up and back, forcing her to look at him.

His tone was that of a black-capped judge passing sentence.

'Until I am certain that you are not lying, I think it advisable that you should have no further contact with the other servants. Clearly you cannot be trusted. You have betrayed your mistress, and that is a very grave matter for which you must be disciplined.'

'But, sir, I was only doing what I thought was right. And I'm not lying, sir. It's the truth, it really is. And I haven't told another soul, sir, honest,' Lucy protested, her voice quivering with fright.

Buxton sneered. 'Honest? That I doubt. But I'll find the truth in my own way and, before I have finished with you, I'll be certain of what is true and what is just a figment of your evil imagination.'

Lucy was about to protest again, but the impact of Buxton's palm on her cheek closed her mouth before any words were released. Tears filled her eyes as she cringed away from him.

Buxton pointed to the corner by the fireplace. 'Stand there facing the wall and do not dare to speak until you are told to.'

Buxton pulled the bell sash and Robert answered the summons within seconds. He looked curiously at Lucy standing, eyes fixed on the oak panelling, shaking with fear, but asked no questions.

'Robert, this disloyal wretch has betrayed her mistress,' Buxton told him as soon as the door was shut. 'She is spreading malicious scandal. I am keeping her separate from the other servants until I determine the truth of the allegations she is making.'

'Yes, sir.'

'I want you to go to the stables,' Buxton continued. 'Bring Tom, the new stable lad, to the house. Do not, on any account, allow him to talk to any of the other staff. Lock him in the cellar until I decide what to do with him.'

'Very good, sir.' The butler accepted the order with no more emotion than if he had been asked to pour more wine. After what he had experienced during the past few days, he had become incapable of being surprised by any request.

As soon as Robert had left, Buxton opened the secret door and picked up the lamp. He grasped the collar of Lucy's blouse and dragged her to the entrance.

'Get down there.'

Lucy hesitated, fearful of what might await her in the darkness below.

'What are you going to do, sir?'

Buxton pushed her roughly in the back and she tripped down the first few stairs, before grabbing at the wall and steadying herself.

'I said you were not to speak until I told you. Don't add disobedience to the list of your crimes,' Buxton replied angrily. 'Now, get down there.'

Scared that one more blow might send her hurtling down the stairs, Lucy did as she was told. She paused in the doorway of the old chapel. Buxton merely placed the sole of his boot against her bottom and sent her sprawling on to the flagstones in the centre of the room. He put down the lamp and busied himself lighting the candles arrayed on the table and window ledges.

As the light slowly grew and she could make out the rings set in the wall and the metal cuffs that now hung from the wooden beam above the leather-covered bench, Lucy's blood chilled. When she noticed the stand and the canes, whips and belts it contained, she felt the hairs on her neck bristle.

'Take off your clothes.' Buxton's tone was coldly matter of fact.

Lucy sank to her knees in front of him.

'I'm sorry I have offended, sir. Truly I am. I won't do it again, sir. Honest I won't. Please don't punish me, sir,' she pleaded.

'Still disobedient, I see,' Buxton calmly observed as he grabbed the front of her blouse and pulled her to her feet, ripping the thin cotton from neck to waist in the process. 'When I turn round, you will be naked.'

Defeated, Lucy took off her torn blouse and then her shoes, stockings, skirt and petticoat, while Buxton carefully considered the range of implements on offer. When he turned to face the shivering girl he held a riding whip in his hand. Without warning he lashed out and the long thin leather slashed across the top of Lucy's thighs. The girl screamed at the sudden searing pain. As she saw her master raise the whip a second time, she turned away. She yelled again as the lash cut into her buttocks.

'Put your hands above your head,' Buxton commanded, and she obeyed instantly.

She felt him close behind her and heard the rattle of the chains above her head being lowered. With one hand, Buxton brought her wrists together and with the other he snapped home the handcuffs. He pulled the free end of the chain until only the very tips of her toes were still in contact with the floor.

Buxton stood facing her. 'You have a good body, Lucy. It seems almost a shame to damage such flawless skin, but I am afraid there is no alternative. I have to go now, but I shall return as soon as I am able. In the meantime, think about your behaviour but, most of all, think about what is to come.'

Buxton emphasised his words by placing the whip, a metal-studded belt and a riding crop on the bench in front of her. Lucy quaked as she looked at them and imagined them striking her tender flesh. She had enjoyed being punished by her mistress, for that had just been a game; something special between them. But this was no game, this was serious, and she was more scared than she had ever been before.

Buxton left a single candle so that all his helpless captive could see once he had left with the lamp were the instruments of punishment on the bench; he left her alone with the darkness and her fears.

Clarissa heard the door open and looked up in alarm, anxious in case Richard had changed his mind about not spending the night with her. One look at his expression made her tremble. Buxton kicked the door shut and advanced towards the bed.

'Get up.'

Clarissa slid further under the sheets, gathering them up round her neck in a pathetic attempt to gain some protection from the aura of menace and anger radiating from her husband. Buxton grasped the top of the counterpane and sheet and in one swift movement pulled it from her.

'I said, get up, slut.'

The venom in his voice and the hatred in his eyes paralysed her. Buxton grabbed her hand and the next thing she knew she was lying in a heap beside the bed and he was snarling down at her.

'I said, get up, slut.'

Clarissa got up and stood before him.

'Richard, what is the matter? What has happened? Why are you so angry with me?'

'Take off your nightdress.'

Despite her fear, Clarissa demurred.

'Richard, I told you, I am not well. Please –'

The back of her husband's hand landed on the side of her head and, for a moment, Clarissa's senses swam as flashing lights blurred her vision.

'I will not tell you a second time.'

Clarissa pulled frantically at the laces which secured the front of her nightgown. She drew it over her head but did not discard it. She held it close against her like a shield, still hoping that she could hide the marks on her body. Buxton tore it from her hands. He looked at the red slashes across her thighs, stomach and breasts. He took hold of her shoulders and spun her round and saw those which criss-crossed her back and buttocks.

'So, our neighbour, the esteemed Colonel, not only fucks my wife but beats her as well.'

He pulled her round to face him and Clarissa trembled at the pitiless look in his eyes and the stern set of his mouth.

190

'Richard? What do you mean? I do not understand what you are accusing me of. I have done nothing to . . .' but her words trailed off as she realised denial was futile.

Buxton placed a hand between her breasts and pinned her against the wall. His cold, calculating tone was even more frightening than his outburst of anger.

'You do not know what I mean? Well, Clarissa, I will tell you precisely what I mean. You have spent the afternoon in bed with Colonel Markham and his son. Do not even try to deny it. Those marks speak for themselves. The ink is hardly dry on the marriage certificate and you cuckold me. You have disgraced your family, soiled its name and reputation and, more importantly, shamed and humiliated me.'

Tears streamed from Clarissa's eyes as she realised the seriousness of what she had done, and the likely consequences of her wantonness. Richard had never wanted to marry her; now he could divorce her. She would become an outcast, rejected by her family and Society, cast adrift to make her way in the world as best she could, with no one caring if she lived or died.

'If you hope that by weeping you will soften me then you do not know me.'

'No, Richard, it is not that,' Clarissa sobbed. 'I am just so ashamed of myself, truly I am. What are you going to do with me?'

Buxton picked up the nightdress and began ripping it into shreds.

'In truth, Clarissa, I have not decided precisely what form your punishment will take. But, until I do, you will remain here. You are confined to this room and you will see no one.'

'Of course, Richard. Whatever you say. But you will allow my maid to see to my needs, won't you?'

Buxton laughed. 'Your maid? You mean the little whore Lucy? It was she who told me about you and the Colonel.'

The revelation startled Clarissa. 'But, she could not have known.'

'She knew. She told. And now she is being punished for betraying you.' Buxton looked at the four lengths of linen that were all that remained of Clarissa's nightgown. 'There, I think these should suffice. Lie on the bed, face down and spread your arms and legs.'

Clarissa obeyed without a word and stayed silent as her husband used the strips to secure her wrists and ankles to the four corners of the bed.

'You can stay like this for tonight. By tomorrow, I will have decided on an appropriate punishment.'

Clarissa made no protest as her husband extinguished the two oil lamps and left the room. All she could think about was not her immediate discomfort, but the terrors tomorrow might bring.

Buxton was crossing the landing, walking back towards the library, when the bell beside the front doors rang. He paused and watched Robert open it. A tall young man, his riding boots and long black cloak spattered with mud, strode into the hall before the butler had time to ask his business. He drew an envelope from inside his jacket.

'I have a letter for Mr Richard Buxton. Is he at home?'

Years of being in service had taught Robert not to prevaricate with a gentleman, but he still had his duty to do.

'If you will wait in the drawing room, sir, I will inquire if the master is at home. Should you wish to leave the letter, I will, of course, ensure that he receives it as soon as possible.'

'I promised to deliver it into his hands and his hands only. And I am in no mood to wait; I wish to be back in Colchester as soon as possible. I shall remain here until he comes.'

'I am Richard Buxton.'

Butler and visitor turned as Buxton descended the stairs and joined them. The visitor clicked the heels of his boots together and bowed stiffly.

'Captain Roger Tremayne, Her Majesty's Life Guards. At your service, sir.'

Buxton took the envelope the young officer proffered. Excitement and anticipation surged through him as he recognised the handwriting.

'Who gave you this, Captain?'

The officer smiled. 'A most extraordinary lady, sir. I am staying the night at the Five Bells in Colchester on my way to Harwich. I met the lady at dinner. She is entrancing, quite entrancing. After we had dined she suggested we play cards. I am a good card player, but my skill was as nothing compared to hers. She took twenty guineas off me in as many minutes. When I had nothing left to stake, she wagered the lot against my agreeing to run an errand for her. I lost again and that is why I am here.'

Buxton laughed. 'I can believe it, Captain. If you will allow me a few minutes, I would like you to take back my reply. Robert, show Captain Tremayne into the drawing room. I am sure he would not say no to a large brandy.'

Seated at the Davenport in the morning room, Buxton read the letter.

My Darling Richard,

I hope you are in good health and surviving the rigours of married life. London is oppressively hot at the moment and I decided the peacefulness and clean air of the country might be good for me. I arrived this morning and will be staying at this inn for three more days. It would be so nice if we could meet, but if that is not possible, of course I will understand.

My love as always,
    Maxine.

So, she had come to him even before receiving his letter summoning her. She did not know it, but her timing was perfect. Buxton's reply was a single line.

'Tomorrow at noon, my love.'

Buxton handed the sealed envelope to the Captain.

'Please hand this to the lady, and do not fret about your loss, Captain. I have a feeling your luck is about to change and you will be wagering more than your money before the night is over.'

When the messenger had departed, Buxton turned to Robert.

'Is the boy locked up?'

'Exactly as you instructed, sir.'

'Good. Tomorrow you will send a trap – no, on second thought the coach – to collect a Miss Maxine Brandside from the Five Bells in Colchester at midday.'

'Yes, sir. And may I enquire how long the lady will be staying?'

'As long as she likes, Robert,' said Buxton happily. 'Miss Brandside is our new housekeeper.'

Robert's shock was plain. 'You want me to send the coach for a housekeeper?'

Buxton grinned. 'Miss Brandside is not just any common or garden housekeeper, Robert. She will bring a new style to The Hall, and therefore why should she not arrive in style? I am sleeping in the guest suite tonight, but in the morning ensure that it is prepared ready for Miss Brandside to occupy.'

'Very good, sir.' After all, Robert reasoned, if a housekeeper was to be collected in a liveried coach, emblazoned with the coat of arms of an Earl, why should she not be put in the guest suite instead of the housekeeper's parlour?

Buxton returned to the library and descended to the chapel. Lucy looked fearfully from him to the whip. Buxton released her wrists from the cuffs, but her freedom was short-lived. Placing her on the settle, he replaced handcuffs with manacles.

'I have decided to postpone your punishment until tomorrow, Lucy,' he told her.

'But you can't leave me chained here all night,' the maid objected. Buxton only laughed as he blew out the candle.

'Haven't you learned by now that I can, and will, do anything and everything I please? And that I will do it how I want, when I want? Dream on that, Lucy. Dream on that.'

An hour, and several brandies later, Buxton lay in his bed and thought about the twists and turns of fate the evening had brought. He had not wanted to spend the night with Clarissa because he had decided to enjoy it with Rebecca instead. But, first the revelations about his wife, and then the letter from Maxine, had changed everything. What surprises she had in store. A new position through which they could be together all the time, a wife tied to her bed awaiting her fate, a lithesome maid chained and ready to receive her punishment and a strapping youth locked in a cellar who would also need to be shown the error of his ways. And then there was the matter of Colonel Harry Markham to be dealt with. If life had anything better to offer than the prospects for tomorrow, Richard Buxton was unable to imagine what it might be.

* * *

The dew had barely dried when Buxton swung into the saddle and cantered across the fields towards The Grange. He had risen with the sun and attended to many tasks before eating a hearty breakfast and setting off to confront the Colonel. He had taken bread and water to Clarissa, waited while she ate and drank and then retied her to the bedposts. He had refused to answer any of her questions and, when they became irritating and the food was finished, had silenced them with a gag made from her own stockings. Lucy received the same fare as her mistress but had had the sense to remain silent while she ate it. Buxton had then ordered Robert to serve an identical breakfast to Tom. When the head groom mentioned the lad's absence, Buxton had told him that Tom was on an errand for him and the man had seemed satisfied with the explanation. Now, all that remained to be accomplished before Maxine arrived was to settle matters with his neighbour.

The Grange turned out to be a large, square, mid-Georgian country house on the crest of a small hill. The broad, wrought-iron gates were locked, but the gateman was quick to answer the bell. He took one look at the tall, immaculately dressed rider sitting on his thoroughbred and did not bother to ask his identity before opening the gates.

The butler was equally impressed by the early morning visitor, but did enquire his name and purpose before ushering him into the hall.

'I am sorry, sir, but Colonel Markham is not at home at present. He is at the lodge, but if you would care to wait, I will send word that you are here.'

'At the lodge, you say,' Buxton mused. 'No matter – I will go there. I have a mind to see the place.'

It took five hammerings on the heavy brass knocker before the lodge door opened. Buxton found himself confronted by a bear of a man, unshaven, naked to the waist and smelling of whisky. The Colonel was less easily impressed than his servants.

'And who the devil are you?' he demanded.

Buxton proffered his card. 'Richard Buxton of The Hall. And you, I presume, are Colonel Markham.'

The name brought a furtive glint to the Colonel's eyes.

'And what can I do for you, Mr Buxton?'

'There are matters we need to discuss, Colonel. Perhaps it would be better if we discussed them inside.'

'Matters?' queried the Colonel suspiciously.

'Concerning yourself, your son and my wife,' Buxton replied evenly.

The Colonel held the door open and Buxton entered.

'A useful little hideaway this,' he observed as he looked round the room. 'Perfect for a lovers' tryst.'

'I do not know what you mean, sir,' the Colonel blustered, but Buxton dismissed his words with a wave of his hand.

'Yesterday, in this place, you and your son rogered my wife. That is hardly a situation I can ignore, Colonel. The question is, what do you propose to do about it?'

The Colonel's lips curled in a sly grin. 'No, Mr Buxton. The question is, what are you going to do about it?'

Buxton leaned against the mantelpiece. 'I believe I am entitled to demand satisfaction.'

The Colonel bellowed with laughter. 'You mean a duel?'

'Of sorts, though not in the traditional sense. I am competent with both pistol and foil, as I am sure that, being a military man, you are too. It might prove interesting but, as the local magistrate, I can hardly be seen to break the law. Also, I am enjoying my life far too much to risk it over a little matter like honour. Should we put on the gloves, it would be entertaining, for while you are bigger than me, I am certainly faster than you. However, broken noses and split lips do not appeal either.'

'Then what the deuce are you suggesting?' the Colonel demanded irritably.

'I believe that you and I have a similar attitude to life in general, and women in particular. I therefore propose a challenge of a very different kind which, I am sure, we will both find enjoyable and stimulating.'

'What sort of challenge?' asked the Colonel, intrigued.

In reply, Buxton took a small, leather-covered book from his pocket and handed it to Markham.

'The text is in French, but the illustrations speak for themselves.'

The Colonel's eyes widened as he flipped through the pages.

'At this moment, the village blacksmith is making me the harnesses and carts. They should be ready within the week. My proposal is simple. We will have a race. My wife against any slut you can find. Winner takes both women. And, to make it even more interesting, why not a side bet of, say, five hundred pounds?'

The Colonel closed the book and returned it to Buxton.

'When I was in the Crimea, I dined one night with a captured Russian officer. He told me that he punished his female servants by harnessing them to just such contraptions and having them pull him around his estate. At the time, I did not know whether to believe him. And you say you will have the equipment soon?'

Buxton nodded. 'But, we will require at least a couple of weeks to train the women. I suggest the last Friday in the month, if that is convenient. Of course, it depends on whether you can find a filly.'

'Come with me.'

Colonel Markham led the way up the stairs and pushed open the bedroom door, motioning for Buxton to enter first.

The girl on the bed had cropped, coal-black hair, large breasts, equally ample buttocks and a mound shaven smooth. All these attributes Buxton could see with a single glance, for the girl's legs were splayed over her head and tied to the top rail of the brass bedstead. He also noticed with approval the lines which criss-crossed her bottom and the back of her thighs.

'This is Margarite,' the Colonel explained. 'I'll put her up against your wife any day. Shall we say a thousand instead of five hundred?'

Buxton held out his hand. 'Agreed. I will have a cart and set of harnesses delivered as soon as I receive them.'

The Colonel shook his hand and sealed the wager. 'I shall look forward to it. And so, I think, will Margarite.'

Buxton looked at the glistening black skin. 'An unusual, er, servant.'

'I was stationed for a year in Jamaica. When I returned, I brought Margarite with me,' Markham explained.

The Colonel stopped as they were about to leave the bedroom.

'I apologise; I am forgetting my manners. Would you care to enjoy yourself before you go?'

Buxton looked at the girl again. It was a tempting offer, but time was pressing.

'Thank you, Colonel. Perhaps another time.'

'Whenever you wish, sir. Whenever you wish.'

At the front door Buxton stopped and handed the Colonel the book.

'You may as well have this. It may give you some tips.'

The Colonel accepted the gift. 'Thank you, though there is little any book or anyone can teach me about training either a woman or a horse.'

Buxton just laughed. 'We shall see, Colonel. We shall see.'

Thirteen

The coach lurched and juddered along the potholed road, swaying from side to side like a boat riding a gentle swell. The coats of the four black horses gleamed in the sunshine, the brasses on their harnesses shining like polished gold. The coachman steered them along the twisting byways, silently cursing his uniform of ankle-length heavy coat and tall top hat as the sweat trickled down his face. Inside, Maxine Brandside lay back against the buttoned velvet upholstery and wondered about the coming hours.

A desire she could not completely understand or explain had taken her to Colchester. The loneliness of recent weeks had gradually become simply too great to bear and, on impulse, she had decided to travel as near as she could to the one man who could fill the void inside her. She had thought as she packed her bags what a very foolish act her whim might prove. At the London terminus she had almost turned back and returned to the world which she had created and where everything was ordered and certain. As the train puffed its slow way through the outskirts of the city and into the countryside, her nervousness had increased with every mile. What if Richard was not at Castleleigh? Even worse, what if he did not want to see her? What if the note she intended to send was opened by his new wife? What if, embarrassed by its contents and angry at her presumption, he sent word for her to leave and never return? By the time she had reached her destination she no longer felt like the dominant, awe-inspiring mistress men and women fought over to kneel before and obey, but rather like a schoolgirl, confused by the feelings inside her and anxious about the reaction of the man she hoped to meet.

Several large brandies in the privacy of her room at the Five Bells had done little to calm the fluttering in her stomach. Only when she spotted the handsome young Life Guards Captain at the next table did her confidence begin to return and the natural authority, which was the core of her being, start to re-assert itself. Here was a challenge she could not resist. He had watched the swell of her bosom more closely than the way she dealt the cards and concentrated more on his fantasies than on the bidding. Once the final trump had been laid, and being a gentleman raised to be true to his word, he had had no alternative but to deliver her letter. The torrent of relief, happiness and excitement which had surged through her when he had returned with Richard's note had made her visibly tremble. The good Captain, believing she was about to swoon, had placed a comforting arm round her shoulder, saying that he hoped the note did not contain bad news. Her reply had been a carefree laugh, as she had taken his hand and led him to her room. As a lover he had proved barely adequate; but as he rode her, she had simply closed her eyes and pretended it was Richard, blissfully content in the knowledge that, in just a few hours, it would be.

She had spent the morning in her room, willing away the minutes, impatient for the town hall clock to strike noon. The knock at her door had come as the echo of the final chime faded away. The sight of the landlord standing outside had made her stomach churn with dread. Richard had changed his mind. He was not coming. He had forsaken her.

'Beg pardon for disturbing you, madam, but the coachman asks when you will be ready to depart.'

The landlord's words made no sense to her.

'What? What coachman?'

'The coachman outside, madam,' the landlord had replied, clearly now as confused as she was.

She had crossed to the window and looked down to see the shiny black coach, its door emblazoned with the crest of the Earl of Brackenhurst, in the courtyard below. She had not understood exactly what was happening but realised that the coach would take her to Richard, and that was enough.

Five minutes later, the coachman was strapping her two bags on to the back of the coach and she was sitting inside, enjoying being the centre of attraction of the small crowd that had gathered in the courtyard and were whispering their ideas about who this important lady might be.

For nearly three hours she had sat and watched the flat Essex farmscape slip past. They had passed through tiny villages that comprised no more than strings of cottages either side of the road, and between seemingly endless acres of fields where the only signs of life had been cattle and sheep and the occasional group of labourers. London might be only sixty miles away, but it could just as well have been in another country. Everything here was different and she knew instinctively that her own life would never be the same again either.

The coachman had stopped once and asked if she wished to break her journey and take some refreshment at the next inn. He was clearly disappointed when she declined on being told that Castleleigh was only one more hour away.

And that hour was now nearly up.

The coach crested the brow of a hill and she looked down over the fields and saw the large house in the valley below. A few minutes later, the coach swung between the huge iron gates, rattled beneath the rows of elms and stopped in front of the impressive facade of The Hall. But she had no eyes for the grandeur of the house, only for the man standing at the top of the steps, hands on hips and the broadest of welcoming smiles on his face. In that instant, she no longer felt a visitor. She felt she had come home.

The coachman helped Maxine down. Though every instinct was urging her to rush up the steps and embrace the man who waited for her outside the open doors of the house, she somehow managed to compose herself and walk normally towards him. Buxton greeted her as protocol dictated.

'Good day, Miss Brandside. I hope your journey was not too fatiguing.'

'Not in the least, Mr Buxton,' she responded with equal formality.

'Robert, see that Miss Brandside's luggage is taken to her rooms.'

At the sound of his master's voice, the butler appeared from the gloom beyond the doors.

'Very good, sir.'

'Oh, and, Robert, Miss Brandside and I have many things to discuss. We shall be in the morning room. On no account are we to be disturbed.'

'Of course, sir.'

Once in the room, Buxton locked the door. He gestured towards a table on which was spread a mouthwatering array of meats, cheeses and freshly baked bread with, in their centre, a bottle of champagne in a silver cooler.

'I thought you might be hungry, Maxine.'

Maxine smiled. 'I am, Richard. Indeed, I am famished, but not for lack of food.'

No more words were necessary. She opened her arms as he reached for her and held him tight as their lips crushed together. She could feel his manhood hardening as he pressed against her. She slipped her hand down to grasp it. He ran his fingers through her hair, tugging her head back as his tongue probed her mouth. His hand slid down her back and his fingers tugged at the buttons of her dress, while she groped for those which were imprisoning the object she desired most in the world.

Buxton released her and stepped back as he kicked off his shoes and pushed down his trousers, while Maxine wriggled out of her dress. He did not bother with his shirt, nor she with her stockings. For a moment they looked at each other: he savouring the fullness of her breasts, the slimness of her stomach and the carefully trimmed triangle between her thighs; she the firmness of his pulsating cock and the tightness of his balls. But only for a moment. Buxton stooped and, grasping her buttocks, lifted her clear of the floor. Maxine threw her arms round his neck as her legs closed round his waist. Buxton pushed her back against the door and Maxine slid down until she felt his tip touching the entrance to her sex. He thrust upwards as she pushed down and both gasped as she took his entire length inside her in one go. It was not a time for pleasantries. Buxton rammed into her and Maxine sighed with every thrust. Her nails dug into his neck as her legs clamped tight around him.

Maxine felt delirious; a mixture of lust and love setting every fibre and nerve on fire. She felt him jerk inside her and her muscles spasmed uncontrollably, forcing the hot fluid from him. She bit his lip and her fingers raked his back as he shot his seed into her and she climaxed continually until there were no more juices left to flow.

Gently he let her down and tenderly kissed her forehead as he brushed away her sweat-wet hair.

'My God, Maxine, but I've missed you.'

Maxine pecked the tip of his nose. 'And I you, Richard. Oh, so very much.'

Buxton smiled. 'A toast to celebrate our reunion.'

He pulled his trousers on and, while Maxine retrieved her discarded dress, opened the champagne and filled two glasses. Maxine took the proffered glass and raised it.

'To our reunion.'

'And to our future,' Buxton added.

'Before you tell me of the future, Richard, tell me about the past. Is being the local Squire as awful as you imagined?'

'Awful, Maxine? It is absolutely wonderful. I would not swap being the Master of Castleleigh for a million pounds.'

Maxine was genuinely intrigued. 'And what makes being stuck out in the middle of nowhere so enjoyable, Richard?'

Buxton pretended to give the question serious consideration before replying. When he did, he counted the blessings by raising each finger in turn.

'Well, let me see. There's Rebecca, and Alice, and Alice's cousin, and Lucy. Oh, and, of course, my own dear wife, Clarissa.'

Maxine spluttered as she sipped her champagne. 'Richard, I don't believe you. Not even you could have bedded half the village by now. You haven't been here more than five minutes.'

Buxton grinned. 'Bedded 'em, beaten 'em and buggered 'em. In addition, there's a very strange and sinful vicar called the Reverend Pimms and a certain Colonel Harry Markham, who is turning out to be a most interesting neighbour. Believe me, Maxine, a night in Castleleigh makes a night in London seem like a church outing. Which is one of the reasons I sent for you. I felt it was selfish to enjoy all the delights on offer on my own.'

'You sent for me?'

Buxton nodded as he topped up their glasses.

'Yes, a few days ago. The letter should be lying on your desk by now, but you pre-empted my request.'

'Richard, I am confused. What request?'

'To come and join me, of course. Even if your business will allow you to stay only a short while, I am sure you will find the time well spent. I can assure you it will be very entertaining. I want you to be my housekeeper.'

Maxine was shaken by the news. 'Your house-keeper? Richard, surely you know me better than that. Me? A glorified servant?'

Buxton laughed. 'Only in the eyes of the world outside. In this house, you will rule. Come with me. Seeing is believing and experience is the best form of explanation. Ask no questions, for all is about to be revealed.'

As requested, Maxine remained silent as they walked to the library; even when he slid back the hidden door and she followed him down the twisting stairs, she asked none of the questions which were clogging her brain. Only when he lit the candles and she saw the girl tethered to the bench did she speak.

'And who is this?'

'This wretch is Lucy. One time Clarissa's personal maid. From this time on she is yours, to do with as you desire,' Buxton explained as he unfastened the straps and yanked the girl to her feet.

'Lucy, this is Miss Maxine Brandside. She is the new housekeeper and, from this moment on, your only mistress. You will obey her in everything, instantly and unquestioningly.'

For a moment Lucy regarded the woman standing in front of her, but only for a moment. Then she lowered her gaze and stared at the floor. She instinctively understood that to look directly at either her master or this new lady would be to invite reprimand. For the same reason, she made no attempt to cover her nakedness. Whatever she did, whatever she said, Lucy knew they could, and would, do whatever they wished with her. It was a knowledge that was both frightening and exciting. She stood and waited, with calm resignation, to learn whatever her fate was to be.

Maxine had seen so many strange and bizarre sights in her life that only very rarely was she genuinely surprised or impressed. This was one such occasion. Slowly she studied the ancient chapel, eyeing the old wooden beams, the iron studded door, the soundproofing stone walls and the rings set into them approvingly. She inspected the array of whips, belts, rods and canes and made a mental note of the instruments she would send for from London to complete the collection. Only when she had finished studying her surroundings did she bother to look at the girl standing so submissively in the centre of the room.

A couple of years off twenty, she estimated. A good age. Young enough to be fit and resilient; old enough to understand what was expected of her. She felt the muscles of the maid's shoulders before running her middle finger slowly down Lucy's spine and sliding it between the cleft of her cheeks, as her others dug into the surrounding flesh.

'She's nice and firm, Richard. She'll be able to take a lot of correction,' Maxine observed.

'So far, she has been little tested,' Buxton replied as he leaned against the wall, clearly enjoying the spectacle. 'That is where you come in. She needs the tuition of an expert.'

'You are as expert as me, Richard,' Maxine remarked. 'No man more so.'

Buxton laughed. 'Perhaps, but I cannot be everywhere all the time. I have other calls upon my time, and my expertise.'

Maxine put one finger under Lucy's chin and the girl raised her head in obedience to its pressure, while still keeping her gaze lowered.

She felt Maxine's hands stroke her face and then slip down past her shoulders and glide with tantalising slowness over her breasts. She could feel her nipples hardening even before Maxine's fingers began to rotate them. Lucy shivered inwardly at the sensations the slow, sensuous exploration of her body was arousing. She wanted those caressing fingers to linger, but they moved on down the flat expanse of her stomach until they reached the small triangle between her thighs.

'Open your legs,' Maxine commanded, and she obeyed.

Maxine's hand covered her mound. Lucy bit her lip to suppress a sigh of pleasure as Maxine's fingers squeezed her button and then entered her. They penetrated no further than a nail's length, but it was enough. Lucy felt herself growing damper by the second and instinctively lowered her hips to drive Maxine further inside.

Abruptly, Maxine withdrew her hand and held it up, smiling at the moisture glistening on her fingertips.

'So, it takes little to arouse the slut,' she remarked thoughtfully before commanding, 'On your knees, wretch. My shoes need cleaning.'

Immediately Lucy sank to her knees and lowered her head. She lifted the hem of Maxine's dress as far as her ankles and began to lick the black leather in front of her, her tongue running up and down each shoe in turn.

'Richard, pass me that cane. No, not the thick one, that willowy one at the back.'

While Buxton did as he was asked, Maxine unbuttoned her dress and pulled it over her head. Buxton handed her the cane.

With her face pressed against Maxine's feet, Lucy's raised buttocks presented an irresistibly tempting target. Maxine stroked the cane lightly over the girl's back and buttocks, in a gesture which told her what was about to happen, but not when. Maxine knew only too well the power of anticipation and how it could heighten the experience for both giver and receiver. Suddenly, without warning, she brought it down straight between Lucy's cheeks. Lucy tensed involuntarily, but stopped herself from crying aloud by pushing her face harder against Maxine's shoes.

Maxine swiped sideways, making a thin red line appear down the side of the maid's left cheek. A backhanded slash brought a matching mark to her right buttock. They were followed by a further six strokes, delivered with all Maxine's considerable strength, to produce an attractive criss-cross pattern.

The pain of the first blow brought stinging tears to Lucy's eyes. The second released them and the subsequent ones sent them flowing down her cheeks until they fell on the leather she was kissing and she licked them away.

When her mistress had beaten her, Lucy had felt a strange excitement she had never experienced before. Now she realised Lady Clarissa was merely an inexperienced amateur compared to the woman she now knelt in front of. Although the physical pain made her cry, she did not care. Inside, she was on fire, with each blow serving only to fuel the flames. When the beating stopped, and she heard Maxine throw the cane aside, she felt not relief, but a strange disappointment.

'You have cleaned my shoes well, slave,' Maxine told her. 'Now let us see how that tongue of yours copes with a more delicate task. Raise your head.'

Lucy threw back her head and looked up. The sight which greeted her made her feel as if she were melting; slipping away, no longer in control of mind or body. She stared transfixed. All she could see was the inside of her new mistress's thighs, the pink lips between them and the dark curls above. All she could smell was the pungent musk of another woman. Like a pagan grovelling before the statue of a goddess, Lucy was both cowed and elated. In that instant she knew that this was what she had always been waiting for; had always longed for. All she wanted was to please this divine being and willingly, joyously, accept whatever was demanded of her. From that instant on, Clarissa meant nothing. It was as if she had never really existed at all. She had been the stuff of dreams, just the immature infatuation of a frustrated girl who knew no better.

Lucy did not need to be told what was required of her. She ran her tongue up Maxine's left leg from knee to inner thigh, skimmed it across her mound and then down to her right knee, then back again. On the return journey, she lingered. She probed the tip of her tongue between the top of her mistress's slit and lapped at her button before moving it downwards and skimming the outside of her cunt lips. The skin was stiff with the residue of Buxton's lovemaking and she eagerly licked away the stains. She pressed her face close against her mistress's body, flicking her tongue in and out, sucking with all the strength her lip muscles could muster at her clit. When the juices began to trickle out, her tongue bowed like a spoon, channelling them down her throat. She could taste both master and mistress, and she had never craved any other food or drink so much.

Maxine bent over and stroked her hair.

'You are good, slut. Very good.'

Such praise! Her mistress had complimented her! She had succeeded in pleasing her. Lucy felt as if she had been rewarded with gold rather than mere words, and in response she licked and sucked even faster and harder. She felt the tremor ripple through Maxine's body and opened her mouth as wide as she could to catch the torrent of warm liquid which poured into it. When it hit the back of her throat it triggered her own climax and she shook uncontrollably as the shock waves tore through her.

Panting slightly, Maxine stepped back and looked down.

'Enough. At least for the present. You have done well, but you still have a great deal to learn. I will teach you.'

Daring to look and speak for the first time, Lucy raised her head and gazed adoringly at the woman who towered over her.

'Thank you, Mistress.'

Buxton had enjoyed the show. Normally, it would now have been his turn to savour Lucy's delights, and while the stiffness in his trousers prompted him to do so, there were other, more important matters to attend to. This had been just a diversion; only the first act of the drama he had scripted.

'Stand up, Lucy.'

Lucy stood, catching the clothes Buxton tossed at her as she did so.

'Get dressed now, Lucy. You will return to your room and stay there. You will talk to none of the other servants. We will send for you when you are required.'

When both Maxine and Lucy were dressed, Buxton hurried them back to the library. As soon as the maid had left the room, Maxine put her arms round his waist and kissed him.

'If that is what is required of the housekeeper at Castleleigh then perhaps the position may not be so tedious as I imagined.'

Buxton poured two large glasses of brandy.

'This will help us keep our strength up. Lucy was simply the hors d'oeuvre, a trifle to whet the appetite.'

Maxine sipped her drink. 'So what, pray, is the main dish on the menu?' she enquired.

Buxton laughed as he put down his empty glass.

'Why, the speciality of the house, of course. Truly worthy of the gourmet I know you to be. Come, I can tell that you are famished.'

Naked, securely bound, blindfolded and gagged, Clarissa lay spreadeagled on top of the bed. How long she had lain there, imprisoned in a world of darkness, silence and immobility, she could not tell. An hour? All morning? All day? She had no way of telling. All she knew was the creeping cramp in her limbs and the ache which came from suppressing natural bodily functions.

She had meant it when she had told Richard that she was sorry for what she had done with the Colonel and his son. With no distractions, and so nothing to do but think, she had reappraised the true meaning of her words. Yes, she was sorry, but not about her actions. What she was truly sorry for was being found out. She had enjoyed herself. For the first time in her life, she had had the opportunity to be true to her innermost desires and she had grasped the chance. She did not feel ashamed. She did not feel humiliated. She did not feel as if she had betrayed her husband. She did not feel as she had always been taught an adulterous woman would, and should, feel. All she honestly felt was fear, not of any physical punishment her husband might decide to inflict – she now understood herself well enough to know that she would probably enjoy that too – but of what the future held. She could accept anything Richard might do, so long as he did not abandon her. Discarded by the only society she knew, she would never survive alone. She pictured herself on a street corner, standing under a lamp selling her body and fast fading charms for the price of a beggar's meal. Destitute, pox-ridden and totally alone.

Clarissa heard the door open and close. Deprived of sight, her sense of smell was more acute. It told her that Richard was close and so too, she sensed, was someone else. The mattress tilted as Buxton sat on the edge of the bed. She felt his fingers pat her head. When he spoke there was no anger in his voice. Instead his tone was conversational, almost matter of fact.

'Well, my darling young wife, there are matters we need to discuss. Serious matters. What you have done has turned my world upside down, you do understand that, don't you?'

All Clarissa could do was nod her head in agreement.

'Things can never be the same again, Clarissa. You have disgraced me. That is something I cannot tolerate, or forget. Do you understand that also?'

Again Clarissa nodded. Yes, she understood. She understood all too well. Why did he not just hurry up and tell her her fate?

'I have considered throwing you to the wolves, Clarissa,' Buxton continued in the same even tone. 'I thought, why do I not just divorce the trollop, kick her out and have done with it all? But then I thought of the scandal. I want to become a respected member of the community and that might prove difficult if my wife, even my former wife, was known to be a whore. Unmasking my neighbour as a woman-beating adulterer would hardly have helped my plans to lead local society either. Also, while your father would certainly have disowned you, my father may well have disinherited me as well. That was perhaps the greatest risk of all. Therefore, Clarissa, we shall remain man and wife, at least in name. Now, before I tell you your new role at Castleleigh, I think it best if I release you.'

Buxton untied the linen strips securing his wife's wrists and ankles. He also removed the gag, but left the blindfold in place. Grasping her arm he pulled her from the bed.

'Stand up straight, Clarissa. Head up, hands by your sides.'

When Clarissa had complied, he continued in the same even, almost conversational, tone. 'That's right. Now, Clarissa, you do realise that you must be punished for what you have done, don't you?'

'Yes,' Clarissa answered, her voice hardly above a whisper.

'Speak up, Clarissa.'

'Yes,' his wife repeated more loudly.

'Good. But you see, darling wife, the problem is that I do not want to soil my hands on you. Therefore you shall submit to another.'

So saying, Buxton pulled the knot of the blindfold. Clarissa blinked at the sudden intrusion of daylight. For a second the brightness blinded her, then she saw Maxine. Her instinctive reaction was to bring her hands across her body to shield her nakedness. Buxton's words sliced the air like a whiplash.

'By your sides, I said. Have you learned nothing about obedience?'

'Richard, I do not understand. Who is this woman? What is happening?'

'Silence! You were not given permission to speak. From now on, you will speak when you are told to speak, and you will say what you are told to say. Is that clear?'

'Yes, but . . .' Clarissa's voice trailed into bewildered silence as her eyes met Buxton's and she realised the futility, and the probable consequences, of questioning his actions.

He nodded approvingly. 'You are learning, Clarissa. Slowly, and it may prove painfully, but you are learning.'

He turned to Maxine, put his arms round her and kissed her passionately. Her response was to fondle his buttocks with both hands and pull him close, sensuously gyrating her hips as she did so. Clarissa could only stand and watch. She wanted to protest, but dared not. She knew this was both a test and a demonstration. With that single kiss, her husband had shown her that she had been supplanted. That she was no longer the sole object of his desire.

Finally, reluctantly, Buxton released Maxine and turned back to his wife.

216

'I apologise, Clarissa. I am forgetting my manners, and that would never do. Allow me to present Miss Maxine Brandside, our new housekeeper.'

Clarissa's eyes widened in shock and disbelief, and this time she could not halt the words of protest.

'Housekeeper! Richard, how dare you show me like this to a common servant? This is intolerable. I am a lady. It is not done. I will not –'

The back of her husband's hand struck her cheek and Clarissa staggered backwards, almost falling on to the bed.

'Understand, Clarissa, that Maxine is neither common nor a servant. And never let me hear you say "will not" again.' Buxton's soft, level voice was suddenly hard edged with anger. 'She commands here now, not you. In public you may pretend to still be the mistress of Castleleigh, you may afford yourself all the airs and graces of being Lady of the Manor, but in private you will be just another servant. Maxine will teach you the finer points of discipline and obedience. You should feel privileged; there is no better-qualified instructor in Britain.'

Buxton handed Maxine the horse crop.

'Maxine, my wife is a slut and a whore. An insatiable trollop who gives herself to any man she fancies. Please show her the error of her ways.'

Maxine turned to the cowering Clarissa.

'On the chaise longue, I think. Elbows on the arm, and that pert little bottom of yours in the air.'

Clarissa hesitated. It was not a sensible thing to do. Before she could struggle or argue, Maxine had clutched her hair and sent her spinning across the room. Before she could properly regain her balance, Maxine had pushed her on to the chaise longue so that she had no alternative but to adopt the required position.

'We shall commence with twenty strokes,' Maxine told her. 'You will shout out the number of each stroke and then say "Thank you, Mistress"; if you fail to do so, that stroke will not count. Do you understand?'

Clarissa could only nod her assent. Her mind was still reeling at the events of the past few minutes. She had expected Richard to beat her. She had even secretly hoped that he would, and that afterwards they would make love and he might then find it in himself to forgive her. She had never dreamed he would degrade her by even letting a servant see her naked, let alone instruct one of the lower orders to actually strike her. Lucy, of course, had seen her unclothed, but then Lucy was her maid. Lucy had satisfied her desires and she had beaten her; that was in the order of things.

Clarissa clenched her teeth as she heard the swish of air an instant before the riding crop bit into her buttocks. She cried out at the sudden, burning pain and buried her face in the leather arm of the chaise longue.

'I told you to call the strokes. And you forgot to thank me. Really, Clarissa, this simply will not do.' Maxine spoke to her like a schoolmistress whose pupil had presented substandard work.

Clarissa! A servant had dared call her by her Christian name. This was intolerable. Clarissa, heedless of the possible consequences, was about to complain when the crop landed again, this time flat across her shoulders. Instead of protesting, she gasped, 'Two. Thank you, Mistress.'

Maxine's approach was still that of the teacher to the slow-witted child. 'Oh dear, Clarissa. What are we going to do with you? Even servants can count. That was not two, that was one, as will this be, and the next and the next, until you get it right.'

The tears streamed down Clarissa's cheeks as the crop smashed into her flesh from the soles of her feet to the middle of her back. But now, after every stroke, she managed to control her sobbing for just long enough to find the breath to gasp the number of each one, and utter her thanks to the woman who loomed so tall, and so impassively, above her. By the time she had said 'twelve' she started to become aware of the changes taking place inside her body. While her mind still found it difficult to fully grasp the humiliating reality of what was happening, her innermost senses were slowly beginning to react in a very different way.

'Twenty. Thank you, Mistress,' said Clarissa, and realised she meant it. Her body was rocking gently from side to side. The tears were drying. She ached from feet to shoulders, but she had not really felt the pain of the last few blows. Instead, she had been concentrating on the quivering inside, the increasingly urgent fluttering deep within her belly, which she knew was the prelude to the most exquisite pleasure of all.

When Maxine told her to stand, Clarissa responded with all the speed her protesting muscles could provide. She stood, head bowed, skin glistening with sweat, in front of the woman she now understood would always be her superior.

Maxine Brandside regarded the pathetic creature before her and smiled with genuine pleasure, as she felt old resentments being rekindled. She recalled her childhood, when she had witnessed her father and mother bowing and scraping to the local lord and his lady, and jumping to carry out the whims of their overfed, spoilt and precocious offspring. She had vowed, long before she had realised the power of the attraction her body held for men and women alike, that she would never kowtow, never bend the knee or eat their humble pie. Instead, they had had to pay for her services, to hand over their money in return for what she could offer them. But this was different. This was not a business transaction that would be over in an hour or so. This was real, and this could go on for ever.

'We'll make a true servant of you yet, Clarissa. Get down on your hands and knees and crawl to the fireplace.'

Clarissa moved to obey but Maxine stopped her by reaching out and grabbing her right nipple between thumb and finger.

'If I tell you to do something, what do you say?'

Clarissa hesitated hardly an instant. 'Yes, Mistress.'

'That is better. But being a servant is not just about saying "Yes, Mistress" and "No, Mistress"; it's about work. Now, do as you were told.'

Once Clarissa was kneeling on the sheepskin rug in front of the hearth, Maxine opened a small door set into the side of the chimney breast from which she took a large china tub of brass polish and a couple of soft rags.

'Really, Richard, your maids are slovenly,' Maxine remarked. 'When, I wonder, was this fender properly cleaned and polished?'

So saying, she placed the tub and the rags on the tiled hearth in front of Clarissa. 'Clean that fender until I can see my face in it,' she commanded.

Clean? Clarissa had never cleaned anything in her life. 'What?' she exclaimed and, in the instant that the word escaped her, realised her error as the riding crop slashed against her already sore buttocks.

'If your master or mistress tells you to do something, you do not argue. You do it,' said Maxine evenly. 'Now, polish that fender. Do not look up, do not look back. Concentrate only on your work.'

Gingerly Clarissa picked up a rag and dabbed it into the polish. She began to rub it along the length of the long brass top rail of the fender. She jumped as once more the crop scored her buttocks.

'Put some effort into it, girl,' Maxine told her. 'You are not stroking the silk of some new ball gown, you are polishing brass. Richard and I have other urgent matters to attend to, and while we do so, I want to see you work. Just like any other skivvy.'

Buxton paid his wife no heed as she complied with Maxine's order. He had removed his breeches and boots and settled himself comfortably in an armchair by the window, gently stroking his erection while he watched Maxine dominate his wife.

He smiled as Maxine removed her clothes and, taking his hand, led him to the bed.

'Ride me, Richard. Ride me stronger and harder than you have ever done before,' Maxine pleaded, and he was eager to comply.

They made love noisily, Maxine shouting with every thrust, using the most coarse language to continually urge him on, shouting out every action of them both in the most graphic fashion. Buxton quickly realised her intent and joined in the game. Both knew that every word, every grunt, every moan, pierced Clarissa like a needle. When they screamed their climaxes they watched her whole body shudder, but she kept polishing the fender and did not look round.

When Buxton had finally spent, Maxine squeezed the lips of her sex together and walked over to Clarissa. She stood, legs astride her back, and let the spunk drop in globules on to the flaming stripes criss-crossing Clarissa's back.

'Some cream to ease the soreness,' she remarked, before turning back to Buxton.

'You told me this was the main course, Richard. But in truth, I am far from sated; in fact I am still very hungry. I think it is time we considered our further culinary needs. May I make a suggestion which will satisfy both our appetites?'

Fourteen

Robert sat in the butler's pantry. It was a small room, sparsely furnished but comfortable. There was a single armchair beside the fireplace, a table with two Windsor chairs, a dresser on which were displayed china plates and cups, plus a desk and stool. Robert sat at the desk, looking through the window which gave a panoramic view of the kitchen.

On the other side of the glass which separated them, Rebecca was busy cleaning the copper. The long pine table, where the food was prepared and the servants dined, was covered with saucepans, pans, bowls and moulds which she was energetically polishing, just as he had instructed her to.

Ever since she had been released from the old chapel, Rebecca had become the perfect servant. She started work each morning early; she was never slow in completing her tasks, yet they were always done so competently that it was impossible to criticise her. She never answered back and she never argued; on the contrary, she always did exactly as she was told. And everything she did, she did well. It was a situation he found both infuriating and frustrating.

He thought back to their time together in the chapel, savouring each delicious memory. Oh, how he had enjoyed whipping the arrogant young bitch who had publicly mocked and ridiculed him on the few occasions that he had visited the village inn. Rebecca Dakins the village whore, as easy to lay as a carpet, that's what everyone said of her, yet when he had asked her to walk with him she had laughed in his face. She had said she did not bother with servants, especially those who thought they were special because they wore fancy uniforms.

Well, she was a servant now, and he was in charge of her and she had to obey him. Since he had beaten her and used her body for his pleasure, she had shown him respect, but only in what she said and what she did. Her eyes told a different story; in them he saw reflected her disdain and contempt – but when she looked at the master, those same eyes shone with admiration and longing.

Rebecca was standing leaning over the table, a position which made her skirt rise above her ankles and her bottom jut outwards towards him. Robert slid his hand down and unbuttoned his trousers; thumb and forefinger circled his half-erect manhood and gently coaxed it to its full, throbbing length as he watched and imagined.

He knew he could take her in an instant. No one else was near and all he had to do was cover the two yards from his pantry door, lift her skirt and force himself home. It would be so easy, too easy. He knew she would not protest; she would simply wait until he had finished. Her silent acquiescence would be a greater rebuff than any words or physical struggle. He could accuse her of any misdemeanour he cared to invent and punish her accordingly and she would accept it; but however hard he beat her he knew he could never whip the contempt from her eyes. When the master had punished her, she had dripped like a sodden sponge, but if he did the same he knew she would stay as dry as a desert.

He would have liked to have felt jealous about this upstart who had become the new Lord of the Manor, but he could not. Unlike the old Earl, the Squire had recognised his abilities and promoted him to what he had always considered his rightful place in the household. Mr Buxton had treated him almost as an equal rather than a faceless dogsbody and had doubled his salary into the bargain. No, it was not the master who was at fault, just this bitch of a game-playing girl.

In the kitchen, Rebecca had stopped working for a moment to bend and tie the laces of her boots. The sight of her skirt raised to above her knee and her plump arse pointing towards the ceiling was more than the butler could bear. Without bothering to button his fly, his erection pushing out straight as a yardarm, he stood up. He would take her this instant and to hell with it. Only the tinkling of the bell stopped him. He looked up at the board and sighed. He was summoned to the master bedroom. Rebecca would have to wait.

The candle the butler had given him had lasted the night but had long since guttered and died. The only light filtered down from a small iron grill set high in the far wall of his cavernous prison. Since they had first appeared, he had watched the small squares of sunlight creep across the floor. By now, he reckoned, it must be early afternoon. He had long since eaten the stale bread and drunk the tankard of water the butler had brought him. He was hungry and cold and very frightened. No one had bothered to tell him why he was being punished; there had been no charges against which he might have been able to defend himself. Without a word of explanation, the butler had come to the stables as he was bedding down for the night in the hayloft, dragged him to the house and thrown him into the cellar. When he had asked what was the matter, the only reply had been a cuff on the ear and a warning to mind his place. Tom sat, head in hands, and for the hundredth time tried to work out what he had done wrong.

Two days before, he had been just another village urchin, scraping a living by earning coppers where and when he could. The Squire had changed all that. Within a day he had risen to have a proper job, working with the animals he loved. From being a nobody, he had suddenly become someone who could hold his head high. Now, just as quickly, he had sunk to being not just a nobody again, but a prisoner as well. He had carried out his duties diligently. He had groomed and exercised the horses, he had cleaned the stables, he had waxed the leathers and polished the brasses. He was certain that it was not his work that had led him to this dark, damp confinement. And, if it was not his work, then it could only be Lucy. She had threatened to have him punished for spying on her mistress, and she had carried out her threat. There was no other explanation.

For a brief while he had thought he loved her. Now he hated her. She had played with him for her own amusement; she had used him and then betrayed him. He knew the Squire would listen to her, not him. She was a lady's maid, while he was just a lowly stable lad. She could tell her master and mistress whatever she liked and be believed. At best he would be dismissed; at worst he would be sent to prison or transported to the other side of the world. Tom wanted to cry, but pride held the tears in check. He would stand tall and face whatever they did to him; they might hurt him, but they would never break him.

Tom lifted his head as he heard the key grate in the lock. A shaft of light shone into the gloom, silhouetting the butler standing at the top of the steps.

'Follow me. You are required.'

Tom rose, clenching his fists to stop his hands shaking. At last, he would discover both charge and sentence.

After she had washed, Lucy lay on her bed and tried to make sense of what was happening to her, and around her. Yesterday, life had seemed so perfect, so organised, so predictable. The passion she had always felt for Lady Clarissa had reached a new intensity when she had finally been allowed to show her devotion physically. True, she had been upset that her mistress had not responded by pleasing her in the same fashion, though that was to be expected of someone of noble birth, but there had sprung within her the hope that someday it might just happen.

She had satisfied herself with Tom. Though he had been a poor substitute for her Lady, he had served his purpose adequately enough. If only he had not told her what he had seen. A few words had turned her whole life upside down and caused her to do something which before she would never have dreamed of doing. She had reacted out of spite, and it had backfired on her. Instead of shaming her mistress she had only succeeded in shaming herself. She had spent the night worrying about her loss, unconcerned for her physical discomfort or the punishment the morning might bring. Then she had met her new mistress, and once again her emotions were in turmoil. Clarissa had become a memory, part of her past. Lucy knew she only wanted one future, a future of servitude to a woman she had met for only a few minutes, but whom she wanted to rule her life for ever. A sharp rap at the door, and the turning of the handle, interrupted her thoughts. The door opened a few inches and Robert spoke through the gap.

'Your mistress wants you. Be quick.'

Lucy slid from the bed and smoothed down the creases of her skirt as she hurried to obey. Her mistress wanted her – but which mistress?

The Reverend Matthew Pimms was finding it difficult to concentrate on writing his sermon. He was torn between two themes: 'So the flesh lusteth against the spirit and the spirit against the flesh so that ye cannot do the things that ye would' and 'Let him who is without sin cast the first stone.' Both had merit, and both summoned up his own particular problems. He, of all people, understood just how frail the flesh was, and how powerful the lust that Satan sent to tempt and torment those with little strength to resist. And, because he understood so well the trials and tribulations the flesh was heir to, he was the perfect person to warn his flock against succumbing to self-gratification and wantonness. But, it was the second verse which really concerned him. Who in Castleleigh, he wondered, was about to cast the first stone, a stone which might in turn start an avalanche which would destroy him? He had never felt threatened by his housekeeper. Mrs Fellows was a simple soul who relied upon him for her board and keep. She needed her position and she rarely mixed with the other villagers. Whether or not she approved of the extra services which were occasionally required of her, he neither knew nor cared. She would do as she was told and keep quiet and that was an end to the matter. Rebecca Dakins and Alice Craddock, however, were fish from a very different kettle. Already he might be the laughing stock of both the manor and the tap room. And what of the new Squire? Could he be trusted? Was he busy with some secret ploy to entrap and expose the vicar whose living he controlled? The Reverend Pimms laid down his pen and sighed; so many questions, so few answers. St Augustine of Hippo had understood when he had written, 'Give me chastity and continence, but not yet.' He doubted his own bishop would share the same view.

The memory of what the Squire, Rebecca, Alice and he had done in the old chapel made him tremble with dread, but it also made him shiver with excitement. He recalled the birch scoring Rebecca's young skin and how the delightful Alice had thrashed the demons from him, before Rebecca had sucked them into her own body.

The Reverend Matthew Pimms leaned on his desk and buried his face in his hands. It was no good, no earthly or heavenly use. He could feel his manhood rising and was unable to check its growth. He tried to concentrate on holy scripture, or call to mind images of the saints, but all he could visualise was Rebecca kneeling before him, her lips squeezing out his juice while the divine Alice swished the birch with such wondrous skill. Had Mrs Fellows been at home he would have summoned her immediately and they would have gone to the attic and she would have chastised him till he bled; but she was away, visiting a sick sister in Dillsbury and would not return until morning.

As the vicar looked up in despair he noticed the calendar on the wall and the ring circling the Sunday after next, the blessing of the crops. It was an important date in village life, not as important as Harvest Festival itself, but still an occasion people looked forward to, not least because of the tradition that, after the service, the Lord of the Manor hosted a thanksgiving lunch for all who might wish to attend. Did the new Squire know of it? If not, he should be told, and the sooner the better.

Alice sighed as Maria's tongue followed the line of her spine before sliding between her buttocks. Alice spread her legs and raised her hips to make it easier for her cousin to kiss the rim of her arse. Maria removed her mouth, licked her forefinger and slowly inserted it up to the knuckle, rotating it as she did so and pushing upwards and downwards with each revolution. Maria's other hand moved round Alice's thigh, the fingers toying with her bush for a moment before starting to squeeze her clit.

'Use the candles, Maria. Please, I need the candles,' Alice begged.

Maria released her cousin for as long as it took to reach across to the little table beside the bed and pick up the implements Alice wanted. One was a candle some ten inches long and fully five round; the other was half that length, but only slightly thinner. The tips of both had been melted and moulded to make penetration easier. The cream and brown stains along their lengths showed that this was not the first time that afternoon that they had been required.

Expertly, Maria guided the smaller of the two into Alice's anus, pushing it to its hilt, making her cousin buck and gasp with the force of its entry. She brought the flat of her other hand down hard on Alice's buttocks as she worked the candle in and out of her body. Alice squealed with pleasure. Maria took the other candle and inserted it two inches between the gorged lips of Alice's sex.

'More. More. Oh God, more,' pleaded Alice, and Maria laughed as she plunged it home.

Maria relaxed her hold on the candles, allowing Alice to roll over on to her back, raising her knees as she did so. Maria knelt beside her and pushed the candles in and out of her body, first one and then the other, like pistons driving a train. With every thrust the momentum accelerated until Alice was writhing and panting and calling out for her to stop. Maria not only ignored her, but worked even faster, her own wrists aching with the effort. Suddenly, Alice's whole body convulsed, her hands grasped the brass rail behind her head and she screamed as her climax engulfed her. Only when she was sure her cousin had nothing left inside her did Maria remove the candles and toss them aside. She bent her head and lovingly kissed Alice's sopping entrance, before moving to lie beside her, one arm across her breasts, her head on her shoulder.

For several minutes neither spoke, Alice because she did not have the breath and Maria because she felt so peaceful and content in her cousin's arms that she had no wish to break the comforting silence. At last Alice turned, put her arm round Maria and kissed her tenderly on the lips.

'That was absolutely wonderful,' she breathed. 'Thank you.'

Maria smiled. 'If it was half as good as what you did to me then I am happy.'

For a while longer they lay in silence, each content to enjoy the soft touch of the other's body, until Maria asked, 'What are you thinking about, Alice dear?'

'Beer,' her cousin replied.

'Beer? What do you mean, beer? You don't like beer.'

Alice sat up, leaning back against the brass bedstead, her hands behind her head as she explained, 'Not my beer. The beer we delivered to The Hall.'

'What about it?'

231

'If they don't keep it proper, it'll go off. In this heat it's bound to. I don't think that Robert knows anything about beer and I'm sure the Master don't.'

Maria was confused by her cousin's concern. 'What does it matter? They ordered it, you delivered it. If they can't keep it right, ain't your fault.'

Alice swung herself off the bed and began donning blouse and skirt.

'That ain't the point, Maria. I got a responsibility to my father. I think I ought to go to The Hall and make sure it's being kept as it should be.'

Maria followed her cousin's example and pulled on her stockings and smock.

'But you don't give a fig for your father, nor his inn, nor his trade.'

Alice laughed. 'That's true right enough. But I does give a fig for Mr Buxton.'

Maria giggled. 'And the fact that he's hung like a stallion ain't got nothing to do with it, I suppose.'

Alice regarded her companion with mock indignation. 'Maria, how can you say such a thing? How can you be so coarse?'

'Suppose it's because I had a good teacher,' her cousin replied. 'Well, come on. We mustn't keep the Squire waiting, nor his tackle neither.'

The crack of the whip reverberated around the clearing, as the long thin leather sliced high through the air. With unerring accuracy it landed exactly on target, scorching a vivid crimson line from shoulder to hip. Margarite screamed and staggered, but paused for barely a second before answering its bidding. Somehow she forced new life into her protesting legs, gripped the chains even tighter and carried on towards the oak tree where, she prayed, she would be allowed to rest.

Colonel Markham admired his marksmanship. It was not every man who could wield a coachman's lash with such precision. But then he did not have six beasts to guide and control – just the one. He was very pleased with the progress his single filly was making. Undoubtedly the red streaks which stood out so starkly against the glistening black skin had played a major part in that progress.

Margarite reached the oak tree and slumped exhausted against its trunk, desperately trying to gulp more air into her bursting lungs.

Markham cracked the whip again and the girl yelped as it cut into her buttocks.

'I did not tell you to stop. Turn round and come back, only faster this time.'

Wearily, Margarite turned and started to lumber towards the other end of the clearing. Sweat streamed from every pore, her legs felt like lead and she feared the bones in her shoulders and arms would be wrenched from their sockets.

The Colonel sat on a tree stump and took another sip of wine as Margarite swayed and stumbled towards him. The contraption he had made was crude compared to the professionally crafted harnesses pictured in the book Buxton had given him, but it was serving his purpose even better than he had hoped. Around Margarite's neck was a milkmaid's yoke; the buckets which hung from it were not filled with milk, but with earth and stones. A chain that attached to a wheelbarrow, from which the two rear supports had been sawn, was looped through the broad leather belt round her waist. The wheelbarrow too was loaded with stones.

Finally, Margarite completed her journey and collapsed at her master's feet, unable to move another yard, however painful the incentive. Her skin shone

233

with the moisture of her exertions. Every sinew was screaming its protest against the almost intolerable strain placed upon it. Her pendulous breasts heaved as she desperately tried to suck in air.

With years of experience gained from schooling the finest horses in the county, Markham knew when hard training needed to be replaced by kindness and reward; when the stick should be laid aside and the carrot given. He unfastened the chain and pulled away the wheelbarrow before lifting the yoke from Margarite's shoulders. The girl remained prostrate on the grass. Markham lay beside her and, resting on one elbow, gently patted her head before lightly stroking her back; just as he would a young horse which had performed better than expected over the jumps.

'You did well, Margarite. Very well indeed,' he told her. 'Between us we will show this young upstart Squire a thing or two. Now it is time for your reward.'

Margarite, still too exhausted and breathless to acknowledge her master's praise, stayed lying face down on the soft grass. All she had the energy to do was smile, spread her legs and await the pleasure her master would give her.

Markham pulled off his boots and pushed down his breeches. He ran his hand over her buttocks and down her legs, gathering the sweat in his palm and fingers before using it to lubricate a cock that had long been stiff and eager from the sights he had so recently witnessed. He positioned himself between her splayed limbs. He ran the tip of his cock slowly down the cleft until he reached his goal and then thrust home.

Margarite's whole body shook as he pushed into her. She reached back and pulled her cheeks further apart to ease his passage. She pressed her face against the ground and chewed at the grass as her master slid inexorably into her, generating that strange combination of pain and pleasure she had come to love so much.

Markham slid his hands under her and clutched at her breasts, forcing her backwards and upwards with every thrust, as he repeatedly buried his entire length into her tightest of entries. Margarite clawed at the earth, her fingernails digging into the soil, as she pushed back against him and felt his balls slap hard against the entrance to her sex. Markham grunted as he came, the final few thrusts the hardest and strongest of all. Margarite screamed as the feeling of the hot liquid shooting into her body triggered her own climax.

As soon as he was fully spent, Markham withdrew and stood up. He walked over to the stream which bordered the field and washed, using Margarite's discarded dress to dry himself. He fastened his breeches and pulled on his riding boots. He looked down at the girl.

'I am very pleased with you, Margarite. Very pleased. Go back to the lodge when you are ready and relax. I shall not need you again today. I have other business to attend to.'

At least, he told himself as he mounted his horse, he would attend to it if the opportunity to do so availed itself. If not, then he would discuss matters further with Mr Richard Buxton. Either way, something told Colonel Harry Markham that a ride to The Hall would not be a wasted journey.

Rebecca scrubbed the utensils till they shone. She was far from happy. First, Robert had suddenly announced that the Squire wanted a full dinner prepared by six o'clock, which had sent cook into a panic. Then she had had to carry it all up to the dining room and lay the table. And now, cook having departed to her room and her gin bottle, she was left alone to clean the pots and pans, and would undoubtedly have to stay and later wash the plates and cutlery as well. She had been told to lay six full settings at table, though who the Master and Mistress's guests might be she had no idea. But, it was not just her domestic duties which made her so irritable: there was also Robert's attitude.

Rather than move round the table, she leaned across it as far as she could, knowing that the action would automatically raise the hem of her skirt to at least her calf. When she needed more water, she did not kneel, but instead bent over the bucket as if she were trying to touch her toes. It was an action which not only had the same effect as stretching along the table, but also drew the cloth tight across her backside. She wiped the back of her hand across her forehead as if brushing away the sweat from her brow and, to accentuate how hot her work was making her, undid the top three buttons of her blouse so that her breasts were almost fully exposed and dangerously close to popping free of her bodice when she bent back to her work. But, whatever she tried, nothing seemed to work.

What was wrong with the man? She knew he was watching her every move, yet he said nothing and did nothing. It was almost as if he was one of those eunuchs in a harem she had heard about. Able to look but not to react. But he was able to react – she knew that only too well. She had felt him inside her and, though she had been too proud to admit it, she had enjoyed it. He had beaten her, and she had relished that almost as much. But since the Master had released her from her prison, Robert had ignored her. He had told her her duties, and she had carried out the tasks as well as she could. She had hoped that such obedience, such willingness to be of service, would please him. And, even if it did not please him, at least he would have the excuse to punish her. However, he had grown ever more distant, treating her not only with disdain, but also with a strange form of respect.

She had been wrong to mock him so often in the past, she realised that now. But his airs and graces had annoyed the village folk and they were her family and friends. To even have admitted that she liked him, let alone have walked out with him, would have made her just as much a figure of fun and derision as him; that she could never have allowed. But her entire life had changed in just a few short days, and Robert had been a key part of that change. Now she wanted him. It seemed a strange sort of retribution on her that he no longer seemed to want her.

Rebecca's hopes rose as she heard the door to the butler's pantry open. She stretched as far as she could across the table and wiggled her bottom but did not look round. A second later the kitchen door closed behind the butler.

Rebecca threw the scrubbing brush the length of the table and kicked over the pail, sending a pool of dirty water spreading across the stone floor. Damn! What did she have to do to attract this man? Was there really something wrong with him? Perhaps when he had taken her he had done so only because his Master had ordered it, not because he had wanted to.

Rebecca slumped in a chair. What was she doing wrong? No man had refused her before. Never. Had she changed? Or was this high and mighty butler more stone than flesh and blood? She thought back to the old chapel. No, he was certainly more flesh and blood than stone, though one part of him had been as hard as granite.

The memory made her smile. Instinctively, her hand reached between her legs and her fingers began to push against the skin beneath. It was a delicious feeling. She closed her eyes and tried to recall every moment of her time with both Robert and the Squire. She pulled her skirt above her knees and her fingertips sought the rapidly dampening fold beneath her bush. One finger slid inside and began to rotate in ever-widening circles. Another joined it as she recalled . . .

'Stop that, slut! You're wanted.'

In the same instant that her eyes flicked open, her fingers were withdrawn and she stood up so that her skirt slid back down to her ankles.

Robert stood in the doorway sneering at her.

'Can't leave it alone, can you? Well, you'll have to. The Master wants you. Follow me.'

Rebecca smoothed her skirt, buttoned her blouse and patted her hair into place. What the Master wanted with her she could not guess, but instinct told her it would be more enjoyable than scrubbing pots and pans.

Fifteen

The early evening sun which streamed through the high, broad windows was outshone by more than a hundred candles which blazed from the crystal chandelier in the centre of the dining room and flickered from the stems of the highly polished silvergilt candelabra spaced along the length of the huge mahogany table. Their light was reflected from the silver cruet coasters, knives, forks and spoons and highlighted the gold edging around the almost translucent porcelain plates and tureens and it danced like diamonds from the exquisitely cut wine glasses and decanters. The serving table at the far end of the room was covered with silver salvers, a tantalising array of smells escaping from beneath their domed covers. Bottles of champagne rested in silver buckets beside carafes of the finest Burgundy. Richard looked at Maxine.

'Well, what do you think?'

'Magnificent, Richard. Truly magnificent. A setting fit for the Queen herself,' Maxine replied.

Richard put his arm round her waist and kissed her lightly on the cheek.

'I'm so glad you approve, my dear. And now on to the evening's entertainment.'

He turned to his wife. 'You may show in our guests now, Clarissa.'

Clarissa stepped from the shadows in the far corner of the room and fell on her knees before her husband.

'Richard, please. Please do not make me do this thing,' she begged.

Her husband looked down at her impassively. It was Maxine who responded to her plea.

'Have I not told you a dozen times, Clarissa? You do what you are told, when you are told. You speak when you are spoken to. That is the role of a servant. Don't you understand what will happen if you refuse? Are you really that stupid? Now, get up and open the door or the food will get cold. You of all people should know that it is impolite to keep guests waiting.'

There was nothing to be done. Clarissa rose slowly to her feet and began to walk towards the door. Clarissa Buxton, Lady of the Manor, daughter of an Earl, opened the door and held it wide for her guests to enter, curtseying as each one stepped past her into the room.

Richard greeted each in person, politely but informally, as if this was just a regular gathering of old friends.

'Robert, glad you could come. Rebecca, I trust you are well. Lucy, I hope you have recovered from your recent uncomfortable predicament. Ah, Tom, good to see you again.'

When they were standing in the centre of the room, he announced, 'Allow me to introduce Miss Maxine Brandside, as from today our new housekeeper. Although she can be a strict taskmaster, or should I say taskmistress, I am confident you will enjoy working with her.'

Maxine smiled at them. 'I am sure we will all get along excellently.'

Buxton turned to his wife, who was still standing beside the open door. 'Don't stand there gawping, girl, show our guests to their places. And shut that door, there's a draught.'

Robert, Lucy, Rebecca and Tom stood in a nervous huddle, gazing in awe at the splendour of their surroundings, which made them horribly conscious of their poor workday clothes and unwashed hands and faces. Whatever they had expected on being summoned to their master's presence, it had certainly not been to be his guest at table. Only Robert, having been instructed to organise the feast, had had an inkling of what might lie in store, but this exceeded anything he had imagined. But it was the sight of Clarissa, as she shepherded each to their seats and dutifully held their chairs for them as they sat, which proved the greatest shock of all. For Clarissa was wearing a plain black servant's dress over which was a heavily starched white pinafore. But, while the material was coarse and the cut severe, it was not a dress most servants would be allowed to wear, or even wish to. Instead of the customary white collar, the neckline was cut provocatively low. Not only that, but the dress was clearly two sizes too small so that it accentuated every curve of her body, forcing her breasts upwards and outwards, while her pert buttocks strained against the tightness of the cloth.

Buxton sat at the head of the table with Maxine facing him at the other end. Rebecca sat immediately on his right with Robert beside her. Tom sat on his left with Lucy between him and Maxine. When all were comfortably seated though, with the exception of the host and hostess, far from relaxed, Buxton addressed his wife without deigning to look at her.

'You may serve the champagne now. Then the soup.'

Clarissa fumbled with the wire around the cork. She loved the taste of champagne, but she had never before been required to actually open a bottle. Buxton and Maxine watched her with amusement, the others with disbelief. Finally Buxton said, 'You are useless. Bring it here before we die of thirst.'

His wife hurried to obey. But the cork was already halfway out of the neck and the shaking the bottle received as she crossed the room completed the task for her. The cork shot towards the ceiling and the golden liquid spurted like a fountain just as she reached the table, drenching Tom and splattering over the plates and cutlery.

'How very careless of you,' Buxton remarked calmly. 'Stand up, Tom, so we can assess the damage.'

Tom stood up. Most of the wine had landed in his lap, soaking the front of his breeches.

Buxton took the bottle from Clarissa and placed it on the table.

'Get a cloth and dry our guest's clothes. And be quick.'

Buxton filled Rebecca's glass and motioned for her to pass the bottle around the table, remarking, 'It appears we shall have to help ourselves. One just cannot get the right quality of servants these days.'

Clarissa took a large linen napkin from the sideboard drawer and returned to stand uncertainly between her husband and the flustered stable lad.

Buxton spoke sharply to her. 'Well, what are you waiting for? Dry our guest's trousers.'

Blushing with embarrassment, Clarissa leaned over and gingerly dabbed at the damp patch.

'Not like that, stupid,' her husband rebuked her. 'Rub harder. And you'll never do it properly from that angle. Just get on your knees and rub, for goodness' sake.'

Clarissa sank to the floor. Her head whirled as she tried to comprehend the full extent of her shame. She was kneeling in front of a common stable lad, one of the lowest members of her household. This must be a dream; surely it was not really happening. She almost fell against the boy as Buxton shoved her in the back. There was nothing she could do, no escape. She scrunched the napkin into a pad and began to mop the front of Tom's breeches.

Tom's cheeks flamed almost as red as those of his mistress and he shifted nervously from one foot to another as she rubbed. But, try as he might, he could not take his eyes off Clarissa's breasts. Looking down, he could see straight between her cleavage. He watched mesmerised as they rose and fell in time with her breathing. The sight, coupled with the vigorous rubbing of the napkin across his crotch produced the inevitable result. Vainly he tried to think of something, any thought which would help stop the rapidly growing erection which was becoming visible to everyone round the table.

Buxton laughed. 'I think our young guest is now sufficiently dry. You had best cease in case he explodes. We shall have cream with the dessert, not before. The soup, if you please.'

Gratefully Tom sat down as Clarissa went to the serving table and returned with a large tureen of mushroom soup. Though she had never served at table before, as she had herself been served every day of her life she knew what to do. Carefully she ladled the steaming liquid into the bowls before the diners and then returned to stand forlornly at the far end of the room, ready to respond quickly to her husband's next request.

The meal progressed from the soup to a main course of roast pheasant and mixed vegetables, followed by a dessert of strawberry tart and cream and then a varied selection of cheeses with fresh-baked biscuits. Throughout the dinner Buxton and Maxine chatted to their guests as if they were their equals. Buxton asked Tom his opinion of the horses and the stables and what should be done about both. He explained to Rebecca the need for more staff and enquired if she knew anyone in the surrounding villages who might be suitable. Maxine talked in similar vein to Lucy and Robert. And both Master and housekeeper discussed their plans for renovating the house and its grounds. All the time, Buxton ensured that his guests' glasses were always full of wine and when the cheese arrived he passed round a decanter of vintage port.

Clarissa had hoped that, by doing as she was bid as quickly and as well as she was able, she would be spared any further indignity. Her husband's words, as soon as the soup was served, had dashed any such hope.

'Clarissa, you sound as if you are wearing hob-nailed boots, not shoes. Take them off.'

She had done so. As the diners had raised knives and forks for the main course, Buxton had sounded almost as if he genuinely cared for her comfort when he had remarked how hot she looked.

'Best get some air around your legs to cool you down. Remove your stockings.'

With every eye upon her, Clarissa had meekly lifted her dress and rolled down her knee-length black stockings. She had cleared away the plates and was about to replace them with the dessert bowls when the next order came. The fact that she expected it made it no less painful to carry out. Her trembling fingers had fumbled the hooks and eyes, but eventually the black dress had slid to the floor and she stood before the company with only the starched white pinafore for protection. It hid little. The top was so low that the outer rims of the light-brown circles around her nipples were clearly visible, while the hem was so short that it barely covered the top of her thighs. As she had walked away from the table she had been conscious that her back, buttocks and legs were bared to all, and with them the angry marks of Maxine's beating.

Buxton enjoyed the pantomime he had directed, and it was clear to him that Maxine was also highly amused by the performance. The wine did its work well and by the end of the meal it was the main reason why his guests were clearly far less nervous, and much more relaxed, than when they had first sat down. When each had a full glass of port before them, Buxton rose.

'Ladies and gentlemen, thank you all for coming. I asked you to join Miss Brandside and myself tonight as a way of thanking each of you for the pleasures we have all enjoyed during the past few days and to toast the future of Castleleigh and the important roles I hope you will all play in that future. I have many great things planned for the house, the estate and for each and every one of you. Therefore, I give you the toast, Castleleigh.'

'Castleleigh!'

Glasses and voices were raised in unison and most of the port drained in a single gulp. Buxton sent the decanter back on its round of the table.

'No doubt you were all surprised to be summoned here,' he continued when the glasses had been refreshed. 'I know some of you expected a far less enjoyable evening. Not only surprised to be here, but perhaps even more so by the presence of our new maid. To all of us in this room, she is just that, a maid. She is a wanton slut with morals which would disgrace a back-alley whore. She has shamed me and no longer deserves to be the Mistress of Castleleigh.

When we have visitors, and in front of the new servants I shall employ, at least until we can be sure of them, you will treat her with all the respect due to the Lady of the house. In private she will do your bidding, whatever that may be, just as you will do mine and Miss Brandside's. Should any one of you mention this outside the house, all of you will be driven from the village and punished by the law. And the law, of which I am the local representative, is far sterner than I can be as your employer. I am sure you all understand my meaning.'

Buxton looked searchingly round the table. Yes, he was quite sure they all understood his meaning. He relaxed and smiled.

'Good. Clarissa, come here.'

Head bowed, his wife went and stood beside her husband's chair. Buxton addressed her as he would any other trainee servant.

'For a first-timer, your efforts at waiting table were not too bad. However, you wasted the champagne, only half-filled the soup bowls, the dinner plates were cold and the tart unevenly portioned. Servants who do not give satisfaction must be punished, and it is only right that they should be punished by those they have failed to serve properly.'

From beneath his chair, Buxton picked up a thick leather tawse.

'Bend over the table, Clarissa.'

She had no pride or protest left in her. Totally shamed, her will broken, Clarissa meekly bent over the table. As she did so, her breasts flopped free from the pinafore for everyone to see.

Buxton delivered six smarting blows across her buttocks, but she hardly winced. They were as nothing to the beating she had received from Maxine. Buxton handed the tawse to Rebecca.

'Go round the table, Clarissa. Six from each, I think.'

Clarissa, her breasts hanging over the front of her pinafore, positioned herself across the table between Rebecca and Robert. Each rose in turn to deliver the required punishment. Neither spared their strength as they brought the leather down across her buttocks and thighs. Rebecca smiled with pleasure at the opportunity of punishing the high and mighty Lady of the Manor, just as she herself had so often been punished, while Robert remained as stone faced as ever. When Clarissa reached Maxine, the new house-keeper waved her on with the words, 'I am not a guest, Clarissa, remember that.'

Lucy was already out of her chair, tapping the tawse eagerly against the palm of her left hand when Clarissa reached her. For a moment they looked at each other and Clarissa saw the triumph in her former maid's eyes before she once again rested her forearms on the table and prepared herself.

'This is in my way,' remarked Lucy, as she unfastened the bows at neck and back which secured Clarissa's last remaining garment. The pinafore fell to the floor, revealing Clarissa's final secret.

Lucy applied the tawse with vigour, relishing every stroke, every quiver of Clarissa's flesh as the leather smacked across her inflamed cheeks and upper thighs and her former mistress gasped at each blow. After the sixth strike, she reluctantly handed the tawse to Tom.

The boy rose unsteadily to his feet. He had never drunk wine or port before and they, together with the richness of the food, the magnificent surroundings and the strange, almost unbelievable events he had witnessed, were making his head spin and his senses reel.

Buxton recognised the signs.

'Perhaps, Tom, you would best remain seated. Our new maid here can perform a different service for you. Clarissa, get under the table.'

'Under the –' his wife began, but her husband's words cut her short.

'Do as you are told. At once!'

Clarissa got on all fours and crawled under the table. She knelt in front of Tom's chair and waited, but not for long.

'You have soaked Tom's trousers and it may be that he is still wet beneath. I see he certainly remains in a state of discomfort. Such a condition can prove painful unless it is relieved. Relieve him.'

As Tom sank back into his chair he felt Clarissa's hands groping at his trousers, flicking free the buttons and releasing his manhood. Then her fingers were tight around its shaft and her lips compressed around its tip. He could not contain the sigh of pure pleasure which escaped as Clarissa's free hand gently massaged his balls.

Everyone round the table was grinning as they watched the expression on Tom's face.

Lucy, happily two-thirds tipsy, said, 'You next, Robert.'

But before the butler could answer, Rebecca laughed. 'No, me next.' So saying, she slid from her chair. Robert made no protest as Rebecca began to do to him what Clarissa was doing to Tom.

Buxton, his own trousers bulging, was beginning to think it might be an idea to invite Lucy to join her fellows when he heard the sound of a horse cantering up the drive. He crossed to the window in time to see Colonel Markham dismounting. He turned to Maxine. 'Excuse me, but it seems we have an unexpected guest.'

With Robert clearly in no fit state to do so, Buxton himself answered the bell's summons.

'Harry, good to see you again. Do come in.'

'I trust I'm not intruding,' said the Colonel as he placed riding crop and gloves on the hall table.

Buxton beamed. 'Not at all, my good fellow, not at all. I am afraid we have finished dinner, but there are cheese and biscuits left and a damned fine port. Do please join us.'

'Answering the door yourself these days? Where's that butler of yours?'

'Oh, he is, how shall I put it? Somewhat preoccupied at the moment. Come along.'

Buxton led the way into the dining room, opening the door at the instant that Tom emitted a series of loud pants as his body jerked in rhythm with the flow spurting from him. By the time the Colonel had taken three steps into the room, Robert was also clutching the edge of the table and gasping as Rebecca's skilful tongue completed its work.

The Colonel stopped and stared in disbelief at the sight before him. Buxton carried on as if such things were commonplace.

'May I present Miss Maxine Brandside, the new housekeeper of Castleleigh. Miss Brandside, Colonel Markham. Colonel Markham, Miss Brandside.'

Still shocked, but too well brought up to forget his manners, the Colonel extended his hand.

'Pleased to meet you, ma'am.'

'And you, Colonel. I have heard so much about you.'

It was only when Maxine released her grip that the Colonel realised he had actually been shaking hands with a housekeeper.

'What the devil's going on, Buxton?' he demanded.

Buxton airily waved his hands. 'Anything and everything I want. Which is more than most people can imagine. Come on you two, get out from under there.'

Rebecca scrambled from beneath the table and seated herself back beside Robert, who leaned across and kissed her spunk-stained lips. More slowly Clarissa, all too aware of the identity of her unexpected guest, crept from the protection the table had afforded her and stood up. She was a mess, but somehow she no longer cared. Her hair was streaked with sweat, her face splattered with come and almost every inch of her fair skin was criss-crossed with red streaks.

To give the Colonel his due, he regained his composure quickly.

'Good to see you again, my dear. All of you.'

Clarissa hung her head as Buxton and Maxine's laugh rang in her ears.

'A sight for sore eyes. Or should that be a sore sight for eyes,' quipped Buxton, and the Colonel laughed as he took the glass of port Buxton proffered.

Buxton addressed the gathering. 'Ladies and gentlemen, no more work will be required of you this evening, so you are free to enjoy yourselves in whatever ways you wish.'

'I think I would like to have a talk with my new maid and Tom,' said Maxine. 'As you know, Richard, I am something of an accomplished rider myself. In my own fashion, that is.'

Buxton turned to his butler. 'I'm sure you and Rebecca also have many things to discuss.'

As the pair rose, Rebecca slid her arm round Robert's waist, while his hand gently patted her bottom.

'Yes, sir, we have. So if you'll excuse us?'

'Carry on. Carry on. But remember, business as usual tomorrow.'

As butler and maid left the room, Buxton turned to his wife, who still stood naked, head bowed, beside the dining table.

'And what's to be done with you, Clarissa?' he mused softly.

'Whatever you wish, Richard,' she answered without looking up.

'Quite so. I think perhaps . . .'

But what Buxton thought, he never said, for at that moment the sound of a donkey cart reached him. He listened as it passed the main entrance and headed for the rear of the house.

'It seems we have more unexpected visitors to attend to,' Buxton remarked. 'And, as my servants seem to be otherwise engaged, I suppose I must see to them myself.'

He turned to the Colonel. 'Harry, please excuse me. I do not know how long I shall be gone, but I would be grateful if, while I am away, you could entertain my wife. You must have many questions which she will be pleased to answer. She will show you the way to our suite.'

Buxton left them and walked briskly down to the kitchen, following the loud clanging of the tradesmen's bell. He opened the door to be greeted by the sight of Alice and Maria, standing just in front of a sheepish-looking vicar.

'He was walking here, sir, so we thought it only our Christian duty to give him a lift,' Alice explained.

'Quite so,' Buxton agreed as he held the door wide and the trio entered. 'Good evening, Alice, Maria, Mr Pimms.'

'Evening, sir,' said the girls together.

'Good evening, Mr Buxton,' said the vicar, taking off his wide brimmed hat and bowing slightly.

'And what can I do for you all?'

251

'We come to make sure the beer's all right,' replied Alice.

'Don't want nothing going flat, do we?' added her cousin with a giggle.

'And you, Mr Pimms?'

'I thought we might discuss some church matters. But I see I have called at a most inconvenient time.'

'Not at all, Mr Pimms. Not at all,' Buxton reassured him. 'All of you, please follow me.'

Buxton led them back into the body of the house and up to the library. He sat in his favourite chair in front of the window and poured himself a large Cognac. His three visitors remained standing in a row before him. After sipping his drink, he put the glass down and pointed to the floor between his legs.

'Maria, here if you please.'

The girl sauntered over. Buxton waved his hand languidly towards the carpet. Maria instantly understood and in a moment was kneeling and unfastening his trousers. As she coaxed his cock free she bent her head and began to suck as hard as she could. Buxton looked at Alice.

'A trifle overdressed for such a warm summer's evening, I think.'

Alice needed no further prompting and quickly shed her clothes. She perched herself on the arm of his chair and blew into his ear while his hand massaged her breasts and then slid between her legs, his fingers nipping at her rapidly swelling button. Buxton looked up at the Reverend Pimms.

'Exactly which church matters did you want to discuss?' he enquired.

The vicar dragged his eyes away from the naked girl and back to the Squire.

'I, that is, well, you see, er, in two weeks' time, it will be the blessing of the crops and I thought . . . but it doesn't really matter. Not now. This is obviously not the right time to talk about such things.'

'On the contrary, vicar. We must always make time for God's work,' Buxton told him. 'Tell me, have you sinned recently?'

'Being of the flesh, I am always sinning,' the vicar admitted.

'Those demons need driving out again, do they?'

The vicar gulped nervously. 'I fear so, sir. Oh yes, I fear it is time to once more pay for my sins.'

Buxton lifted Maria's head clear of his throbbing cock.

'This girl too has sinned, as you have just witnessed. Perhaps it is time we all paid our dues.'

Buxton pulled up his trousers but left them unbuttoned. He walked to the bookcase and opened the door.

'This way to salvation.'

Five minutes later, in the centre of the old chapel, all four were naked. Buxton moved the leather-covered bench to one side and suspended both the vicar and Maria by their wrists from the chain hanging from the ceiling. He took a piece of rope and drew it tightly around the pair so that their bodies were pressed hard, one against the other, Maria's breasts crushed against the vicar's chest, his member flat against her stomach, his balls buried in her pubic hair. Buxton stood back to assess his handiwork.

'One final adjustment, I think,' he observed thoughtfully.

Mr Pimms and Maria were almost exactly the same height. Buxton glanced around and found the answer to his problem in the shape of a pile of old hassocks. He placed two under each of the girl's feet, an operation which brought the vicar's cock in line with the entrance to Maria's sex. Despite being pressed against one naked girl and the sight of another standing beside him, it was still a sorrowfully flaccid affair. Buxton handed a vicious-looking plaited whip to Alice.

'I think a little encouragement is called for, don't you?'

Alice stood aside and cracked the whip high through the air. The vicar yelled as it tore into the flabby muscles of his back, but the action added a good inch to his member. The second lashing produced a similar response and by the third, it was visibly beginning to harden into something which might prove useful. Buxton held up his hand, motioning Alice to stop. He took the vicar's prick and found it was just stiff enough to push into Maria's already moistening hole. When two inches were inside, Buxton kicked away the hassocks and, as Maria's feet returned to the floor, so every inch the vicar possessed disappeared inside her.

'With a will, Alice. With a will.'

Alice was only too pleased to oblige, slashing the long length of leather again and again across the vicar's back and buttocks. Every time it landed, Maria jerked as the vicar grew longer and thicker inside her.

'Maria, you are not doing a great deal to help our poor reverend friend. Now, move that little arse of yours,' Buxton instructed.

Maria could not have kept her arse still if she had tried, for the next moment the thinnest, whippiest cane in Buxton's collection cut into both cheeks. Maria's 'ow' coincided with an involuntary wriggle of her hips.

Alice and Buxton took it in turns to thrash the helpless pair, she scoring broad red lines across the vicar's back and buttocks, he thin, but no less painful, horizontal streaks across the girl's perfectly rounded, ultra-tight globes.

Maria threw back her head and howled as the beating progressed, pushing down on the length inside her, swaying her shoulders so that her nipples were rubbed raw against the vicar's coarse chest hair, constantly pushing down to ensure every millimetre of him was inside her. When Buxton roughly pushed his hands between her legs, his fingers came out wet and sticky.

The vicar shouted quotations from the Psalms, passages from Revelations concerning sin and eternal punishment and called upon the saints to forgive him. Suddenly, he stopped shouting, his eyes opened wide and his whole body went rigid. For the first time in his life, his seed had penetrated a woman via the entrance designed for it.

Maria gasped as she felt him begin to come. Then she brought her face to his and kissed him as passionately as she had ever kissed a man, gnawing at his lip before driving her tongue between his teeth. One final swipe from Buxton's cane and she exploded too.

Buxton threw aside his cane and Alice her whip. He took her hand and pulled her to the leather-covered bench. There was no foreplay, both were too desperate, and already too stimulated, to require any. Alice spread her legs wide and Buxton rammed into her. His fingers entwined in her hair as her arms enfolded him, her fingernails clawing the skin from his back. They came in the same instant, bucking and shouting as the feelings convulsed their bodies and senses.

When, at last, their bodies had stopped shaking and their breathing had returned to normal, Buxton withdrew. He sat on the corner of the bench smiling down at the now totally relaxed Alice.

'You are amazing, Alice. Truly amazing.'

'You ain't so bad yourself, sir. And that's the truth.'

Buxton began to dress. 'I had almost forgotten that I have a house full of guests and I do not wish to be seen to be a poor host. Tell me, Alice, have you ever seen round The Hall?'

Alice too started to put her clothes back on. 'No, sir. I only ever been to the kitchens, and here of course.'

'Then come, I will give you a guided tour.'

Alice nodded towards the vicar and her cousin. 'What about them?'

Buxton shrugged. 'They'll still be here when we get back. Can't see them going anywhere, can you?'

Outside the library, Buxton pondered which direction to take. Finally he decided, 'I think we will start with the servants' quarters.'

If the sounds which floated towards them when they reached the corridor leading to the butler's bedroom left little to the imagination, the sight which greeted them when Buxton opened the door left nothing at all.

Rebecca was kneeling on the bed, Robert behind her, his cock half inside her anus. In his hand he held the tawse he had taken from the dining room. Every thrust was carefully calculated so that each one took him only a fraction further into her quivering body. And with every thrust he struck. Rebecca's body jerked as the leather slapped hard against her shoulders and was swung sideways to smack against her hanging, swaying breasts. Robert looked round as the door opened, but Buxton just waved.

'Carry on, Robert. Sorry to have disturbed you.'

Buxton closed the door and turned to Alice. 'The guest bedroom next I think.'

On entering the guest suite, an even more bizarre sight confronted them. Tom and Lucy were naked on the bed, he lying on his back, she astride him. As she rose and fell, so too did the lash in Maxine's hand, scything across back and breasts like a whirlwind.

Buxton walked over and kissed Maxine lightly on the cheek. 'Keep up the good work.'

'And this is?' Maxine enquired, looking at Alice.

'Hopefully a new recruit to the household,' Buxton replied. 'I will tell you more later, in bed.'

The connecting door between the guest rooms and the master suite was already ajar. Buxton pushed it wide.

Clarissa hung tethered by silk scarves to two uprights of the four-poster bed. Her body shone with sweat and her breasts, stomach and thighs clearly displayed the results of a very recent leathering. Jewellery glinted from her body. Gold and silver earrings, encrusted with emeralds, diamonds and sapphires, were clamped to her nipples, the lips of her sex and hung from her clit.

Clarissa was pleading with the man who stood before her.

'Please take me. Now, Harry, please. Have me now.'

Colonel Markham turned as Buxton and Alice entered.

The Colonel greeted him jovially. 'Hello, old man. Hope you don't mind. Seemed a pity to let the filly go when she was on heat. And who, may I ask, is this pretty little thing?'

'This is Alice, Colonel, a dear friend. Say good evening, Alice.'

Alice stared at the huge naked figure, or rather she stared at the enormous, pulsating cock which jutted true and straight from a jungle of black hair.

'Evening, sir,' she managed to say at last.

Buxton turned back to her. 'It seems, Alice, that the good Colonel may require some assistance with my wife. I wonder, would you be good enough to help him?'

Alice continued to gaze in awe at the Colonel's massive weapon, the biggest she had ever seen.

'Please, sir,' she replied.

'Good, then I'll leave you all to it. See you all later.'

Alice was already half out of her dress before Buxton reached the connecting door. In the guest room, Maxine was now sitting on Lucy's face and at the same time sucking Tom's cock, all the while encouraging him by sliding a finger in and out of his back passage. Buxton merely nodded to them as he passed through.

Back in the dining room, he refilled his glass with champagne and strolled out on to the terrace. It was a perfect summer's night. The sky was like a rich dark-blue umbrella on to which someone had sewn a million sparkling sequins. The harvest moon hung like a great yellow balloon high above the horizon. The air was heavy with the sweet fragrances of a thousand flowers. Somewhere in the copse a nightingale began its serenade.

Squire Richard Buxton, Lord of the Manor, Master of Castleleigh thought about all that was happening below and above him, smiled, sipped his champagne and raised his glass towards the stars in a toast to the future. The future of Castleleigh.

NEXUS NEW BOOKS

To be published in September

DISPLAYS OF PENITENTS
Lucy Golden
£5.99

In this, the third volume of tales from Lucy Golden, the lives of ordinary people are turned upside down as they submit to the allure of a totally new experience. It may be a medical examination. It may be a drinking game with very wet forfeits. It may be a bet. It may be an encounter with friends, family, neighbours or colleagues that takes a turn for the bizarre. Whatever the circumstances, whatever aspects of pain, pleasure, domination and submission are encountered, these tales explore every facet of the wide world of perverse eroticism with a haunting power and intensity.

ISBN 0 352 33646 3

TEMPER TANTRUMS
Penny Birch
£5.99

Natasha Linnet has a weakness for dirty old men – hence her relationship with wine buff and accomplished spanker Percy Ottershaw. When Percy visits a former colleague, the louche Dr Blondeau, in France, Natasha tags along. Blondeau, figuring correctly that any girlfriend of his perverted old friend must be a willing submissive, has extreme ideas of his own, for which he considers Natasha fair game. Natasha sees right through his wiles, of course. But how can she give in, and still have the last laugh?

ISBN 0 352 33647 1

DARK DESIRES
Maria del Rey
£5.99

Sexual diversity is the hallmark of Maria del Rey's work. Here, for the first time in one volume, is a collection of her kinkiest stories – each one striking in its originality – with settings to suit all tastes. Fetishists, submissives and errant tax inspectors mingle with bitch goddesses, naughty girls and French maids in this eclectic anthology of forbidden games. A Nexus Classic.

ISBN 0 352 33648 X

To be published in October

CAGED!
Yolanda Celbridge
£5.99

Tucked away in the Yorkshire Dales is a women's corrective institution where uniforms and catspats are the order of the day, the first often shredded by the second! But are the bars and fences to keep the women confined, or the locals out?

ISBN 0 352 33650 1

BEAST
Wendy Swanscombe
£5.99

Without time to draw breath from the indignities already heaped on them, the three sisters of *Disciplined Skin* – blonde Anna, redhead Beth, raven Gwen – are plunged into the new tortures and humiliations gleefully devised for them by their mysterious leather-clad captor Herr Abraham Bärengelt. Putting its heroines through ordeals that range from mild to perversely bizarre, *Beast* is sure to confirm the reputation its author has already established for surreal erotic depravity that entertains as much as it arouses.

ISBN 0 352 33649 8

PENNY IN HARNESS
Penny Birch
£5.99

When naughty Penny is walking in the woods one day, she is surprised to find a couple pony-carting. Penny is so excited by watching this new form of adult fun that she has to pleasure herself on the spot. Realising how keen she is to discover for herself what it is all about, she begins to investigate this bizarre world of whips and harnesses. Will she ever be able to win the highest accolade in their world of kinky games – the honour of being a pony-girl? A Nexus Classic.

ISBN 0 352 33651 X

If you would like more information about Nexus titles, please visit our website at www.nexus-books.co.uk, or send a stamped addressed envelope to:
  Nexus, Thames Wharf Studios,
  Rainville Road, London W6 9HA

BLACK LACE NEW BOOKS

To be published in September

CHEAP TRICK
Astrid Fox
£5.99

Super-8 filmmaker Tesser Roget is a girl who takes no prisoners. An American slacker, living in London, she dresses in funky charity-shop clothes and wears blue fishnets. She looks hot and she knows it. She likes to have sex, and she frequently does. Life on the fringe is very good indeed, but when she meets artist Jamie Desmond things take a sudden swerve into the weird. Her outsider lifestyle is threatened by disgruntled ex-lovers, big-business corruption and, worst of all, cinematic sabotage of her precious film. With all this on the go, and a libido that craves regular attention, Tesser is a very busy girl.

ISBN 0 352 33640 4

GAME FOR ANYTHING
Lyn Wood
£5.99

Fiona – Fee to her friends – finds herself on a word-games holiday with her best pal. At first it seems like a boring way to spend a week away. Then she realises it's a treasure hunt with a difference. Solving the riddles embroils her in a series of erotic situations as the clues get ever more outrageous. It's a race to the finish with people cheating, partnerships changing and lots of the competitors shagging. Fiona needs an analytical mind and an encyclopaedic knowledge of sex to be in with a chance of winning. And she can't do it all on her own.

ISBN 0 352 33639 0

FORBIDDEN FRUIT
Susie Raymond
£5.99

When thirty-something divorcee Beth realises someone is spying on her in the work changing room, she is both shocked and excited. When she finds out it's a sixteen-year-old shop assistant Jonathan she cannot believe her eyes. Try as she might, she cannot get the thought of his fit young body out of her mind. Although she knows she shouldn't encourage him, the temptation is irresistible. To Jonathan, Beth is a real woman: sexy, sophisticated and experienced. But once Beth and Jonathan have tasted the forbidden fruit, what will happen? A Black Lace Special Reprint.

ISBN 0 352 33306 5

To be published in October

ALL THE TRIMMINGS
Tesni Morgan
£5.99

Cheryl and Laura, two fast friends, find themselves single. When the women find out that each secretly harbours a desire to be a whorehouse madam, there's nothing to stop them. On the surface their establishment is a five-star hotel, but to a select clientele it's a bawdy fun house for both sexes, where fantasies – from the mild to the increasingly perverse – are indulged. But when attractive, sinister John Dempsey comes on the scene, Cheryl is smitten and Laura less so, convinced he's out to con them, bust them or both. Which of the women is right?

ISBN 0 352 33641 2

WICKED WORDS 5
ed. Kerri Sharp
£5.99

Hugely popular and deliciously daring, *Wicked Words* short story collections are a showcase of the best in women's erotic writing from the UK and USA. Hot, upbeat, fresh and cheeky, this is fun erotica at the cutting edge.

ISBN 0 352 33642 0

PLEASURE'S DAUGHTER
Sedalia Johnson
£5.99

It's 1750. Orphaned Amelia, headstrong and voluptuous, goes to live with wealthy relatives. During the journey she meets the exciting, untrustworthy Marquess of Beechwood. She manages to escape his clutches only to find he is a good friend of her aunt and uncle. Although aroused by him, she flees his relentless pursuit, taking up residence in a Convent Garden establishment dedicated to pleasure. When the Marquess catches up with her, Amelia is only too happy to demonstrate her new-found disciplinary skills. A Black Lace Special Reprint.

ISBN 0 352 33237 9

NEXUS BACKLIST

This information is correct at time of printing. For up-to-date information, please visit our website at www.nexus-books.co.uk

All books are priced at £5.99 unless another price is given.

Nexus books with a contemporary setting

ACCIDENTS WILL HAPPEN	Lucy Golden ISBN 0 352 33596 3	☐
ANGEL	Lindsay Gordon ISBN 0 352 33590 4	☐
THE BLACK MASQUE	Lisette Ashton ISBN 0 352 33372 3	☐
THE BLACK WIDOW	Lisette Ashton ISBN 0 352 33338 3	☐
THE BOND	Lindsay Gordon ISBN 0 352 33480 0	☐
BROUGHT TO HEEL	Arabella Knight ISBN 0 352 33508 4	☐
CANDY IN CAPTIVITY	Arabella Knight ISBN 0 352 33495 9	☐
CAPTIVES OF THE PRIVATE HOUSE	Esme Ombreux ISBN 0 352 33619 6	☐
DANCE OF SUBMISSION	Lisette Ashton ISBN 0 352 33450 9	☐
DARK DELIGHTS	Maria del Rey ISBN 0 352 33276 X	☐
DARK DESIRES	Maria del Rey ISBN 0 352 33072 4	☐
DISCIPLES OF SHAME	Stephanie Calvin ISBN 0 352 33343 X	☐
DISCIPLINE OF THE PRIVATE HOUSE	Esme Ombreux ISBN 0 352 33459 2	☐

MAIDEN	Aishling Morgan	☐
	ISBN 0 352 33466 5	
NYMPHS OF DIONYSUS	Susan Tinoff	☐
£4.99	ISBN 0 352 33150 X	
THE SLAVE OF LIDIR	Aran Ashe	☐
	ISBN 0 352 33504 1	
TIGER, TIGER	Aishling Morgan	☐
	ISBN 0 352 33455 X	
THE WARRIOR QUEEN	Kendal Grahame	☐
	ISBN 0 352 33294 8	

Edwardian, Victorian and older erotica

BEATRICE	Anonymous	☐
	ISBN 0 352 31326 9	
CONFESSION OF AN ENGLISH SLAVE	Yolanda Celbridge	☐
	ISBN 0 352 33433 9	
DEVON CREAM	Aishling Morgan	☐
	ISBN 0 352 33488 6	
THE GOVERNESS AT ST AGATHA'S	Yolanda Celbridge	☐
	ISBN 0 352 32986 6	
PURITY	Aishling Morgan	☐
	ISBN 0 352 33510 6	
THE TRAINING OF AN ENGLISH GENTLEMAN	Yolanda Celbridge	☐
	ISBN 0 352 33348 0	

Samplers and collections

NEW EROTICA 4	Various	☐
	ISBN 0 352 33290 5	
NEW EROTICA 5	Various	☐
	ISBN 0 352 33540 8	
EROTICON 1	Various	☐
	ISBN 0 352 33593 9	
EROTICON 2	Various	☐
	ISBN 0 352 33594 7	
EROTICON 3	Various	☐
	ISBN 0 352 33597 1	
EROTICON 4	Various	☐
	ISBN 0 352 33602 1	

Nexus Classics
A new imprint dedicated to putting the finest works of erotic fiction
back in print.

------- ✂ --------------------------

Please send me the books I have ticked above.

Name ....

Address ....

....

....

.... Post code ....

Send to: **Cash Sales, Nexus Books, Thames Wharf Studios, Rainville Road, London W6 9HA**

US customers: for prices and details of how to order books for delivery by mail, call 1-800-805-1083.

Please enclose a cheque or postal order, made payable to **Nexus Books Ltd**, to the value of the books you have ordered plus postage and packing costs as follows:
   UK and BFPO – £1.00 for the first book, 50p for each subsequent book.
   Overseas (including Republic of Ireland) – £2.00 for the first book, £1.00 for each subsequent book.

If you would prefer to pay by VISA, ACCESS/MASTER-CARD, DINERS CLUB, AMEX or SWITCH, please write your card number and expiry date here:

....

Please allow up to 28 days for delivery.

Signature ....

------- ✂ --------------------------